Before sacr[...], Geraint Anderson was a long-haired hippy and left wing idealist. His dream of becoming a trinket-selling global traveller was cruelly dashed when his brother got him an interview at a French bank in the City, which would set him on the rocky road to destruction and despair. He is the bestselling author of CITYBOY: *Beer and Loathing in the Square Mile* and a regular media commentator on the financial world he once inhabited. He now lives a quiet life, with his family, exploring the planet and failing to learn how to surf.

Praise for Geraint Anderson:

'If you found *The 39 Steps* short of sex and drugs, Geraint Anderson, aka Cityboy, has kindly corrected John Buchans's oversight . . . an affable romp' *Telegraph*

'[Steve Jones'] exciting journey is guaranteed to have you racing through every page! Brilliant' *Closer*

'*Cityboy*'s author revives the excesses of this world in a laddish and memorable style' *Star*

'Superb . . . and with the added 'bonus' of plenty of banker bashing' *Lancashire Evening Post*

'His timing couldn't be better . . . London's pernicious financial world reveals itself in all its ugliness' *Daily Mail*

'Excruciatingly candid' *Sunday Times*

'As a primer to back-stabbing, bullying, drug-taking, gambling, boozing, lap-dancing, this takes some beating' *Evening Standard*

'Engaging, timely and important . . . an effective indictment of the narcissism and decadence of City life' *The Times*

'An undeniably slick and entertaining read' *Sunday Business Post*

By Geraint Anderson and available from Headline

Cityboy: Beer and Loathing in the Square Mile
Cityboy: 50 ways to Survive the Crunch

Just Business

JUST BUSINESS

Geraint Anderson

headline

First published in 2011 by
HEADLINE PUBLISHING GROUP

First published in paperback in 2012 by
HEADLINE PUBLISHING GROUP

1

Cataloguing in Publication Data is available from the British Library

ISBN 978 0 7553 8173 9

Typeset in Hoefler by Avon DataSet Ltd,
Bidford-on-Avon, Warwickshire

Printed and bound by CPI Group (UK) Ltd, Croydon, CR0 4YY

HEADLINE PUBLISHING GROUP
An Hachette UK Company
338 Euston Road
London NW1 3BH

www.headline.co.uk
www.hachette.co.uk

To the most beautiful pot-bellied
moustachioed dwarf in Abergavenny

Acknowledgements

The following people deserve major thanks – Martin Fletcher at Headline for having faith in me, Nancy Webber for being an extremely patient editor and my agent Lizzy Kremer at David Higham who didn't lose hope even when I forgot to contact her for seven months. Anyone who read the book when it was in a rough state should get a special mention and that includes Laura West at David Higham, Jamie Tall Pills and my lovely wife Emma. Big thanks to Bridget Harrison who allowed me to rant every week in the pages of *thelondonpaper* and Sophie Lodge who made me a lovely website (www.cityboy.biz) and almost started my pop career. Apologies and thanks to Toby, Warren, Razzall, Angus and Uppy, Al Maguire, Camilla and Craig who once again found their gags stolen and used in this book. Huge thanks to my parents who still haven't disowned me despite the terrible embarrassment I've been causing them all my life.

Finally, I need to thank my wife once more . . . for being the best partner in crime a man could hope for.

If you have any thoughts regarding this book please contact me on geraint@cityboy.biz.

Prologue

November 2008

I WAS SITTING ON THE beach watching the two guys hassling the hippy and desperately trying to remember why I should be scared. Even from afar, the two figures looked vaguely familiar, but a dope-fuelled haze prevented me from reaching a vital conclusion straight away: if I didn't leave immediately there was every chance I'd be dead within a minute.

I stood up in as nonchalant a fashion as possible and put my sunglasses on. The two heavily tanned, dark-haired men, one short and squat, the other tall and angular, were showing old Dave a photo and asking questions. Although I couldn't hear what they were saying their manner was menacing. Even from this distance I could tell that Dave was nervous.

Juan and Diego had made some effort not to stand out amongst the westerners lying around on sarongs by wearing baggy beach shorts and ill-fitting, garish Indian T-shirts.

However, their tidy moustaches and well-maintained hair-cuts were most certainly out of place amongst the travellers on this particular beach. It was finally dawning on me that these two men had followed me halfway round the world to kill me.

I turned my back on the sea and began walking towards my battered motorbike feeling the hot sand beneath my feet, my eyes never leaving the two men who were questioning Dave. They stood over him, twenty short paces to my right. Without looking down, I unzipped my bum bag and started rooting around for the bike key even though the Enfield was still many yards away. My heart was pounding like a bass drum and I was sweating profusely. Beneath my artificial calm, I prayed over and over again that the two guys would not look over in my direction.

Suddenly Dave glanced towards me. The eyes of my two would-be assassins instinctively followed his and immediately widened with recognition. Without a moment's pause I broke into a sprint. Leaping on to my bike, I flicked up the stand and after two nervous, frantic attempts finally managed to slip the key into the ignition. I twisted it to the right but the Colombians were already running towards me. Juan was reaching into his bag for something – something I didn't need to see to know what it was.

I now had about five seconds to start my ever-unreliable Royal Enfield Bullet. I tried to steady myself but I was shaking like a leaf. I slammed my right foot down on the kick start but it slipped off the greasy pedal, tearing a gash in my ankle. I lost my balance and the bike almost toppled over, but I ignored the pain, stamped the pedal down again, pulled the throttle back and heard what at that moment was without doubt the most beautiful noise in the world – the deep, popping sound of the 350cc four-stroke engine starting up. I pulled the clutch in, clunked into first gear and went heavy on the throttle. I roared off along the sandy dirt track and turned round to see my two assailants shouting obscenities at heaven, but the feeling of relief was momentary – a second nervous glance into my one remaining wing mirror showed them running towards two nearby Hondas, both holding keys in their hands . . .

I haven't told anyone what really forced me to leave the City in late 2007 and, believe me, the press reports got it all wrong. Admittedly, they mainly got it wrong because of the misinformation I drip-fed them – something I had to do in order to protect my bony arse. Now I'm going to tell you what really happened and it's a story so outrageous that even I can barely believe it, yet all of it is totally true. An insane moment of greed set in motion a series of events that turned my life upside down and means that I will never feel safe again. I have endangered my life and the lives of those I love, and for what? A quick buck in a sick world.

Everything that we've witnessed over the past three years reveals just how out of control things have become in the world of finance – the lunatics truly have taken over the asylum. Hardly a day has gone by without some selfish degenerate striving to outdo his twisted banker mates with some appalling act of self-serving greed. For the first few months of my forced exile I could hardly believe what I was reading on the internet. But each callous feat of fathomless avarice seemed to be superseded by the next and I, like most of the dumb schmucks on this planet, grew numb to them. Jérôme Kerviel's €4.9 billion 'trading loss' looks like a rounding error compared to the $50 billion Ponzi scheme organised by Bernie Madoff. Meanwhile, those charmless scumbags at Goldman Sachs keep proving themselves to be the most repugnant cocksuckers this world has ever seen. Amazingly, despite bankers' best efforts to bring pain and suffering to their fellow man whilst lining their own silk pockets, finance remains relatively unregulated and the despicable sluts are still raking in bonuses so vast they bring tears to the eyes of all right-thinking people.

Most Cityboys lie, cheat and steal every single hour of their lives as they strive to accumulate ever more wealth. But I went even further. I loathe the hideous chaos that my former colleagues' tireless greed has created but I am in no position to judge them, for I am as bad as they are, maybe worse. The only difference between me and the Armani-clad gangsters who plunged the world into recession is that I didn't get away with it. It's going to be payback time for the rest of my sorry life.

Because just one stupid fucked-up decision can destroy everything.

Part One

- In 2007 the outgoing chief executive of the City regulator, the Financial Services Authority, admitted that insider trading was 'rife'. The FSA's own annual analysis concludes that 'suspicious share price movements' took place prior to 29 per cent of the public takeovers that occurred in 2009. The FSA was created in 1997 and according to a *Times* report in 2009, in its first decade of existence it failed to secure a single criminal conviction for insider dealing.

- In 2004 President George W. Bush justified not increasing taxes for the wealthy by claiming that 'the really rich people figure out how to dodge taxes anyway'. In 2006 the National Audit Office revealed that 30 per cent of the UK's largest 700 companies paid no tax at all. In February 2009 the Trade Unions Congress published research stating that tax avoidance by wealthy UK residents through tax havens cost HM Revenue & Customs £4 billion every year.

- Despite the trillion-pound bank bailout, City bonuses in respect of 2009 reached close to £8 billion – an increase of almost 50 per cent relative to 2008. So far virtually no concrete changes to financial regulation have been implemented in the UK despite universal recognition that it was bankers who almost brought about the collapse of the global economy.

One

September 2007

'WELL, YOU ONLY GET ONE shot at the title, and she blew it,' I lied through a coked-up rictus grimace. The banging house music made decent conversation almost impossible but my clients and I were way too wired to dance properly and so had little choice. Anyway, it didn't really matter much because conversation with these clowns was always going to be macho horseshit and tiresome oneupmanship at the best of times. We huddled together on the luxurious cushioned seat just feet away from the dance floor, our eyes darting around checking out the fit young East European gold-diggers. On the low table in front of us were two bottles of Grey Goose vodka, a huge bucket of ice and a shedload of different mixers. All this would set me, or rather my bank, back £500. Seeing as we'd already blown well over a grand on cocktails at Fifty St James and a meal at the Wolseley, this night of debauchery was certainly going to take some explaining to the expenses department. Still, a couple of these hedge fund boys were bound to give me some man-sized orders the next day so I'd almost certainly get away with it, again.

'Well, I'm bored with talking about me . . . so how about you guys talk about me for a while?' I joked, trying to steer the conversation away from the fact that I had recently been binned by an amazing girl I was still utterly besotted by. I knew I'd fucked up and I was really suffering. I was in the grip of the growing realisation that I'd possibly just lost the love of my life for an office fling that didn't even get past first base. But the last thing I wanted to mention to these pricks was something 'vulnerable' that would detract from the image of God-like invincibility that everyone around the table sought to project. Anyway, the lads were focusing their saucer eyes on some particularly slinky mover, who must have been all of about nineteen. She looked like your standard, slender, barely legal Lithuanian hooker. We all stared at her for a bit and then proceeded to follow the predictable routine of commenting on her attributes in a way that would confirm to each other our rampant hetero-sexuality as well as our boundless virility.

'Fuck me, check out the buns on that slapper! You could break fucking coconuts on her arse!' exclaimed Richard, the richest and evidently the most erudite of the clients I had the dubious pleasure of entertaining that night. 'And there's only one thing wrong with her face . . . it ain't covered in my muck,' he added with a disgusting leer. Richard was the sort of self-satisfied, loathsome tosspot who didn't just think the world owed him a living, he damn well knew it did. I had spent four long years buttering up this offensive deviate and it was paying off.

'Hell's bells! She's got a set of Bristols on her that just ain't quittin',' shouted Brad, virtually foaming at the mouth such was his manufactured excitement. He was another foul, depraved human being and was most certainly not the sharpest tool in the box. In fact, we three others often joked that he'd find it difficult to chew gum and walk at the same time.

'Mate, he who hesitates masturbates . . . why don't you go and have a boogie with her? Show her some of your moves? Otherwise you're just gonna spend another night cranking yourself to sleep,' laughed Dimitri, a diminutive, pox-ridden, sleazy whoremonger whose dilated pupils betrayed the fact that he was buzzing his nuts off.

'Yeah, come on, Richard, stop giving it the Terry Big Spuds and strap a pair on, you fucking Wendy,' added Brad.

'Yeah, in your own time, Richard, while we're still young . . . this side of Christmas would be nice,' said I, joining in with the general ribaldry.

'Christ alive! I'm getting advice on picking up girls from the thumb-it-in-soft posse? Fucking hell, I might as well get anger management lessons from Russell Crowe! I'm gonna call up Leslie Ash right now to ask for her advice on cosmetic surgery. Chaps, I don't wanna be rude or anything but the only reason you sick onanists ever get laid is because you never leave home without a stash of Rohypnol and a load of Viagra, so please don't give it large.'

Ah . . . we were slipping into the old familiar routine. Good, the evening was going as planned. Although Richard's little speech sounded angry, which as the hosting stock-broker meant I initially felt a little concerned, a quick glance in his direction assured me that he was merely playing a role, and was very happy to do so. Richard rarely talked, he just held forth, and today was no exception. Of course, I wanted everything to go smoothly tonight but in this con-text 'going smoothly' meant non-stop childish banter that only to the uninformed observer was aggressively hostile. I sat back happy in the knowledge that this false bonhomie would soon translate into some serious commission.

We had spent the earlier part of the evening talking shop over our overpriced dinner and Richard had even been kind enough to share some inside information with us about a transport company that was going to be acquired on Monday at a 25 per cent premium. All of us had virtually promised him that we'd be getting our long lost aunts, great-uncles and anyone else who wasn't directly connected to us to invest shedloads in said company at the break of dawn. I planned to punt my usual unit size of £100,000 via a cabal of five old school friends and was looking forward to the twenty grand winnings that my three-day 'investment' would garner after my pals had each taken their usual £1,000 costs.

Funnily enough, now that the 'business' was over, I was

almost having fun. This was a pleasant surprise considering the company I was keeping and the fact that the Eurotrash losers at Chinawhite that night were generally at least ten years younger than me – making me feel once again like the worst paedo in the paddling pool. Still, by late 2007 I'd been partying with obnoxious clients for over a decade and faking sincerity had become second nature. Shit, these smug, charmless idiots probably thought I actually liked them.

The drinks were being downed at a rate of knots, and since my main role that night was simply to ensure that my clients never had an empty glass in front of them, whilst providing them with enough toot to keep things rocking, I lined up four more triple vodka and tonics and, as we clinked glasses, proposed a toast of sorts: 'The liver is evil and must be punished!'

My faithful stooges laughed and repeated the mantra. Richard, seemingly annoyed that I, and not he, had raised a titter, decided he would add further to the general hilarity: 'A weekend not wasted is a wasted weekend!'

Pleasingly, Brad and Dimitri didn't laugh quite so heartily at his piss-poor gag. It didn't make much sense anyway because, as usual, we were having our knees-up on a Thursday – the traditional night for client entertainment. All Richard's inane joke succeeded in doing was to remind me that it was a school night and I had to be in the office at 6.55 a.m. tomorrow, which was approximately six hours away. My brain quickly calculated that we had at least a gram and a half of wallop left and that meant I didn't have a chance in hell of leaving the club before it closed at 3 a.m. So, if I was lucky I'd get two hours of moody kip, max. I felt something I'd been feeling increasingly over the previous couple of years: I was getting way too old for this tiresome bullshit.

Richard suddenly stood up and with an extremely unsubtle beckoning hand movement motioned that he was after the Boutros.

'Oi, pecker breath, quit talking and start chalking. Hand over the ticket now. You've been hanging on to it way too long. If you're not gonna shit, get off the fucking pot!' He sneered in a dismissive manner which reminded me once again, just in case I'd forgotten, that he was the client and I was his simpering bitch. After numerous years at the beck and call of arrogant clients I instinctively jumped to it and pulled the wrap out of my shirt's breast pocket.

'Richard, it really is a total pleasure to see you again,' I said for the benefit of any security guards who might be clocking our moves as I shook his hand and slipped the contraband from my palm into his.

'Whatever,' he muttered as he marched off to the toilets, an unmistakable purpose in his stride.

When he got back he looked edgy.

'Steve, Steve . . . is my tie on straight?' he said, wiping his top lip frantically. This was our code for whether there were traces of Charlie deposited around the nose.

'Nah, mate, you've got nostril wings to die for!'

We then repeated the preposterous charade of shaking hands and I transferred the wrap on to the knee of Dimitri, who was chomping at the bit like a Glasgow smack addict. He immediately jumped up and strode towards the bogs.

'God's teeth! If I have another line of that speedy gak they're gonna have to peel me off the *fucking* ceiling!' shouted Richard, his grinding jaw making his words blend together. 'Anyway, muppet boys, it's time for you to watch and learn from the master.' And with that he moved off towards the slinky girl who was still dancing nonchalantly in her skintight white catsuit. As he did so he rocked from one foot to the other. I imagine this was meant to be some kind of funky move but in fact he just resembled an embarrassing uncle dancing at a wedding, complete with 'white man's overbite'.

Brad and I watched his jerky, spasmodic dancing with amusement. There was no way in hell he was going to get anywhere with the chick and I secretly delighted in the fact that his clumsy attempts to make eye contact with her and garner a smile were being soundly ignored. As soon as Dimitri came back from his nasal mission, gurning as if he was auditioning for *My Left Foot*, I made my own way to the gents.

It was whilst I was in the cubicle racking up a fat line that I decided I definitely would write a column about this torrid gathering. I'd been thinking about doing so all evening, because tonight clearly had all the ingredients required to keep Londoners amused whilst confirming all their prejudices about Cityboys and their insatiable hunger for debauchery. Of course, I'd omit to mention our drug consumption or the insider trading, as those aspects wouldn't do any of us any good if my identity were ever revealed.

I'd started writing the column for a laugh. A London-based free paper had come into existence in September 2006 and an old school friend happened to be its deputy editor. She'd told me two weeks before the newspaper's first edition that they wanted a weekly column exposing the excesses of the City and I'd leapt at the opportunity. Every week I could vent my spleen – anonymously – about the job I'd accidentally fallen into to the half-million or so commuters who read the newspaper. I soon found that publicly revealing my internal struggle with my job acted as a kind of therapy for me and helped me overcome my guilt about 'playing for the wrong team'. Over time, and much to my surprise, the column garnered a cult following.

I'd got away with it for a year but there was every chance I'd be rumbled soon. There'd be quite a few colleagues and clients amongst the bored drones on the tube who read *thelondonpaper* every Friday afternoon and if one of them recognised the tale I recounted then I could be done for. I was fully aware that I'd lose my job if anyone at my bank could prove I was 'Cityboy', and though I desperately wanted to leave the City before I morphed into a rotund, red-faced alcoholic facing my third divorce, I wanted to do it in my own time and certainly not before this year's bonus, which looked likely to be disgustingly huge. That bonus alone would almost certainly be enough to finally make me give up my bullshit career and start living La Dolce Vita on a tropical beach. Truth be told, it was only the image of me smoking a fat joint in a hammock in the cool shade of a palm tree that kept me going through all this relentless two-faced drudgery.

The rest of the night proceeded in a horrifyingly predictable way. The conversation became ever more edgy and the trips to the bogs ever more regular. At some point Dimitri proposed that we pick up some hookers and head to either the Dorchester or the Mandarin Oriental but, I'm pleased to say, that idea was quickly dismissed. The boys were obviously feeling particularly morally upstanding that night. Predictably, none of us managed to pull. The fit, Gucci-clad, Eastern European gold-diggers must, for some unfathomable reason, have decided that their future didn't lie with four sweaty, wide-eyed buffoons who could barely string a sentence together without first rushing off to the gents. A baffling decision if ever there was one.

When the club signalled the end to the night's fun by turning on the all too bright lights we filed out with the rest of the punters, trying not to let the bouncers see our horribly dilated pupils. We briefly discussed sharing cabs home and I secretly rejoiced that no one lived in my direction. After allowing my three clients to pick up the remaining taxis idling outside the club I had to wait five minutes before another black cab rolled by. As I entered the taxi I felt a warm glow of relief envelop me as I took on board the fact that I wouldn't have to kowtow to anyone for at least four hours.

It was whilst my cab was rocketing down a deserted

Bayswater Road that an idea I'd been flirting with for several hours began to announce itself more loudly in my psychotic cerebellum. I knew I'd soon be passing close to Jane's flat in Queensway, and now I decided to call her to see if there was any chance of a late-night rendezvous. Jane was a graduate trainee who'd been with us for a year. She was the confident, sassy 22-year-old Oxford grad I'd embraced in a nightclub whilst pilled off my head. She was the pretty, sexy Lolita who had cost me my relationship. It wouldn't have been so bad, but after we'd kissed she'd promptly gone home alone despite my overly eager protestations at the taxi rank. It was my bad luck that Gemma's cousin had spied us leaving the club together and informed her of my misdeed. That was two weeks before and Gemma was neither taking my calls nor letting me cross her threshold. Our terse, brief conversations had all been via the intercom. It seemed that no amount of reasoned voicemail, Interflora bouquets or impassioned email was going to disabuse my beautiful girlfriend of the view that I was a grotty little toerag who had 'snogged the help' and couldn't be trusted. That ocean-going, copper-bottomed fuck-up was why I faced the world alone again.

I'd just lost someone really special but, I thought, my crime should at least have been worth it. I should try to take something from this catastrophe. I stared at my BlackBerry. I had about a minute before I passed Jane's road. It was 3.25 a.m. on Friday morning and she'd be getting up for work in about two and a half hours. She had been formal with me at the office since our 'encounter' and had indicated in no uncertain terms over the last fortnight that dipping your nib in the company ink is never a good idea. She almost certainly wasn't remotely interested in her burnt-out, depraved boss who was thirteen years her senior and was rapidly developing such large bags under his eyes that one amusing secretary referred to them as 'suitcases'. I took all these persuasive points on board . . . and then rang her. Of course, I was sure to dial 141 before her number so she couldn't see it was me.

The ring tone sounded once, then again. My heart began to quicken. After six rings she finally answered. 'Hi, it's Jane Saint here—'

I interrupted her way too enthusiastically. 'Listen, it's Steve. I know this is crazy, but I'm in the area and . . .'

'I'm sorry I can't get to the phone right now so please leave a message after the tone.'

On arriving home in Shepherd's Bush I spent five drunken minutes trying to remove my contact lenses, only stopping when I remembered that I'd had laser surgery at the beginning of the year and hadn't worn lenses for over six months. I slumped into bed wishing desperately that I had barely more than two hours of coked-up, restless sleep ahead of me.

TWO

'**P**LEASE DO BE FUCKING QUIET, James,' hissed Chuck through clenched teeth, spitting out each individual syllable. My fifteen fellow research department MDs seated at the boardroom's impressive oblong table all looked at poor James. Most had a slight smile that betrayed the joy they were feeling at their colleague's obvious discomfort. Whilst the boss was berating someone else, they could momentarily rest easy . . . and Chuck's diatribe wasn't finished.

'Stop being so damn negative and start offering me solutions, not problems, OK? This little sub-prime issue is going to blow over and most of the people around this table will still be getting a decent bonus this year and hopefully next year too. However, some of you, especially those who are telling all and sundry that Geldlust bank is in big fucking trouble, might not even be here to receive said bonus – so let's start being a little bit more positive, OK?'

There it was again. I was feeling like a leprous crack baby

on cold turkey, but even through my debilitating, soul-destroying hangover I knew there was simply no way in hell it was just my imagination. My boss, Chuck, had blatantly singled me out with his steely stare when he produced that last little threat. The fat fuck was on my case. The malicious, power-hungry cocksucker was going to do me – it was just a question of when, not if. This was definitely not a delusion, unquestionably not just a product of my fetid, addled brain. The simple fact was that I'd been slapdash. On a couple of occasions I'd sent my column to *thelondonpaper* from my work email address rather than my hotmail account by mistake. Everyone knows that work emails are randomly checked by Compliance and I remember thinking at the time that I was probably done for.

Then there was the little fact that two of my colleagues had recently found out what I was up to. About two months before, my secretary Claire had found a column that I'd left on the printer during an especially virulent hangover. She'd soon put two and two together and no amount of bullshit was going to persuade her that I wasn't the increasingly notorious columnist 'Cityboy'. Benjamin, the oil team's graduate trainee, had also worked it out after I'd made the mistake of drunkenly recounting a story to him about bumping into two clients at a fancy dress party I'd attended at a stately home in Shropshire. When he saw the same tale appear in *thelondonpaper* two weeks later he didn't have to be a rocket scientist to work out my dual identity. I'd taken both Claire and Benjamin into what I referred to as 'my inner circle of trust' but the simple fact is that no one keeps a secret in an office. Clearly, one of them had got arseholed at some work knees-up and word had now reached Chuck – probably via the secretary network. If you want to know anything at Geldlust bank, or any major firm for that matter, first port of call should always be the secretaries.

If I was right, then this was truly appalling. I understood exactly what Chuck's evil little game was. It was September and I'd been working my arse off all year. He obviously knew about my column, so he'd probably checked out my website too. That meant he would have seen the backlog of articles I'd written – some of which were scathing about Geldlust and, indeed, him. Christ, I'd written one entitled 'Herding Cats' in which I'd mocked an appalling, ineffectual management chat he'd delivered a few months before. I'd actually referred to him as 'a failed broker who was too expensive to fire' and even mentioned the old adage that the scum always rises to the top. Make no mistake, I was in big effing trouble.

As I sat there among the other MDs, with a film of nervous, toxic sweat rapidly spreading over my forehead, my mind went into overdrive trying to anticipate Chuck's likely agenda. It soon became clear that he was going to do the old City trick of sacking me just before bonus day. That way his department would benefit from all the commission I generated until the last possible moment without reducing the firm's bonus pool one iota. No doubt the flabby, vicious wanker was looking forward to the look of shock on my face when he handed me a P45 instead of half a million quid.

Of course, any objections I might raise would be totally pointless as I'd clearly broken about three contractual restrictions. If Chuck wanted to play hardball there was every chance I wouldn't just be kicked out but also be classified as a 'bad leaver'. That would mean I'd forfeit nearly all of the equity in Geldlust bank that I'd accrued over the years. A third of my previous three bonuses had been paid to me in Geldlust shares that I wasn't able to touch for three years and those would automatically not vest if it could be proved that I had in any way badmouthed my former employer. That wasn't going to be too hard to do seeing as there was a year's worth of columns out there stating what a bunch of worthless scumbags Cityboys were.

I cursed my stupidity at having started writing the column in the first place. My egotistical urge to spill the beans on the financial world was going to cost me not just my job but also about three hundred grand. The column might have been a kind of confessional for me, allowing me to get off my chest the countless misgivings I had about my chosen career, but now it was going to hit me where it hurt most – my wallet.

I sat there in the hallowed directors' boardroom on the eighth floor playing with my food, feeling far too rancid to even consider eating the rich, creamy dish festering in front of me. I'd only been a managing director for just over a year and was happy not to get involved in the tedious point-scoring discussion that was taking place around me. There seemed to be an unofficial competition going on amongst my colleagues as to who could spend the longest licking Chuck's sweaty, pock-marked arse. They were being so enthusiastic that Chuck was going to think he'd accidentally ordered a colonic along with his beef stroganoff. It was the same story at every one of these 'quarterly performance meetings' but, of course, this time it was even worse than usual as bonuses would be being decided within a month. James had clearly screwed up big-time by querying how Geldlust was going to be impacted by the sub-prime crisis that had caused a run on the Northern Rock Building Society just the week before.

I took no pleasure from his obvious distress. He was just another mindless drone sleepwalking his way towards a bloated middle age of varicose veins, gout and coronary embolism. At least the poor bastard actually gave a shit about his job. For years I'd viewed my pinstriped drudgery as nothing more than an unpleasant stopgap that I had to endure before I could trip the light fantastic. The non-stop pretence that I actually harboured any ambition other than the procurement of sufficient cash to be able to waltz around the planet whilst still young enough to know the steps was tiring me out. I just needed to survive one more bonus round – one more officially sanctioned robbery from the unsuspecting shareholders of Geldlust bank – and then I could spend my remaining years sucking the marrow out of this all too short life.

I remembered how I'd promised myself that I'd only

throw away five years chasing the dollar before pursuing something more worthwhile, something I vaguely believed in. The day before I started at a piss-poor French investment bank I'd ceremoniously removed my silver hoop earrings, ponytail and goatee beard – the last vestiges of my previous hippy identity. That had been over ten years ago. After five years of selling my soul my annual pay packet had hit £350,000 and friends and parents alike had convinced me that, in the absence of a serious alternative, I should keep milking the system. My elder brother, a fund manager at a sleepy mutual who'd conned some greedy salesman into giving me my first job, had left finance himself but even he had argued that I should cling on to the gravy train with all my might while it was still steaming along. He and most of my senior colleagues had been saying for years that the party was going to come to an end soon and that chaps like me needed to make hay while the sun shone. Christ, my whole life had been dictated by a series of tiresome clichés! But now the end was in sight – just one more big score and then I could start living . . . really living.

'I was only trying to say that there's gonna be a lot of resentment . . . from equities, corporate finance, commodities and bonds . . . if the bonus pool for all is hit just because the boys in structured finance . . . well, specifically, in mortgage-backed securities . . . screwed up big-time,' spluttered James, trying to sound confident but failing dismally. That one ill-thought-out comment was probably going to cost him about forty grand come December and he knew it. He was flapping badly and the other MDs could hardly disguise their glee at his schoolboy error.

'As I said,' replied Chuck through gritted teeth, '*most* of the people around this table are gonna be all right. *Most*, but not all.'

Oh, Christ, I swear he looked at me again. I was clearly going to be fired and almost a million pounds less well off than I'd estimated come January '08. I could feel the colour drain out of my face as I took on board this new financial reality.

'Are you OK there, Steve? You're looking a little peaky,' sneered Chuck.

I was feeling absolutely shattered and the black rings under my bloodshot eyes were signalling to anyone who had the misfortune to survey my blotchy face that the previous night had been disgustingly debauched.

'Er . . . truth be told, I'm not a hundred per cent. I've got this nasty flu that's been going around. But I came in because I didn't want to miss this important meeting and because my clients really need guidance in these tricky times. Anyway, I just want to say that I, for one, am not concerned about this Northern Rock thing – my customers are still trading and I know that Geldlust will reward those who bring home the bacon.' Phew.

After another fifteen minutes of meaningless wibble Chuck indicated that the meeting was over by simply standing up and saying, 'OK, that's it. Keep up the good work, guys.' Before he reached the door he turned round and said, 'I hope to see you all at the next meeting in three months' time . . . though who knows who will be here and who won't, eh?' He was looking at me again, the sadistic wanker. He was smiling but it was the evil grin of a concentration camp warden about to fire a bullet into my brain. The game was surely up. He wasn't even being subtle now. I was doomed.

We all followed Chuck out towards the lifts, a couple of our number asking tiresome sycophantic questions as we did so. I sidled off from the group to the toilets and splashed water on my face. Then I stared at my pale, sickly countenance in the mirror and took several deep breaths. After a few minutes of garbled introspection I headed down the stairs to the trading floor to see my trader for our usual Friday afternoon chat about what the next week held for the ever-exciting utilities sector.

This was, after all, an integral part of my job as a research analyst at Geldlust – a mid-tier German investment bank with all the long-term prospects of a turkey on Christmas Eve. These deluded Continental firms kept on trying to compete with the American bulge bracket banks like Goldman Sucks and Organ Stanley but were merely wasting their shareholders' capital in the pursuit of an impossible dream. We Cityboys simply wanted to rinse these European dimwits of their cash before their misguided executives realised that they didn't have an icicle's chance in hell of beating the big boys. Fortunately, my team of analysts was a big fish in a small pond. We had a solid reputation for advising our clients to invest in sensible stocks and were one of the highest ranked teams at Geldlust. Day in day out we told fund managers across the world whether shares in the thirty or so listed European electricity, gas and water companies were good bets or bad ones, and for some sick reason they took us seriously and executed many of their utility share trades through us. Geldlust made about €15 million of commission annually from trading utility shares and the whole team hoped to see some of that come December . . . unfortunately, I was becoming ever more doubtful that I'd see a penny.

I tentatively pushed open the glass doors to the vast trading floor. I had spent the morning cocooned in the research department desperately avoiding any contact with salespeople, traders or clients, and I was immediately overcome by the sheer energy that now faced me. As I entered the humming, buzzing heart of Geldlust investment bank a wave of nausea swept over me but I suppressed the urge to run away and resolutely stumbled towards the far corner where the traders sat. I passed row upon row of desks behind which sat hundreds of men and the occasional woman shouting into phones, all looking as if they took their job extremely seriously. Someone was talking on the mike about an explosion at an oil refinery in Nigeria and its impact on the oil price. Salespeople were shouting clients' orders at the traders: 'Fifty thou BP to sell at 546', 'Hundred thou Next at 954 to buy', and so on. All the commotion was causing my headache to intensify exponentially. I kept my head bowed as I negotiated my way past the salespeople chatting away excitedly to their clients, praying that no one would draw attention to my plight.

''ello, 'ello, 'ello – what have we here? Everybody, look what the cat dragged in! Shit, Steve, either you had a massive one yesterday or I just accidentally entered the space–time continuum and am meeting a version of you that's twenty years older! Fuckin' 'ell! What did you get up to last night?' shouted my ever-thoughtful trader Gary for all to hear. Everyone within about twenty feet who wasn't on the phone turned round and stared at me. Several nudged their neighbours who, on looking up, giggled to themselves. It's at times like these that you find out about yourself.

'Dude, you're not looking too hot yourself. At least when I wake up tomorrow morning I'll be back to being my gorgeous self but you, my friend, will still be a fat, ugly bastard!'

'Oooh,' trilled Gary's fellow traders at my journeyman riposte.

'Mate, that's not what your missus says to me when she's whisperin' sweet nuffinks in my ear every night.'

'Well, I did tell her to get her eyes looked at . . . and anyway, she's a *Star Wars* fan and always had a thing about Jabba the Hutt,' I replied half-heartedly.

'She's told you what she calls my knob?'

'Yeah . . . she's told me a few names: Tiny Tim, the angry inch, the acorn . . .'

I suspect both of us were no longer finding this verbal

banter much fun and were only continuing it because we had an audience and didn't want to lose face. One of us had to bring the nonsense to an end or it could go on for ever. I decided to do the honours.

'Anyway, enough of that horseshit. I've got something even more interesting to talk about than your penis – the European utilities sector.'

Gary's fellow traders saw that the game was over and swivelled round in their ergonomically designed black leather chairs to assess what had happened to the stocks they traded in the previous twenty-five seconds.

I proceeded to bore Gary about the potentially price-sensitive events that were to occur in my sector over the upcoming week. But as I banged on about 'a pre-closed-season trading statement from United Utilities' and 'a merger update from the Spanish electricity regulator' I could sense myself feeling more and more uneasy. My mouth continued talking shite, but my mind drifted off to what lay in store for me come December. *I'll be fucked if I'm gonna just sit around on my bony arse waiting to get the chop*. I needed to have it out with Chuck there and then and find out what my fate was to be. There was no way he was going to just string me along paying me a measly £10,000 a month until December and then promptly give me a zero bonus and sack me. If he thought I was gonna sit back and give him that pleasure he had another fucking think coming.

I'd always had a tense, difficult relationship with Chuck. I'd once made the mistake of beating him at squash and he'd never forgiven me. I despised him and the bank he worked for and I think he sensed this. The only reason he tolerated me and paid me half-decent bonuses was because I was bringing in the commission and corporate fees. The more I thought about his smug demeanour the more I refused to just sleepwalk blindly towards my dismissal. I could see he was going to love humiliating me and ruining my plans for a better life. I just needed that one big bonus and I'd reach the two million savings target that I'd made when I first entered this shady business. If I could just last another four months more I could leave this job a winner with my head held high. I could prove my doubters wrong whilst showing my colleagues how to quit whilst ahead as they had all promised themselves a hundred times. If Chuck had his way I'd leave with my tail between my legs with no prospect of ever getting another job in the City. If Chuck had his way I'd not only forfeit my bonus but lose all my Geldlust equity as well. As my spiel drew to a close I vowed that I would confront Chuck right then about my situation. Since Gary's eyes were beginning to glaze over, it was probably no bad thing.

'Suzie, I need a quick word with Chuck,' I said with all the false authority I could muster.

'Oh, Steve, I'm sorry but he's just left for Heathrow. He's on the six p.m. flight to New York. Back on Tuesday,' she said, fluttering her eyelids as she always seemed to when we spoke. Suzie was an attractive thirty-year-old Essex girl with bobbed dark hair and big brown eyes. She was the kind of bubbly, fun-loving person who'd have joined the Spice Girls without a second's thought had there been a vacancy. She'd probably have been called Happy Spice or Giggly Spice or some such bollocks. There had always been a funny vibe between us ever since we'd had a lashed-up snog at the previous year's office Christmas party. We'd been sharing a cigarette outside and suddenly she'd lunged for me. I seem to remember that it was actually a lot of fun but it hadn't gone any further and neither of us had mentioned it since.

'Shit,' I said without thinking and turned round to consider my options, which essentially involved calling him on his mobile or waiting until Tuesday.

After I'd taken a few steps away from Suzie I suddenly stopped dead in my tracks and slowly turned round. An idea was forming in my confused brain.

'Listen, Suzie, I didn't really come up here to talk to Chuck,' I lied. 'The truth of the matter is that I came to see you.'

Her eyes visibly widened and she seemed to blush slightly. She looked around to make sure she had no audience and said, 'You're having a laugh, intcha?'

'Not at all. In fact, I was wondering if you're free tonight for a drink. I think we should leave this hell-hole at half past five sharp and get properly bladdered together. Maybe go for dinner at Nobu or something . . .'

After a moment's pause she smiled sweetly and said, 'That doesn't sound such a bad idea . . .'

Three

'DARLING, PASS THE CIGARETTES, WILL you?'

'Oh, "darling" is it now? You say the occasional word to me for nine months and then suddenly it's all lovey dovey. You really are a card, you are!' cackled Suzie as she leant over to get the fags, the top of her pert arse revealing itself briefly from under the covers.

The night had worked out perfectly. The first vodka and tonic at the Fine Line had begun the process of making me feel almost human again. As I got steadily drunker, the feeling that my soul had been ripped out of me by Beelzebub himself gradually became a distant memory. We were genuinely having a proper giggle and even managed a little kiss in the back of the cab on the way to Nobu in Mayfair. Over black cod in miso and a two-hundred-quid bottle of champagne I mentioned that I thought it would be wise if we went back to mine, since she lived in darkest Essex and my place was only twenty minutes away. Somewhat to my surprise, she concurred. As soon as we were back, after more drunken snogs in the back of the cab, I led her upstairs.

It was the next morning, when we were both still a little befuddled, that I decided to try to extract the information necessary for my nefarious plan to work.

'By the way, it's Chuck's fiftieth birthday next month, isn't it?' I said, lighting two cigarettes and passing one to her, the ashtray balanced precariously on my chest.

'Yes, October the twelfth.'

'Well, some of the MDs and I want to do something a little bit different for Chuck this year. We've been talking about it for a while now. Basically, we want to make a special birthday presentation pack. We'd like to use PowerPoint and we're thinking several of the sheets should have a photo of him and his wife or kids on them. We'd also like to compose a few funny graphs showing Geldlust's stellar profit growth since he joined and that kind of bullshit. The problem is that none of us have got any photos of him . . . but I know there are loads on his computer, since its screensaver shows a whole gallery of them on loop, doesn't it . . .'

'Yessss . . .' There was already a certain suspicious tone in her voice.

'Well, I know it's a bit tricky, but if you gave me the password to his computer then I could get those photos off it and we could get this special birthday presentation pack made and—'

'There is no way in hell I'm giving you his password!' she exclaimed with a look of utter horror on her face. My heart sank, my hopes of breaking into his computer and discovering his bonus plans for me rapidly fading. Fortunately, before I had to resign myself to simply waiting until December to find out my fate, she relented . . . a little.

'But it is a lovely idea – quite a surprise really, coming from you guys. Didn't know you had the heart. What I will do is go with you on Monday and we'll get the photos together, OK?'

'Yeah, absolutely. That's fine. It's just about getting the photos on to a memory stick, that's all.'

'Well, OK. Now let's see if that's a memory stick you got down there or if you're just pleased to see me . . .'

So, on Monday at precisely 7 p.m., as we had planned, I stood up and walked nonchalantly towards Chuck's office for my secret rendezvous with Suzie. The weekend had been a lot of fun and when she'd left after a boozy pub lunch on Sunday I'd felt a genuine affection for her. But this was business and I needed to forget emotion for the time being.

I studiously avoided eye contact with my diligent co-workers, who sat at their desks fretting over balance sheets that didn't balance and lives that suffered from the same defect, and passed two junior analysts around the water cooler chatting about their weekend. One was an officious, limp-dicked little creep who'd always struck me as having some sinister agenda, whilst the other was a boorish, rugby-playing thug who foolishly believed brute force would make up for his lack of brain cells. When they saw me they lowered their voices and then dipped their heads in an unspoken acknowledgement of my presence. The almost imperceptible nod with which I responded asserted my superior status, as was appropriate for an MD. My heart was quickening and, despite my best efforts, I could feel my gait becoming stiff and unnatural. Fortunately the last few desks before Chuck's office were bereft of life.

'Hello, my dear, how are you?' I whispered conspiratorially when I finally reached Suzie's domain.

'Oh, not too bad. I spent the weekend with this right joker and he put a smile back on my face.'

'Really? I'd like to meet him. He sounds pretty damn cool.'

'No, not really . . . and he was rubbish in bed.'

'Yeah, well, that's the way the cookie crumbles. I'd advise you to meet a real man at some point – stop wasting your time with these pencil-neck losers! Anyway, let's implement plan X.'

Suzie looked around somewhat nervously and saw that there was no one in the immediate vicinity. Her desk was just outside Chuck's office, which was in the far corner of the research floor. There were two other offices between it and the open-plan area; it was relatively well concealed. Like two mischievous schoolchildren breaking into the head-master's office we sloped in as unobtrusively as possible. My heart was pounding away despite the fact that we had a perfectly legitimate excuse should we be caught. Once we were in and the door had closed behind us Suzie immediately grabbed me and planted her lips on mine. After acquiescing for a few seconds I pushed us apart.

'Come on, gorgeous, we need to be a bit careful now . . . If you get caught having a snog with me your reputation really will be ruined.'

Suzie raised her eyebrows with a look of mock surprise at my caution. She was clearly enjoying the danger but for the moment I definitely had bigger fish to fry.

We both crept round Chuck's huge desk. It was covered in files, documents and a photo of Chuck with his wife and kids in a park. I'd met Mrs Johnson at a couple of work events and she ticked all the boxes of a classic investment banker's wife – well manicured, expensively dressed, extremely polite and never a hair out of place. Anna Wintour with a gnarly stick up her arse.

As Suzie fired up the computer and reached the screen demanding a password I theatrically covered my eyes with my left hand and turned my head to the right. Of course, I ensured that there was a slight gap between my thumb and my face so that I could just see what she was typing through the bottom corner of my left eye: R – – L I – G – T O – – S.

Bollocks! I didn't catch it all. She had touch-typed the password and it hadn't been easy to pick up even those letters. Still, it gave me something to work on. All I needed to do now was go through the charade of putting Chuck's photos on to a memory stick and then I could come back later and sort out the rest. As soon as I'd downloaded the photos I left, having told Suzie that I had to see my parents for dinner. In fact, I went straight to the nearest pub, which as always on a Monday was virtually empty, settled into a dingy corner with a pint of wifebeater and a pen and paper, and began trying to work out what the hell Chuck's password was.

Rillingtons . . . Religiontones . . . Reliving tonnes . . .

I began to curse my inability to do crosswords or any kinds of word games. After about twenty frustrating minutes I was seriously considering going home when I suddenly spied something on the television suspended high on the wall to the left of the bar. It was tuned to MTV as usual, and playing some black and white footage of the Beatles performing on the Ed Sullivan show. I sat back and enjoyed their rendition of 'I want to hold your hand'. Just a minute! What was Chuck always saying about the Beatles? Ah yes, that only choirboy fags liked them, and that the Rolling Stones wiped the floor with them. Of course! Chuck was always banging on about his favourite rock group despite being frequently told over a few glasses of Sancerre that he should consider listening to musicians who'd been on this earth for less than sixty years. If Chuck wasn't waxing lyrical about the Rolling Stones he was boring everyone senseless about how there had never been a better guitarist on this planet than Jimi Hendrix.

With a big grin on my face I left the pub and walked back to the office, swiped my way through the security barriers and took the lift to the research floor. I'd already prepared the excuse that I'd forgotten my bag should I bump into any colleagues who might otherwise have been surprised at my new-found diligence.

Much to my horror, and despite its being around 8 p.m., Jane was still at her desk. Jane was outrageously conscientious despite the fact that her family connections meant there was simply no way she was ever going to be treated badly. Her uncle was a large American bank's overall chief of investment banking whilst her father had just been appointed head of the Financial Services Authority – the City regulator. She would have got her job had she merely succeeded in gaining a third in Land Economy at Loughborough Poly. As it was she had managed to leave Queen's College, Oxford with a starred first in economics. Still, there were plenty of smart cookies trying to enter investment banking in the boom year of 2006 and the fact that she had got her foot in the door was mostly due to good, old-fashioned nepotism. Hell, at least a third of the people in our department had got their initial entry into this money machine via a friend or relative. Yet for some sick reason, despite her virtually invulnerable position, she still worked like a Trojan day in day out.

I desperately racked my brain for something 'appropriate' to say. (This was the first time we'd been alone since our little tryst.) She looked beautiful as she worked away at her spreadsheet. Her long auburn hair rested on her shoulders and there was something very attractive about seeing her so intensely engrossed in her work. A familiar feeling stirred in my loins. When I was within about ten feet of our shared desk she lifted her head and fixed me with her green, feline eyes. She was clearly shocked that I was in the office at such an ungodly hour.

'Hi, Steve ... erm, have you forgotten something?' She hardly even pretended not to be astonished that I'd turned up at such a late hour.

'Hi, Jane. Working late, eh? Well, keep it up ... I remember at your stage in my career I was often in the office until ten,' I lied. I felt self-conscious – this was after all *my* grad and I was *her* boss and this conversation was taking place in *our* office. Our previous encounter had been completely by chance. We'd met at a club in King's Cross and after the initial embarrassment of bumping into a colleague when we were both clearly off our heads on Ecstasy we started really enjoying each other's company. We managed to lose our pals and before you could say 'sexual harassment' our lips met during a somewhat incongruous slow dance whilst everyone around us jumped around to some nose-bleed techno. We had melted into each other, and aided by the elephantine quantity of MDMA I'd consumed, my feelings for her grew stronger with every kiss. After about ten minutes she pushed me away and told me she had to go. I'd followed her out like a lost puppy, and I'd lost my beautiful girlfriend as a result.

'Really?' She didn't look convinced. 'By the way, I got a call on Friday at around four a.m. I don't suppose you know anything about that, do you?'

She was staring directly into my eyes, seeking out any indication of guilt. Fortunately, I had prepared for the question and so looked suitably unfazed as I responded: 'Me? Call you three hours before you're due at work? I don't think so. What could I possibly want with you at the dead of night?' I grinned.

'No . . . I didn't think it was you. Probably just a wrong number.'

There was an awkward silence. We both looked at the floor and then Jane started moving some documents around in the filing cabinet next to her desk. I sat down opposite her and wondered how I could excuse myself and then walk into Chuck's office. I logged on to my computer and checked a few emails. It would be so much easier if she'd just leave. My heart wouldn't stop pounding; a film of sweat appeared on my forehead. After another few minutes of pretending to work it was time for decisive action. I logged off and stood up.

'I've just remembered I left the EDF file in Chuck's office. We were talking about pitching for the placement. And I might use the phone when I'm in there . . . there's a confidential chat I've got to have with the head of sales in New York. If you're not here when I come back I'll see you tomorrow.'

'No probs. See you later.'

As soon as I was in Chuck's office I locked the door behind me, then crept to his computer and pressed 'Ctrl', 'Alt' and 'Delete' together until a box appeared in the centre of the screen requiring a user name and a password. The username was, as always at Geldlust, the first six letters of first name and surname together – so 'chuckjohnso' in this case. I typed in the password 'rollingstones' and smiled to myself as Chuck's computer leapt into action. If I searched around his work email inbox and maybe checked out the latest spreadsheets he'd been working on I was pretty sure I'd find out if I was going to get a polite 'fuck off' or half a million quid come December. My fingers were actually shaking with nervous excitement. This time, if I was caught, there'd be no easy excuses.

After about ten minutes I hadn't found anything relevant to me. However, I had discovered a lot of extremely interesting things about a possible merger with another bank, a forthcoming job cull in the corporate finance department and some concerns the chief executive had about Geldlust's exposure to the sub-prime issue.

Frustrated, I decided that it was worth checking whether Chuck had a roving email account, since that was more likely to contain something juicy than his work one, which, of course, was monitored just like mine. I double-clicked on his internet explorer icon and then used the history button to discover what he'd recently been accessing. After Google, the work intranet and a skiing holiday company's website there was hotmail, which looked promising, but when I double-clicked another password was demanded. My shoulders slumped with disappointment, and I was about to go back to Chuck's spreadsheets when a moment of genius touched me.

I typed in 'jimihendrix'. Bingo! I now had access to all of Chuck's personal emails.

I felt like a spy as I read his personal emails to his wife, his kids and his friends. I was becoming more nervous with each passing moment, and kept looking up from the computer half expecting to see Chuck march in all guns blazing. Suddenly, after another five minutes of trembling excitement, I came across the email I was looking for . . . or at least the one I feared existed. It had the word 'Cityboy' in the title and was from the overall head of investment banking.

The Compliance Department has confirmed that Steve Jones wrote an email to someone at a News International email address with an article attached that two days later appeared in the anonymous column 'Cityboy' that features every Friday in *thelondonpaper*. This is definitely a sackable offence as he has criticised the bank in numerous articles (and for that matter you – read about yourself and Geldlust on his website www.cityboy.biz). Although he has not named Geldlust our legal department tells me it still constitutes 'criticism of parent company'. Compliance has also confirmed we will be fully justified in defining him as a 'bad leaver', which will mean that he forfeits all his vested equity (approx. £350K). As discussed, taking into account the cost-cutting we need to do before the end of the year, firing Steve seems like the best course of action. So I think we should include him in December's pre-bonus 'unlucky list' but it's up to you. If you don't want to do that because he's bringing in the commission we could just warn him and demand he stops writing the column.

The only words in the reply from Chuck were 'Steve goes on 15 December'. I could envisage him licking his lips with unconstrained pleasure.

I slumped down in Chuck's seat. Christ almighty. My life was falling apart. I'd lost the love of my life. I was going to get fired before bonus time. I'd also never get another job in the City, which was the only type of work I was remotely qualified for even if I found most of it desperately tedious. Worse still, I was going to forfeit all the share options and equity I'd accrued over the previous three years. My plans to sail away into the sunset next year safe in the knowledge that I had enough cash to last for decades out there were disintegrating around me. What should I do? I couldn't let that slimy bastard Chuck win this game.

I don't know why I decided to read some more of Chuck's emails. I had nothing better to do and, as *The Art of War* written by the sixth-century Chinese warlord Sun Tzu (required reading for any would-be stockbroker) claimed, informational advantage is vital in any battle with a superior opponent. I was not going to take this lying down. The war was not over yet.

I began reading through his recent emails. It was the seventh I checked out that would change everything.

Four

From: Gabriel Llosa (Gabriel.llosa007@hotmail.com.co)
Sent: 18 September 2007 08:16:25
To: chuckgordonjohnson@hotmail.co.uk

Mr Johnson, we are interested in buying 200,000,000 shares in Unilever (sterling not euro). As usual, the payment currency will be US dollar. The settlement date will be 15 October. Commission will be the standard 20 per cent. Please contact us to finalise this trade. Gabriel.

What the fuck was this? To the untrained eye it could be a perfectly normal email but on closer scrutiny it didn't make sense. First of all, a head of research should not be taking orders from clients – especially not using his hotmail account. Second, this seemed too large an order to be conceivable from a single individual. I happened to know that Unilever had around three billion shares in issues, that its shares traded at around £17 and its market capitalisation was hence about £50 billion. So Mr Llosa's order was theoretically worth £3.4 billion. This would effectively mean that some comedian was buying almost 7 per cent of a massive multi-national corporation. Third, settlement date is normally T+5 i.e. five days after the order has been made and not almost a month away. Finally, commission is generally 0.2 per cent so what was this nonsense about 20 per cent? This was really fucking weird.

I decided to forward the email to my hotmail account, and I also printed it out. I was becoming increasingly nervous in Chuck's office: the longer I was there the greater the chance that I'd be caught. After restoring everything to how I'd found it I crept out and quietly closed the door, but as I walked back on to the open-plan office floor I saw that Jane was still working away. My God! It was now around nine o'clock and she was still at the computer. *What is wrong with her?* I froze and wondered what the hell to do. Jane looked up from her spreadsheet and her eyes caught mine. I had to style this out, but my steps were stilted as I walked towards her.

'Well, looks like we're in with a chance with the EDF placing. Brad in the New York office thinks there's huge institutional interest and that the French government owes us a favour so fingers crossed. Great news, eh?'

Jane ignored my bluster completely. With an assurance way beyond her years, she said, 'How about we go for a drink?' I was flabbergasted. Superficially, this could just have been a friendly colleague wanting a quiet chinwag in the pub, but there was something in her manner that told me we weren't going to be discussing free cash flow yields. This was a Lauren Bacall/ Humphrey Bogart moment if ever there was one.

'A . . . a drink?' I stuttered. 'A drink would be . . . er, interesting.' I had to play this cool. I was after all her boss and thirteen years older than her. I was supposed to be the one in charge here.

'Good. Let's go then.' She logged off her computer and we gathered our stuff and left without uttering another word. I had no idea what to expect. She could be about to express her undying love for me . . . or, more likely, try to pick my brains about her potential career path. For the moment I could forget my impending financial disaster – there were more important things to think about.

'So, you're sure it wasn't you who called me? Because Friday morning, excuse me for saying this, you didn't look too hot. You looked like you had been up until at least four a.m.' She giggled. A perfect, sophisticated little laugh. She was worryingly sexy and she knew it.

'You're putting two and two together and making five . . . but . . . what if it had been me? What if I had wanted to come and see you then?'

The fifth pint of wifebeater was clearly beginning to make its presence felt. There was no way I should have been saying this kind of thing. But we had been flirting outrageously prior to this gambit. She'd matched me drink for drink and our gazes were beginning to linger longer and longer. We were becoming more tactile. Her hand had rested on my knee several times for way longer than necessary. I had almost forgotten my woes.

'Well, that depends . . . on whether I already had a man in my bed or not.'

Fuck me! This looked like game on.

Suddenly she changed the subject. She was totally in charge of the situation. 'Anyway, what were you really doing in Chuck's office? I happen to know Geldlust pulled out of the Electricité de France pitch last week. So why don't you tell me what you were really up to?'

I looked into her eyes for what seemed like hours and then thought what the hell. I suppose I wanted to embroil her in my recent discovery and, in so doing, create a kind of confidential intimacy. The devil's urine was most certainly encouraging me to make impulsive decisions.

'If you wanna know the truth . . . I was spying on Chuck. I think he's up to no good. Check out this email. To tell the truth, I don't know what it's all about but I'm going to find out. OK, so here's your test for the day. First, why does this email make no sense, and, second, what the hell is he up to? I'm going to the bog and I expect an answer on my return.' As I swerved my way to the toilets I smiled. I was enjoying the brief return to the master/student relationship that should theoretically always exist.

After an enormously satisfying horse piss I sauntered back in. Jane was studying the email with a look of concern on her face. When I sat down opposite her she looked up, somewhat startled. She had clearly been completely absorbed by what she'd read.

'Well . . . this doesn't seem to make much sense at all. Chuck isn't likely to be taking such big orders and the commission rate and settlement date seem wrong.'

'Well done. That was the easy part. Now, what the hell does it mean?'

'I haven't a clue. Maybe it is just a massive order. Maybe it's totally legit? Why don't you ask him?'

'Whoa there! And reveal that I've been snooping in his office? No, this is something dodgy. I'm going to get to the bottom of it first and then I'm gonna confront him.'

'Well, I think you're probably barking up the wrong tree. Seriously, I think you need to be very careful with this. Don't go around making wild accusations, or you could come a cropper. Anyway, I've just remembered I'm on the mike tomorrow chatting about Red Electrica. Shouldn't be too hungover for that – it's only the third time I've addressed the trading floor.'

'Come on, fuck it! Stick around. Let's have a laugh.' I couldn't believe she was about to head home. Everything seemed to be going swimmingly. Surely all our flirting was leading somewhere?

'Nope. Must dash. I'll see you tomorrow.' She got up to leave. I stood up to follow suit. 'No. Finish your pint. There's no point.' There was something unfaltering and imperious about the way she uttered those last three words. It was clearly no use whatsoever trying to persuade her that I should accompany her home.

I sat down, feeling deflated. But suddenly she did something that lit up my night, my week, my whole fucking year! She looked around the near-empty pub and, on seeing no one from the office, bent down and kissed me on the lips. A full, deep kiss. And with that she left.

I was stunned. I wanted to follow her out but I was stuck to my chair. I half stood up but then pulled myself down. I did nothing.

Jane had left the print-out of the email on the table. I picked it up again. The answer lay there somewhere. I just needed to focus, but the Stella wasn't helping matters. I nursed my pint and went through it again for the tenth time.

Suddenly through my bleary alcoholic blur I noticed the suffix to Señor Llosa's hotmail account. It was '.com.co'. Taking into account the Hispanic name I guessed that he was writing from Colombia. Now, I couldn't remember much about the bi-annual computer-based test the compliance department obliged us to do about the mechanics of money laundering (especially since that year I'd got Jane to do it for me) but I did recall some parts of the one-hour compliance seminar on the subject we had to endure each year. I remembered that Colombia, along with Nigeria and various former Soviet republics, was notably high risk when it came to that particular crime.

OK, so if that's Chuck's game what did the rest of this

email mean? What was it that Unilever did? I knew it was a big global company and I also knew that it had its fingers in many pies. I immediately googled it on my BlackBerry and checked out Wikipedia's description. The first sentence made everything crystal clear.

> Unilever is an Anglo-Dutch multinational corporation that owns many of the world's consumer product brands in foods, beverages, cleaning agents and personal care products.

Unilever was one of the biggest providers of *cleaning products* in the world. Oh yes, I get it! Unilever was the perfect code word for someone who wanted to launder cash. It also had a dual listing in England and Holland and so had shares traded in both sterling and euros – making it easy to state which currency was the preferred option. I looked again at the email. Suddenly, everything fitted into place. This had nothing whatsoever to do with Unilever. Mr Llosa wanted to launder 200 million US dollars by 15 October. Despite a lack of incriminating evidence I suspected that this cash had not been earned by selling cookies door to door. In fact, seeing as I was a major investor in Colombia's finest export myself, I had an intuitive feeling that this was drug money. The final part of the email suggested that Chuck and whoever else at Geldlust was in on the scam would be receiving a fee of 20 per cent for this transaction. That meant Chuck and his dubious colleagues would be sharing $40 million for providing this service. Nice work if you can get it, I thought.

I sat there wide-eyed, trying to compute this unbelievable information. What the fuck was Chuck up to? How greedy had he become? Who else at Geldlust was in on this dodgy dealing? My God, this was truly mindboggling . . . this was inconceivable . . . this was an opportunity.

It was at that moment that I formulated my genius plan . . . one that couldn't possibly go wrong.

Five

'HI, SUZIE. COULD I HAVE a quick word with Chuck, please?' Despite the fact that I sat only thirty yards from Chuck's office I used the telephone for this enquiry so as to remove the need to chat face to face with Suzie. I really didn't want that situation to complicate what was now the main agenda.

'Hello, lover boy. I'm afraid he's in meetings all day. He's also jet-lagged like a bastard cos he arrived at Heathrow on the red-eye at seven o'clock this morning. Frankly my dear, unless you want to have your arse bitten off I'd contact him tomorrow.'

'I've got something pretty damn urgent I need to speak to him about. It will only take a couple of minutes. Surely there's a space in his diary at some point today?'

'Well . . . if you came just before his lunch appointment at around one twenty-five he might be able to squeeze you in. Talking of squeezing you in, how about a rematch tonight? I think I might have a space in my busy diary between about nine o'clock and midnight . . .'

'Yeah . . . why not? Sounds like a sensible idea. Oh, shit. Sorry, I just remembered . . . I've got a dinner party I've got to go to. Let's make it tomorrow, OK?'

'OK, tomorrow it is. See you then, lover boy.' Cool. I think I actually got away with that lie.

At precisely 1.24 p.m. I arrived at Chuck's door. I'd been watching the clock for the previous two hours. Suzie was on her lunch break, which was lucky as I definitely wasn't in the mood for banter. I could see through the glass door that Chuck was ranting away on the phone. He looked stressed and tired. I remember thinking that this might not be the best time to carry out my plan and turn what already looked like a bad day into a considerably worse one.

Chuck's phone call seemed to go on for ever and he made no effort to terminate it despite acknowledging my presence with a dismissive wave of the hand. After about five minutes of standing around like a spare prick at a wedding I swallowed my brave pills and knocked on his door. He looked up angrily but still deigned to beckon me in, and I entered his office trying to maintain my composure despite feeling an anticipatory nervousness that was unrivalled by any exam, fight or drugs bust that I'd ever had the misfortune to experience. The damp patches beneath my armpits were expanding by the second.

As he was winding up his clearly stressful conversation I went through the spiel that I was about to lay on him in my head. I'd already revised it several times over the previous twelve hours and I'd hardly slept a wink since coming up with my plan. I gave myself a little pep talk:

OK, treat this like a business presentation to a hostile client. Take control of the situation from the word go and do not let him get a word in edgeways. Show him who the boss is from the off. Make him understand immediately that I hold all the cards and that there is only ever going to be one winner from this confrontation. Make sure—

'Listen, Steve, I haven't got time for this. I was supposed to be at a lunch with the board ten minutes ago. Whatever you want to chat about will have to wait.' He pushed past me, straightening his tie as he did so.

OK, if that's the way you want to play it, motherfucker! I was fuming, having prepared myself mentally for a massive confrontation and finding that all my nervous tension now had no means of escape. I went to Suzie's desk, found a piece of paper and scrawled on it in big block capitals, underlining certain key words for emphasis:

CHUCK, YOU <u>WILL</u> CALL ME <u>IMMEDIATELY</u>. I KNOW <u>EXACTLY</u> WHAT YOU'RE UP TO AND I DON'T THINK ANY OF US WANT THIS TO GET <u>NASTY</u>. STEVE x4523.

I put the note in an envelope and left it prominently on Chuck's desk with the words 'CHUCK – READ THIS' printed on its front. It was now simply a question of waiting for him to come to me. Muhammad and the mountain and all that . . .

The rest of that day was spent tapping my fingers and glancing up towards Chuck's office. He'd returned from lunch at about 3 p.m. looking even more tense and from then on I'd barely dared to go to the bog such was my debilitating state of anxiety. Every time my phone rang I jumped and looked at the caller ID. For three hours all I received were calls from salesmen and clients and each time I tried my damnedest to get them off the phone as quickly as possible just in case Chuck attempted to get through. As the hours rolled by I began to question whether I was doing the right thing, whether I was being rash, whether I should reconsider the whole plan. I'd almost given up hope that Chuck would actually bother contacting me when suddenly my phone trilled and his name flashed up on my caller display.

'Steve, this better be *fucking* good because I am not in the mood for any *fucking* bullshit.'

'Oh, I think this will be a priority for you, Chuck. I'm coming over right now.' And with that I slammed the phone down and marched towards his office. My heart was totally out of control by the time I'd reached his door. I barely acknowledged Suzie and didn't even knock before striding in. As I shut the door behind me I was clenching my jaw so hard that I felt my teeth squeak.

'OK, what is this all about? If you've heard some bullshit rumour that I'm trying to edge you out you can rest assured right now that it's got nothing to do with reality. OK, a few of the salesmen think you're soft-pedalling at the moment but you're still delivering the goods and compared to some of the fuckwits I have to deal with you're vaguely diligent. Look—'

'This ain't got anything to do with what I'm up to and everything to do with what you're up to. I broke into your computer yesterday—'

'*What?* You fucking did *what?* You'd better be fucking joking, you slimy little pigfucker! I will rip your fucking eyeballs out and skull-fuck you! You . . .'

Chuck's face had turned absolutely puce and he was shouting so loudly that I knew Suzie and anyone within about thirty feet would have heard him. I had to calm everything down or I was going to blow this.

'Look, Chuck,' I hissed through gritted teeth, 'I strongly suggest that you shut the fuck up because I know all about the money laundering.'

I have never seen such a rapid change of expression in all my life. The colour literally drained out of Chuck's face and his chin dropped to his chest in an almost cartoon-like fashion.

'I don't know . . . what you're talking about!' But his face betrayed the fact that he knew exactly what I was talking about and that he knew he'd exposed himself. Still, even a man blessed with the best poker face in town would have probably given the game away.

'OK, this is the deal.' I was beginning to relax. 'You don't need to concern yourself about why I broke into your computer but rest assured I did. Your log-in password is "rollingstones" and your email password is "jimihendrix". During my exploration, I found some damn interesting files that I think the police would be extremely excited about,' I lied. In fact, I'd only found the one email but I assumed there would have been others if I'd bothered trawling around. I thought that if I made out I had a few he'd assume the case for the prosecution was even more watertight than it actually was.

'Here, for example, is one that I think they'd really like to check out.' I smiled triumphantly as I held aloft one of the copies of the Gabriel Llosa email that I'd printed out the day before. There was something enormously gratifying about watching the feared tyrant transform into a frightened mouse in front of my very eyes. I was almost beginning to enjoy this. I handed the print-out to him and he took it from my grasp gingerly, his hand visibly shaking.

'An investigation by the Financial Services Authority into the laundering of two hundred million dollars for some Colombian coke dealer may not be hugely beneficial for your career prospects. In fact, it may not be massively beneficial for your prospects of not getting royally buggered by tattooed nutters whilst residing at Her Majesty's pleasure for the next ten years of your life.' I was laying it on thick because I wanted Chuck to think that I was a ruthless bastard. Without that perception there was no chance my gambit would work. I had to project the image of a callous swine to assure him that I meant business. In reality, my stomach was in knots and my heart felt as if a coronary was imminent.

There was a long pause. It seemed like an eternity. I let the sheer horror of his situation sink in. His forehead was furrowed and his eyes were screwed up. He looked like Clint Eastwood just before he blows away the bad guy – an almost quizzical mixture of anger and contempt. He continued staring at me with a look of utter disbelief on his face. Except he wasn't really focusing on me; he was looking straight through me. He had a Vietnam vet 'thousand mile stare' if ever there was one. He was obviously trying to assess the situation, work out if there was any point in denying his wrongdoing and calculate any possible counter-moves. At last he spoke.

'OK, let's just say hypothetically that you're right. What are you after?'

'You know and I know there's no fucking "hypothetical" here. The FSA are desperate for a money-laundering conviction to prove they're not the toothless pinheads everyone assumes they are. If I throw them a bone they are gonna be all over you like a cheap suit and no matter how careful you've been they're gonna find out your game and come down on you like a ton of fucking bricks. Make an example of you. What I want is very simple . . . I want to keep my job – yes, I know about your plan to fire me in December – and I want you to pay me a three-million-pound bonus. I'll be out of your hair after that. There, that's it. That's all I want and that's what you're gonna give me.'

'You have got to be fucking joking. There is no way that the board are ever going to let me get away with that . . . that's six times what you got last year. Even if I wanted to I couldn't—'

'Mate, I'm not mucking about here and I don't think you're in any fucking bargaining position right now. I want that money. What I'm doing is no different from what every other wanker here does to increase their bonus around this time of year. It's just another form of office politics, OK? Half the fuckers in this bank are shafting each other, stealing colleagues' thunder, trading on inside information, spreading false rumours . . . doing whatever they have to so they can look pretty when it comes to B day. Come on, don't fuck me around . . . I'm just being a little more . . . a little more direct.'

'Steve, that's as may be but I'm telling you I simply won't get away with it. They'll ask tricky questions that I won't be able to answer.' I'd feared he was going to say something like that. That's why I had a plan B.

'Well, you'll just have to give it to me out of your own pocket, then. Yeah, fuck doing it via Geldlust. You can give me ten per cent of what you and your low-life mates are gonna make on this one deal. That shouldn't even touch the sides for a man of your means . . . fuck knows how many of these dodgy trades you've done in the past. You boys are making forty million dollars on this deal alone and I want a tenth of it. So you can just give me four million dollars out of your own pocket. At today's exchange rate that's about three million quid. Yeah, that should do it. I want three million quid, untraceable in a Swiss bank account, all that shit you see in the movies.'

What I was doing didn't seem out of order to me. The geezer was a total wrong 'un and I was just taking a small portion of his ill-gotten gains. He had drawn first blood by choosing to fire me. I was just upping the game. I wasn't prepared to allow him to throw me away like a piece of rubbish and screw up all my 'retirement' plans. He was not going to have the last laugh; I was.

'So you're simply blackmailing me now. You know that's a criminal offence, don't you?' Chuck had a slightly smug expression as if he'd just pulled a crafty chess move. I couldn't let him feel in the ascendant.

'Call it what you will, I don't give two shits. You've got three days to give me your answer or I go straight to the boys in blue. I've got copies of all the relevant files and emails. This is just business, Chuck, OK?' After a suitably pregnant pause I said, 'I'll see you later,' and strolled out of his office. The puzzled look I got from Suzie as I closed the door behind me revealed she'd definitely heard Chuck's shouting. I didn't have the time or inclination to explain, and simply walked off.

In the lift heading back down to the ground floor I breathed a truly massive sigh of relief. There seemed to be no reason my ruse wouldn't work. I had Chuck by the short and curlies and he knew it.

Six

GABRIEL WAS FEEDING HIS ALLIGATORS when the underling came to get him. Several of the prehistoric creatures floated in the pool with their eyes barely above the water line whilst others rested on the artificial beaches like felled logs. To the left of the pool was the lion enclosure and to the right the tigers' cage. The tranquillity was occasionally broken by a low growl or an angry roar from one side or the other.

Gabriel was throwing crudely chopped-up lumps of raw chicken and pork to his pets, and every time a piece of meat landed within about ten feet of one of them it would show a surprising turn of speed as it claimed it. Occasionally, Gabriel would purposefully aim the lumps of flesh between two of the beasts in the hope that they would fight each other for it, and if they did a look of childlike glee would cross his face and he'd shout encouragement. Such was his clear enjoyment of his activity that his honcho was visibly scared to disturb him.

'Er . . . Don Llosa . . . so sorry to interrupt. We have him. We found him in a small village just outside Bogotá. The men have hurt him but he's still alive. We've managed to get another couple of names out of him. I don't think he has anything more to say. What shall we do?'

'We shall do to him what we do to all informers. Bring him to me now. Tie him on one of our hospital beds, bring the doctor and a set of the sharpest tools our infirmary has to offer.'

Soon Gabriel's wishes had been fulfilled. The informer was wheeled to the pool on the hospital bed with his hands and feet handcuffed to the metal bars at each corner. He was naked but for a pair of stained, dark green Y-fronts. His body and face were covered in bruises and dried blood, and his puffy eyes stretched wide open with the sheer horror of what faced him. A gag was stuffed in his mouth, for Gabriel wanted this to be a one-way conversation.

'OK,' he said, as if he were just about to start a business meeting, 'we're going to play a little game I like to play sometimes with scum like you. First of all, we're going to cut off your hands. Then we're going to cut off your feet. Then your *cojones*. If by some miracle you haven't died from blood loss by then, we'll move on to your forearms, your lower legs and so on. We're going to feed each appendage to my pets in front of you and we're not going to discriminate against any of them. The order of lunch service will be lions, alligators, tigers, panthers, jaguars, hyenas and then back to lions. But I doubt very much we'll achieve a full circle before you die.

The record so far is to reach the jaguars, but we must aim high. Just think, unlike during your pitiful little life, you may actually achieve something in death.'

And with that Gabriel nodded at the doctor who, somewhat incongruously, was wearing a green medical smock and mask. The doctor took a medical saw from a hospital trolley covered in a dark green cloth upon which was laid out a variety of surgical cutting tools, neatly arranged in order of size. The prisoner was squirming on his bed, trying to scream, his eyes wide with terror.

The doctor put on a pair of latex gloves and began sawing into the prisoner's right ankle with an air of studious concentration. After about fifteen seconds he had successfully removed the foot. He applied a tourniquet to the lower leg to stop the prodigious blood flow and then picked up the already white foot by the big toe and showed it to the prisoner, whose hideous screams were muffled by the gag. He handed the foot to Gabriel, who by this time had also put on medical gloves and a mask. Gabriel looked at it quizzically for a moment and then lobbed it towards his favourite lion – the male he called Brutus. Gabriel's accuracy was impressive and Brutus simply opened his mouth and snatched the flesh out of the air. Gabriel smiled to himself and signalled for the doctor to continue.

The prisoner managed to hang on to life as far as the jaguars, but much to Gabriel's irritation he died during the short journey to the hyenas. Gabriel began shouting obscenities at the doctor, demanding that he find better ways of stemming the blood flow and insisting that there must be drugs that could help maintain life after the removal of several limbs. The doctor, petrified that he would be the next course, proffered endless apologies and promised that he'd do better next time. Gabriel walked back to his vast mansion enraged by his inability to beat the record.

During the slow, measured walk to his hacienda, Gabriel's mind wandered back to the first man he had killed: Cesar Vallejo. He remembered how much pleasure he had taken from repeatedly sticking the rusty ice pick into the astonished eye of the fat, greasy policeman who ruled his village. Gabriel had always hated the corrupt, vicious bastard, who tyrannised all the small businesses in his area. Every week he came round and, with a disgusting, false bonhomie, collected his 'protection money'. Gabriel could sense the fear that his father felt on the morning of each visit and couldn't bear to see that proud man subjected to the weekly humiliation. The cop would ruffle Gabriel's hair as he waddled into his father's shop and Gabriel would only just resist the temptation to bite the pig's hand.

Gabriel first noticed the strange glances the filthy pervert gave his elder sister one day when his father was in hospital with dysentery. His father had given Gabriel the respon-sibility of handing over the weekly bunch of pesos and had made him promise that he would do so politely and without scowling. Cesar had stumbled in drunk and slumped down in the chair next to Gabriel's beautiful sister, who was darning her father's socks. Whilst counting the notes, the policeman had begun to scan Lupita's young, lithe body with his bloodshot, drink-addled eyes. After a few minutes he had asked Gabriel to go and buy him a cold beer from the next village, and Gabriel had had no choice but to obey him. He ran there and back but on his return had found the front room empty. He heard muffled noises from the yard and crept to the back door, to see the plump, uniformed body of the man he despised jerking furiously against his sister's tiny frame. Cesar's trousers were by his ankles and one of his large hands covered little Lupita's mouth.

Gabriel smiled to himself. Even now he was surprised by the speed with which his younger self had acted. The look on the man's face as he turned round to see Gabriel with the ice pick raised at eye level was something he would never forget. The blood had spurted out on to his sister's white dress and Gabriel had been more concerned about the mess he had made of Lupita's frock than the life he had just extinguished.

When Gabriel Llosa had protected his sister's virtue he was just nine years old.

Seven

CHUCK LOOKED AT HIS WATCH for the fifth time in an hour – it was 3.45 a.m. It had been without doubt the most appalling ten hours of his life. All he could do was stare into the middle distance contemplating his fate. He sat at his huge, antique desk in the office on the fourth floor of his vast Holland Park home and went through all the decisions that had led up to this unbearable situation. He thought all the way back to his days as a young graduate trainee, and analysed the career path that had led to his becoming head of research at Geldlust bank. He remembered his move from one leading bank to another and his progress up the research analyst rankings along the way. His colleagues at his last bank had been surprised when he'd lowered himself to Geldlust, but he had felt flattered to be offered the prestigious role of head of research at the tender age of thirty-seven. The three-million-pound two-year package had also been . . . acceptable.

He recalled the first time he'd been approached about

the possibility of making money on the side. George, who had been in the same batch of graduate trainees, had called him out of the blue in May 2004 and asked him to come out and see him in Monaco. George had moved around private equity and hedge funds and had eventually ended up in some God-awful Brazilian bank. Chuck remembered wondering why such a talented guy was wasting his time in such a backwater. George and Chuck had been good pals for a couple of years and had got up to a fair amount of naughtiness together on various business trips. They had visited brothels in Paris, Zurich and Frankfurt and traded inside information with each other on a regular basis. They hadn't met since George had moved to South America but they still had the occasional chat, though these were generally excuses to impress one another with their respective success. Their friendship was still intensely competitive, more like an extended game of oneupmanship than anything else.

For the meeting in Monaco, George had pulled out all the stops to ensure that Chuck knew who the daddy was. His twelve-seater private jet picked Chuck up from City airport on Friday evening. In Nice Chuck was met by an extremely attractive blonde chauffeuse who escorted him to an orange Lamborghini Countach and drove the twenty-four kilometres to George's palatial cliff-side apartment in record time. Chuck estimated that George's pad was worth at least $20 million and some of the art work within it was worth another ten. They had dinner on George's eighty-foot yacht, which must have set him back another $5 million. Chuck's intense rivalry with his mate was piqued by every new indication of George's superior status. How the hell had his old pal become so rich? Chuck had to know. This just wasn't fair. The explanation arrived over brandy and a fine Montecristo cigar as they rocked gently under a starry sky in Monte Carlo's harbour.

Chuck set the ball rolling by asking just how George had done so damn well. It was the question he'd wanted to ask for hours and the one George had been waiting for since Chuck's arrival. George smiled – now he could get on to why he'd brought Chuck over and done everything he could to impress him. George needed Chuck so that he could make even more money.

George took a puff on his cigar and then began to explain in detail about a virtually risk-free way of making vast amounts of untaxed cash. Yes, it was money laundering, but it was so simple. It merely required two legitimate banks, a senior executive at each bank and a few back office staff on the team. It really was money for old rope and the risks were minimal. His argument was extremely persuasive and Chuck, who had always played fast and loose anyway, required little persuasion. His receptiveness was heightened because he'd married an extremely high maintenance American lawyer and was mortgaged up to the hilt on three properties – his vast Holland Park mansion, another in Florida and another in Barcelona. His third child was on the way and the Harrow school fees most certainly weren't going to be chicken feed either.

Chuck remembered how George had so cleverly justified money laundering as a 'victimless crime'. The guys he was working for weren't terrorists, pimps or white slave traders. They just sold a bit of coke to the west. Shit, they were simply providing a service for loaded westerners who liked a cheeky buzz. In fact, they were bringing some much needed hard currency into their shitty little countries. 'Anyway, Chuck, don't tell me you've never had an after dinner livener!' he'd laughed. He went so far as to say that if the money wasn't laundered it would be used for even more nefarious purposes. Only clean money could be used to reinvest in legitimate businesses so if it wasn't laundered you were virtually helping to perpetuate criminal activities. He went on to employ other intellectual justifications for his activities. He argued that anyone who believed in capitalism would understand that money that was not allowed within the legitimate economy was wasted capital that was failing to contribute to the never-ending growth that capitalism requires. Hell, listening to George made Chuck feel that not accepting his proposition would virtually be a communist act. George had finished by telling him that laundering money was 'just business' and that Chuck had a week in which to respond.

Chuck had called George up after a few days and told him he was on board. He had wrestled with his conscience but it hadn't put up a good fight. His boundless greed was way too strong for such a weedy opponent. He was in this business to make money and this latest scheme wasn't so different from some of the other dodgy dealing he'd got up to. It was just higher risk . . . but the reward was much higher too. George had clearly benefited handsomely from the enterprise and he'd never even had a close shave with the authorities, who were just a bunch of incompetents. It simply had to be worth it, and after the first few highly lucrative transactions were completed without any hiccups Chuck was convinced he'd made the right decision.

Until now.

Chuck thought about paying up, but that was a mug's game. He didn't know if Steve had told anyone else, and he knew that Steve would simply keep coming back for more once he had paid him the first bundle. No, he'd talk to Gabriel and then he'd decide what to do.

He leant forward and placed his tumbler of twenty-year-old whisky on the desk in front of him. His office contained all his favourite art work – an early Lucian Freud, a David Hockney, even some sketches by Picasso. He gazed around him at all he'd achieved, everything that was now under threat. He had to deal with the situation like a man.

He stared at the cheap mobile in his hands. It was an untraceable pay-as-you-go phone he'd bought with cash and only used for calls to Colombia and Brazil. It would be past 10 p.m. in Colombia now. He would call Gabriel and explain the situation. He had never met him but he felt certain he was a reasonable man. He would simply make it clear that this pending transaction would have to wait and that all future operations must be held back until a solution was found to the problem.

He took a deep breath and dialled Gabriel's number. After three rings someone picked up.

'*Si, diga.*'

'*Habla Señor Bond. Favor de comunicarme con el señor Llosa,*' Chuck said in his stuttering Spanish. He'd learnt most of it over twenty years ago during a gap year spent bumming around beaches in Central America and his recent exchanges with various Colombians had allowed him to improve it a little. Señor Bond had been his bright idea for a code name; he'd thought that calling himself James Bond was fairly amusing when George had instructed him to adopt one. It didn't feel quite so amusing now.

'*Bueno. Esperame tantito, señor.*'

Chuck's heart began to race. He knew it was late but this was an emergency. He also suspected that Gabriel was probably in possession of a formidable temper. After what seemed an interminable wait he heard muffled voices. Eventually the phone was picked up.

'Ah, Señor Bond, 'ow are we today?' said Gabriel in his deep voice. Chuck had spoken directly to Gabriel only four times in the last three years and had managed to wangle his way out of his invitations for a face-to-face meeting at his hacienda. He'd been nervous each time he'd spoken to him and each time he'd tried to terminate the conversation as soon as possible. Calling a Colombian gangster from his Holland Park home with his wife and kids asleep downstairs felt . . . terribly wrong.

'Well, erm, Don Llosa, not so good, actually.' And after a long pause: 'We have a . . . situation.'

'Ah . . . we 'ave a situation?' Gabriel rarely gave anything away and often did the trick of simply repeating what Chuck said. This had the desired effect of making Chuck feel even more edgy.

'Yes . . . erm . . . we have been . . . compromised. An individual has found out about the transaction due for settlement on the fifteenth of October. I strongly recommend that we cancel all pending business until further notice.' Chuck was happy with his terminology. It was formal and would surely not be incriminating on the off chance that this telephone conversation was being bugged. There was another long, ominous pause.

'Señor Bond, so sorry but thees ees no possible. These transactions are *necesario*. The money to be raised 'as already been committed to several projects. Please explain the situation. I am sure there will be a, 'ow d'you say, an alternative *solución*. Who is this "individual"?' Gabriel's voice was so horribly menacing that Chuck found himself trembling.

'I'm so . . . so sorry but I can't tell you who he is.' Chuck didn't want any unwanted repercussions from an ill-thought-through admission. He knew that things could get nasty very quickly. He was not willing to be complicit in murder.

'Well, Señor Bond, if you cannot tell me who eet ees who has compromised this deal then I can only assume eet ees you. I don't think you want me to do that . . . so I ask again, who ees the "individual" who 'as compromised us?'

Chuck realised he had not prepared himself adequately for this conversation. He'd hoped it would be over by now. The clock was ticking and Gabriel was not a man to be kept waiting. Finally, after much internal deliberation, he heard himself whisper almost inaudibly, 'Someone at the bank.' He immediately regretted it.

'And it's just one man?'

'Yes.'

'You are sure?'

'Yes.'

'And 'ow 'as he made it clear that he knows?'

Chuck was in too deep now. He should never have got as far as explaining details. He took another deep breath.

'He broke into my computer somehow. He says he has picked up some files and emails you and I have sent to each other. He showed me one of your emails and seems to know exactly what's going on. He wants three million pounds or he's going to get the police involved.'

'Ah, I see. He does not sound like an honest man, thees . . . "individual". Now tell me, ees there any way some-one else can get to the information that he obtained?'

'No . . . no, I've deleted the email account. But he says he has copies of the files and emails and he's smart so I'm sure he's not lying.'

'OK . . . well, I would not worry about thees dishonest man . . . I'm sure he can be persuaded to reconsider his plan.

What is his name, please? Don't worry, we won't do anything . . . *tan pesado*.' 'Too heavy'? What the hell did that mean?

Chuck was perspiring. He was pacing back and forth across his office. Everything was not going according to plan. Somehow Gabriel had manipulated him into disclosing information he'd really not wanted to reveal. He felt like a junior analyst who'd been outsmarted by a more experienced client – except the stakes were infinitely higher. He was either going to anger a man who surely should not be angered or put a colleague, albeit a dishonest, manipulative little fuck of a colleague, in a seriously dangerous situation.

'OK . . . his name is Steve Jones. He's a team leader in my department. What . . . what do you propose to do?' Chuck's voice was trembling with emotion.

'Please, Señor Bond, do not worry about that. We will deal with thees. Eet ees just business.'

Chuck was left listening to the dial tone.

Eight

ON FRIDAY I DECIDED TO call in sick again. I'd stayed home Wednesday and Thursday, being way too jittery to go to work and pretend to all and sundry that everything was just tickety boo. There was simply no way in hell I was capable of phoning obnoxious clients and interacting with aggressive traders in the state I was in, let alone facing Suzie and the half-promised 'rematch'. I was hardly sleeping and questions were raging around my fretting brain: would Chuck call? Would he accept the offer? Would he try to negotiate? If he did try to negotiate what was the lowest amount I should accept? Would I actually go to the police if he called my bluff? Until these questions were answered all I could do was stay at home and wait.

On Tuesday evening I'd given Chuck three days to give me his response to my 'business proposal'. He could decide to call me at around 6 p.m. today if he chose to define a day as a 24-hour block and still not be in contravention of our agreement. It was now 11.30 a.m. I could be sitting here for another six and a half fucking hours. I wished I'd been more specific in the deadline I'd given him. I was beginning to regret the whole thing. What the hell was I doing black-mailing my boss . . . and for three million fucking pounds? I hadn't thought this through properly and I simply didn't have the stomach for it. I wasn't made for this kind of shit; I was a nice middle-class Cambridge-educated boy. How the hell did I get myself into this mess?

I stared at the television. It was some dreadful horse-shit involving various obese families voluntarily being ritually humiliated by a condescending, loathsome host. Fortunately for my teetering sanity the volume was turned right down. The landline phone lay on the coffee table in front of me next to my BlackBerry. I hadn't specified which one Chuck should call so both had to be within my grasp. They sat there staring at me, mocking me, making me feel pathetic. I hardly dared go to the kitchen for a glass of water.

Suddenly the landline rang. I jumped slightly before I steadied my frayed nerves and put the receiver to my ear. 'Hello.' My voice was the husky whisper I used when answering the telephone during a sickie just in case someone from the bank was calling.

'Steve, it's Jane. Just wondering how you are. Are you OK?'

'Oh . . . not too bad, I suppose. Just can't get rid of this damn flu. Erm . . . what's up at work?' I wheezed.

'So you're really ill, then? This has got nothing to do with the email you showed me, has it?'

'No, not at all. I swear I'm in a whole world of pain here.' My voice went even more husky to reinforce my blatant lie.

'Oh . . . that's a shame. I was thinking of popping over and . . . erm . . . bringing you some grapes . . . or something. Are you going to be in tonight?'

'Yep, but perhaps make it tomorrow – hopefully by then I'll be feeling a bit better.'

'OK, I'll do that. By the way – I've been thinking about that email. I don't think it's anything and I think you could get in a lot of trouble if you admit to breaking into Chuck's office. Industrial espionage, stealing confidential material, trespassing and all that. They'll throw the book at you. I'd seriously just forget about the whole thing.'

I mumbled something and after a hurried goodbye put the phone down. I couldn't pretend everything was OK. I'd call Jane tomorrow, tell her I was better and see if we could take things past first base then. In the meantime I had this shit-storm I'd created to deal with.

I waited. And I waited. And I waited some more.

I was just heading for the lavatory when I heard the familiar sound of my BlackBerry vibrating on the table top, and rushed back to the living room. I snatched the BlackBerry, which was now beginning to trill, and without even checking who was calling put it to my ear and pressed the answer button.

'Hi, Steve. It's Chuck.' That's all he said. There was something strangely morose about the way he said those four words. He sounded as if he was about to top himself.

'So, Chuck, what's the deal?' I said, trying to sound as confident as possible.

'Look, Steve . . . things have . . . things have gone terribly wrong. Look . . . we have to meet up. Right now. I'm not joking. This is . . . this is all fucked up.' What? He sounded as if he'd been drinking. He sounded off his head. This was not someone who should sound like this. This was wrong . . . but maybe it was a ruse.

'Listen, Chuck, don't give me that bullshit. I've made a very simple offer and all you have to do is decide whether you want to be slightly poorer or to spend a lot of your life making sure you don't drop the soap in the shower. So what's it gonna be?'

'You don't understand. Steve . . . I didn't mean this to happen, but I told the man who I work for about you. I didn't mean to. He got it out of me . . . and he said he's going to deal with it. He's not a man to be messed with. I told him early Wednesday morning. I don't know what he plans to do. I think he might send people over to . . . to . . . deal with you. I genuinely didn't mean for any of this to happen.'

'You are fucking joking, aren't you?' But even as I said it I knew he wasn't. There was a combination of fear, regret and sheer nervousness in his voice that the greatest actor in the world would have struggled to replicate. Oh, Christ! This was real. There was no doubt that this was fucking real. My stomach turned to water. Finally I managed to pull myself together a little.

'What do you mean, "deal with me"?'

'Look, Steve, these people don't muck about. You've really got to lie low for a bit. Seriously, I'm not joking . . . this is really, really fucked up. Look, I've managed to get together a hundred grand in cash. It will help you hide for a while and then . . . then . . . we can contact each other again. Come over to the communal gardens by my house . . . you remember where it is, don't you?' His voice was tremulous with nerves. He definitely wasn't bluffing.

'Yeah. It's only a few hundred metres from my parents.' My mind was going into overdrive now and I was in a kind of trance. I felt as if someone had injected a gram of coke straight into my brain – yet strangely other-worldly.

'OK. Use the Ladbroke Grove entrance. The combination on the street gate is 4738X. You have to press C to clear it first. I'll see you in an hour. I'll wait for you in the hut near the tennis court. There shouldn't be anyone around. I'm so sorry for all this . . . I never meant—'

'OK . . . I'll see you then,' I said, cutting him off. I wrote down the combination number and turned the television off with the remote control. Staring at the bleak painting above my fireplace, I examined my options. Adrenalin was coursing through my veins. I had to treat this situation like a seemingly intractable research problem – perhaps think of it as a particularly tricky bit of office politics. Analyse my opponents' motives and their means and outsmart them. I'd done it before . . . though the stakes were a lot higher this time. Christ, my life might be in danger. I felt like being sick again. My analysis was hasty:

1   There is an 80 per cent chance Chuck is telling the truth.

2   The people Chuck laundered cash for were almost certainly some kind of Colombian drug cartel. Chuck had not denied it when I bluffed that I knew it to be the case. If my surmise had been incorrect he would not have been so scared because he would have felt my information was incomplete.

3   Drug cartels deal with obstacles by eliminating them. I'd seen enough documentaries and films to be sure this was true.

4   Drug cartels that export coke to the west would have lots of contacts in those countries with which they did business. A simple phone call and someone over here who owed them a favour would step to it.

5   Chuck and the bank had all my contact details, inlcuding my home address.

6   Chuck had discussed the issue with the gangsters over forty-eight hours ago. These boys had a lot to lose and were likely to want to deal with the situation ASAP. Shit, they could be outside my house right now.

7   *I am in big fucking trouble*.

What to do? What are my options? Which offers the highest reward whilst entailing the lowest risk? Shit, I undertook risk/reward analysis day in day out in that soul-destroying job. Despite my pounding heart I had to employ it now. I had to get a grip.

1 Do nothing. Ridiculous – if I stayed still I could be a dead man by sunset.

2 Go to the police immediately and tell them everything. They might charge me with industrial espionage and attempted blackmail, but maybe that was a price worth paying? They might put me in protective custody until the problem blew over. But would it? I'd just be a marked man for the rest of my life. Some Albanian motherfucker would probably blow me away in about two years' time whilst I was having a chilled drink in a local pub. I'd never have peace. No go.

3 Go on the run right now and don't meet Chuck. It could be a trap . . .

4 Meet Chuck, take the cash off him and find out about what I'm up against.

I couldn't make a decision with the data I currently had – I needed to quiz Chuck first. Maybe I'd bite the bullet and go to the police after I'd got all the facts, but not before. *I'll see Chuck . . . but I'll be fucking careful*.

I went and had a piss. As I was washing my hands I looked at myself in the mirror. 'You can do this. You can do this. You can do this.' That's all I said to myself, again and again. I said it so many times it lost all meaning.

I took my scooter key from the mantelpiece and was about to leave the house when I was suddenly gripped by paralysis. They could be out there already. I felt my stomach tie itself in knots. I ran upstairs to my bedroom, crept to the bay window and holding the curtain very slightly to one side scanned the street. There was nobody around. A polystyrene cup blew down the far pavement. The distant rumble of traffic on the main road was the only noise to be heard. My red Vespa was parked directly in front of my house, fortunately with its back to me.

I crept almost silently down the stairs. I picked up the bike helmet, put it on my head and fastened up the strap, my hands visibly shaking. I planned out exactly how the next ten seconds would go. I'd open the door with the scooter key already between my right thumb and forefinger. I'd slam the door behind me and not double-lock it as I normally would. I'd open the gate, leap on to my scooter and rush off on to the Uxbridge Road. Any killer out there would have to be damn fast to even think of catching me.

I prepared myself and executed the plan. No fumbling. No problem. Literally within fifteen seconds I was doing forty-five down Uxbridge Road heading towards Holland Park. I estimated I'd be at the Ladbroke Grove entrance to Ladbroke Square within four minutes. Just as I approached Shepherd's Bush Green I saw the familiar flash of the speed camera that had caught me twice before. You fucking idiot! But actually who cared? There was some much, much more serious shit to deal with.

Soon I was heading down Holland Park Avenue, past my parents' house. I turned left at Ladbroke Grove and passed the police station. I parked the bike illegally on a yellow line but a potential parking ticket fine of forty quid was the least of my worries. I walked to the ominous black gate that led into Ladbroke Square.

I punched in the combination number and started walking the few hundred metres to the tennis court, which was on the other side of the garden. I'd been to this square hundreds of times as a kid – playing kiss chase or football, smoking cigarettes and then, a little later, toking joints. And here I was, a supposedly fully grown adult walking towards an unknown fate. I had to stop thinking like a kid. This was grown-up shit. I'd got myself into this mess; surely I could get myself out of it? I followed the gravel path through the wooded area and emerged into a large open space. The tennis court was on my right and the green wooden hut that Chuck had chosen as our meeting spot was on my left. It was octagonal and almost the size of a small house. Three-quarters of it had wooden walls but two of the eight sides were open to the elements. I remembered as a kid I used to relax in there to escape the rain or my parents. I took a deep breath and entered.

It was quite dark, but I could see Chuck sitting in the gloom on the built-in wooden bench that followed the edge of the floor around. He was wearing the flat cap that he often sported and his head was bowed, almost resting on his left shoulder. He looked as if he was sleeping. My God, what the fuck was he doing taking a nap at a time like this?

I stepped towards him. I said, unnaturally quietly, 'Chuck. Chuck . . . are you OK?' My throat was dry and my voice was croaky. I stepped closer and repeated his name a little louder. He still didn't stir. This was getting ridiculous. I took one more step and, quite angrily, placed my hand on his shoulder and shook him.

Wet. My hand was wet. What the fuck? I looked down and saw the familiar red-brown colour of blood. My hand was covered in it. I instinctively wiped it on the right side of my chest, where it left an unmistakable smear on my light yellow shirt. As I looked at him in horror Chuck slumped over to his left. His head hit the bench with a thud and he didn't move. His face was sheet white. His eyes were open but had a glazed look on them. His mouth was agape and his tongue lolled out. There was not a doubt in hell. He was definitely dead.

Nine

OK. BE CALM. OK. THINK. Think fast. Think *fucking* fast.

Only one thought. Get the fuck out of here as soon as possible. Don't even bother to check if the hundred grand is there. I hadn't seen any bag. Chuck's killer would have surely nicked it had there been one. I never wanted to see that face again as long as I lived.... which if I didn't run immediately would probably be about ten seconds. Chuck had been there at most fifteen minutes. There was every chance the killer was still close by. Fuck, he could be watching me right now.

I crept to the entrance of the hut and peeped out. It was a sunny Friday afternoon and there weren't many people around. A couple in full tennis whites were knocking balls back and forth to each other, warming up before a match. A young mother lay on a rug with her kid on the far end of the green towards the Kensington Park Road exit. A man walked slowly round the perimeter path, seemingly lost in thought. He had short dark hair and wore chinos and a collared T-shirt. He did not look like a killer. He looked like an off-duty banker.

Two choices: one – run as fast as humanly possible to the nearer entrance, get out on to the road and then circum-navigate the garden and get back to the scooter, avoiding having to go down any long shady paths surrounded by menacing bushes that could easily hide a hitman. There was a wooded path between me and the nearer gate but it was only short – perhaps forty foot long.

Two – run back almost the entire length of the garden to the gate I came in by, risking the heavily vegetated path.

Initially, the first option seemed by far the more sensible choice and I prepared to sprint for it, but suddenly a compli-cation entered the equation. Chuck – that's dead Chuck lying ten feet away from me with his throat cut wide open – had seemed quite insistent that I come through a specific gate with a specific code. There was every chance that each gate had a different code. When I used to come here as a kid you had a key, none of this code bullshit, so I had no idea what the deal was. If I ran to the nearby gate and couldn't open it then I was almost certainly a dead man. I supposed I could try to climb it but it was at least eight feet tall and my climbing skills weren't what they used to be. But the long run via shady paths was even more daunting. Fuck it, I decided to go for the shorter one.

I pulled out the piece of paper I'd written the gate code on and tried to commit it to memory: 4738X. I repeated the number in my head until there was no doubt it was filed. Then, like a sprinter about to run the hundred metres, I steadied myself and crouched down.

After a deep, full breath I burst out of the hut and started sprinting like a maniac across the green towards the woman with the kid. She lay almost directly between me and the path that led to the nearer gate, and both she and the kid were staring at me with utter astonishment. The kid, I seem to remember, was actually pointing at me and had a quizzical, confused look on its face. As I ran by the woman she grabbed her son as if I was about to try to stamp on him. I didn't have time to explain. There was every chance some fucker was pointing a telescopic sight at my bony arse at that very moment.

I ran up the path towards Kensington Park Road, relieved that there was no sign of any heavily built, fedora-wearing, gun-toting motherfucker . . . so far. I breathlessly punched in the number and tried to twist the locking mechanism to open the gate. No dice. I frantically punched the code in again: 4738X. Nothing. What the fuck? My face twisted in panicked anger. Through gritted teeth I screamed in pained anguish, '*What the fuck?*'

Suddenly I heard a noise behind me. It was footsteps on gravel. Someone was coming towards the bend in the path. Oh, Christ! God! Why hast thou forsaken me?

The footsteps continued at an almost unbearably slow pace. This killer was taking his time. He was in no rush, but even so he was about to appear round the corner. It looked as if I had no choice but to try to climb the seemingly insurmountable gate. The footsteps were getting ever closer.

All of a sudden I remembered something – something that could save my life. *You have to press C to clear the mechanism before you punch in anything else, you witless retard!*

I typed in C4738X and twisted the lock. To my sheer delight this time the locking mechanism turned smoothly all the way round. I wrenched the gate open, stepped out and slammed it shut. Then I turned round and punched in a few random numbers on the panel. If the killer wanted to open the gate he'd have as much trouble as me.

Just before I set off on my long run back to my scooter a figure emerged round the corner. It was the pensive chino-wearing guy I'd clocked earlier. He looked up, seemingly as shocked as I was.

He was about as likely a killer as I was a gangster.

Ten

'STEVE, YOU'VE GOT TO GET out right now. I'm sorry, but after what you've just told me I simply can't have you round here. I can't have this shit on my doorstep. Not now. Not ever. You've got to go!'

'But . . . please. I've got nowhere else to go. Just let me stay here for an hour or so and I'll be on my way. I need to gather my thoughts . . . work out what to do.' Every word I spoke was filled with desperation.

Gemma took a deep breath and stared into my eyes. She seemed to soften. After a suitably long pause she broke the silence. 'OK . . . OK. Don't get comfortable, but you can stay for a little bit. So what are you going to do?'

'That is the six-million-dollar question.'

After my breathless sprint round the perimeter of Ladbroke Square I had jumped on my scooter and set off up Ladbroke Grove. I was in such a desperate state that I forgot my helmet, and even when I realised my error I did not stop to put it on. I didn't know who was out there, who was watching me.

A police car passed me on the other side of the road; my eyes actually made contact with those of the officer who was driving. He had a look of almost comic surprise on his face. I suppose it's not every day you see some helmetless arsehole on a scooter wearing a shirt covered in blood a hundred metres away from a major police station.

Without checking to see what the police car was doing I turned left into the confusing one-way system near my parents' house. I don't know exactly why I did this – I suppose I was panicking. Maybe I'd subconsciously realised that my situation might look a little . . . incriminating to police eyes. With hindsight, I would have saved myself a hell of a lot of shit if I'd just allowed those coppers to arrest me there and then. After driving around like a man possessed for about five minutes and making sure I'd lost the policemen, I found myself on Bassett Road. Something subconscious had guided me to it. Then it came to me – Gemma lived in a basement flat on Bassett Road. Ah, Gemma. The girl I'd had a massive argument with not two weeks before. The girl who had unceremoniously dumped me after seven months together just because her cousin had seen me leave from some moody nightclub in King's Cross with a graduate trainee.

Without further thought I raced to her flat, which was at the far western end of the road. I was about to park the bike directly outside the house when I changed my mind. The police or a CCTV camera might have registered my number plate. I scootered round the corner, put the bike on its stand and called Gemma's home number whilst still sitting on it. This call would later prove to be an error. A massive error.

Gemma was an artist who hadn't had a grown-up office job for over a decade. She had large beautiful brown eyes that dominated a Mediterranean face. Her thick, straight, almost black hair fell long past her shoulders, and despite being only five foot three she exuded a powerful presence. She had told me early on that the identity of her grandfather was a bit of a mystery, but judging by her looks and her fiery temper the smart money had to be on the Spanish sailor rather than the Welsh lord. She had a biting wit, a razor-sharp brain and a magnetic personality. She was a boundless ball of kinetic energy who didn't suffer fools gladly.

We'd met high as kites at the previous year's Glastonbury, introduced by mutual friends. I'd felt an instant attraction, though if Gemma shared my feelings she certainly didn't show it. In fact, that first meeting and the ones that followed it were characterised by a gentle, but relentless, mockery of my pathetic attempts to impress her. She'd got my number after about three minutes and it took a long time to disabuse her of the view that I was a Cityboy wanker whose ego needed deflating. It was several months before she deigned to come out on a date with me. After she'd finally accepted I had agonised over whether to take her to Quaglino's and risk being dismissed as a flash tosser, or the local pub and risk being regarded as a cheapskate. In the end I compromised and took her to a Soho tapas bar, and after a few early hiccups we started having a beautiful, relaxed, fun time together. We'd had a truly mind-blowing surfing holiday in Mexico where she'd spent her year off, and slowly but surely had grown into each other. On several occasions I'd thought about popping the question but some residual childishness, some persistent commitment-phobia, would suddenly reassert itself. It was clear to me that what we had built together had ended prematurely, that I had lost someone very special.

Much to my delight she was at home when I called and despite her surprise she clearly sensed the panic in my voice and told me to come round. As I pressed her bell, I was shaking. It wasn't just Chuck's recent execution and my own potential murder that was making my pulse race. Gemma was a fun-loving, stunning, sexy, intelligent woman. She ticked all the boxes. This was going to be our first face-to-face meet since our split. I'd been in a pit of despair for the last two weeks and had only been coping with the knowledge that I might have lost the love of my life through a combination of vast quantities of chisel and my pathetic flirtation with Jane. My recent genius blackmail ploy had helped take my mind off the sheer horror of my romantic calamity. I wondered whether that was part of the gambit's attraction. Would I have done such a rash, outrageous thing if I had been enveloped in a loving relationship? Surely I wouldn't have had the stupidity, the insanity, the sheer fucking lunacy to try what I'd tried if I'd had the hand of a good woman nestled in mine instead of a rolled-up twenty?

Gemma turned her head and looked out of the French windows leading from the kitchen to her small terraced garden. Her voice was subdued.

'You have to go to the police. You have no choice.'

'OK, but let's think about this. Let's say I do that, let's look at things from their perspective. On Tuesday several employees hear my boss shouting at me. I then take a few days off work. Today, there is a phone conversation between me and Chuck which they'll have a record of. An hour later I'm caught by a speeding camera racing towards where my boss is just about to be murdered. Ten minutes later I'm seen running away from a hut with blood on my shirt. My boss's very recently murdered body is later discovered in that same hut. I'm then seen by pigs driving my scooter like a fucking nutter without a helmet on and with blood smeared on my shirt. I clearly see that the police have clocked me and choose to escape them. They might even find the threatening note I left on Chuck's desk. It doesn't look good. It doesn't look good at all. In fact, it's a fucking open and shut case if ever there was one.' My voice was cracking with emotion.

There was a long pause. Gemma looked as if she'd finally understood my predicament.

'I've been a complete fucking idiot. This is what you get for being a wanker. Karma. That's it. Fucking karma!' I spat out the last two words. All my plans to start really enjoying life had been shattered by a single reckless gamble. I'd only put up with ten years of suited servitude to Mammon on the strict understanding that I'd soon be sipping tequilas at Mexican fiestas without a care in the world. I just wanted what everyone wanted – enough money to mean it was no longer a worry and the time to spend it while I was still young enough to appreciate it.

Suddenly, without warning, I felt tears welling up, and started sobbing like a lost child. All the emotion I'd been storing up for the last half-hour was released. I couldn't stop myself.

Gemma came and sat next to me. She looked into the middle distance and said nothing. I saw us both reflected in the mirror above her fireplace. Her expression was quite hard but it couldn't disguise some tenderness. Tentatively, she put her arm round me. I bowed my head and held it in my hands. I kept repeating, 'I've been such a fucking idiot.'

After hugging me for a minute or so she removed her arms and said slowly, 'OK, stay here tonight. Just one night, all right? And on the sofa bed, mind. We'll work this out.'

I looked into her eyes. Was it my imagination or did I see the old Gemma looking at me? There was something more than sympathy in her gaze. There was love. I could see it. She still loved me. She knew that we'd had something special. I decided to be brave.

'Whatever went wrong with us?' There was pleading in my voice.

'What went wrong, Steve, is that you shagged your fucking grad!'

'*What?* I did not shag her,' I almost shouted. There was righteous indignation in my voice.

'Look, Rachel saw you share a cab home with her. I'm not fucking stupid. I know how you operate. One of the few nights I'm not with you and you piss off with the help. How can I trust you when you fall at the first hurdle? For all I know, you've shagged her before, too.'

'I had a loved-up snog with her for about two minutes. I told you we just kissed at the Egg. I'd done about forty-seven pills and half a gram of K. Christ, I was gurning for England and could barely see cos my eyes were rolling so far back in my head. I escorted her to a cab and took one home myself. I swear I kipped alone round at my gaff. You can ask the cleaner . . . she woke me up when she came in. Rachel's just stirring shit. She was probably jealous of the good thing we have . . . I mean had. Fuck me . . . it all makes sense now.' It was about then that I remembered I'd given Suzie the good news merely a week before. I frantically pushed that thought to the back of my mind, justifying it by reminding myself that Gemma and I had split up before then and I'd only done it to get at Chuck's computer. I had to be careful because if there was even the slightest hint of deception on my face Gemma was bound to pick up on it . . . as she had always done.

There was another long pause. It looked as if what I said made sense to Gemma. I didn't know much about her relationship with her cousin but I knew they weren't close. Gemma had once told me a story about how they'd both pursued some guitar-playing surfer dude down in Devon when they were in their teens. Apparently Rachel had never forgiven her for winning that particular battle. I bet she saw an opportunity to get back at Gemma fifteen years later and break up a relationship that meant something to her.

'Look, there is no way on earth I would have jeopardised what we had just for a meaningless bunk-up. You mean the earth to me. The last two weeks have been an absolute nightmare. I miss you so much. I can't tell you how much. You were the one. You are the one. Life without you . . . life without you is . . . bollocks.' I stared at her and she looked at me. I could almost see the cogs of her mind operating, trying to compute all the new information.

'Rachel always has been tricky with me, so maybe you didn't go home together. But you still snogged someone else when only the day before you were expressing your undying love for me. OK, maybe you were mashed but I still count that as a betrayal of trust. But . . . I suppose I didn't give you a chance. I was so convinced you'd shagged Jane that I just couldn't be bothered to talk to you. I just couldn't bear to hear you try to lie your way out of it. But . . . I believe you. I'm sorry . . . I've been a fool too. I . . . I . . .'

I didn't need to wait to hear what she said. I just pulled her towards me and kissed her. I kissed with every cell in my body. I hugged her so hard I must have almost hurt her but I couldn't help it. As we kissed I felt tears flowing down my face. It was when I realised they were hers as well as mine that I knew everything was going to be OK. Everything was more than OK. Everything was fucking outstanding.

The Colombian contract killer situation . . . that piffling trifle . . . could wait until tomorrow.

Eleven

I AWOKE TO THE SOUND of birds singing. The late September sun was streaming through the French windows. I wasn't at home but the room was familiar – Gemma's living room! I remembered her beautiful, snug duvet. I remembered the sweet, fresh smell of the sheets she'd placed on the sofa for me – always clean, unlike mine. She hadn't allowed me to sleep with her but we'd talked long into the night and things looked . . . hopeful. Oh, it doesn't get much better! Everything is so damn beautiful. She'd said that she still 'kind of' loved me and . . . *I'm about to either get fucking murdered by a contract killer or do twenty fucking years for killing my boss!*

I jumped bolt upright and grabbed my head with both hands. Shit, shit, shit! That's right . . . I had to get my shit together. I had to think of a plan . . . a business plan. If you have a plan you're the man. Failing to plan is planning to fail and all that bullshit. There was even a chance the police might come round to Gemma's place at some point. OK, we were no longer officially girlfriend and boyfriend but eventually they would follow up all leads – no matter how loose the connection.

I stood up and quickly threw my clothes on. I knocked gently on Gemma's bedroom door and getting no response opened it slightly and peeped round. She was still sleeping. Her long dark hair was splayed out round her head. Her gentle, regular breathing seemed so calm. I could just see the smooth, flawless skin of her face although it was mostly buried in the pillow. I crept in and sat on the bed next to her and placed my hand on her arm. She was definitely awake now. Even though I was behind her and couldn't see her expression I knew she was smiling. Soon our hands found each other, and held on for a few seconds. I didn't want this moment to end. I knew I had to bring up the rather important matter of my impending doom but first I wanted to confirm that yesterday wasn't just a dream.

'I love you.' My voice was tremulous.

'I love you too.' No hesitation. No uncertainty. Nothing. Fucking back of the net! 'But don't think you can just rush back into my life – that it's straight back to how we were. We have got things we need to talk about. You've got to prove to me you're not a gutless sleazebag . . . that you can be a decent, faithful man. Believe me, you are most certainly not out of the doghouse yet.'

I clenched my teeth. This was . . . disappointing. Well, OK, it was going to take a bit of time, but . . . at least we'd established that we were virtually back on – kind of. If I didn't fuck up, surely we'd be able to make it? We just needed to discuss how to ensure that there was a chance of our spending more than a couple of days together before I was either killed or incarcerated.

Over a glass of freshly squeezed orange juice and strong coffee in the kitchen Gemma, sitting in her baggy, moth-eaten pyjamas, explained her thoughts. The television was on, volume down, in the background.

'Look, Steve, you have to go to the police. What's the alternative? Going on the run? How far are you going to get? If the police are after you you won't be able to leave the country because they'll be on the lookout for your passport. If you explain to them exactly what's happened they'll surely find evidence of the laundering and your story will seem plausible. You might be remanded in custody before the trial but . . . you've just got to hope the British justice system works. You're innocent until proven guilty . . . and you *are* innocent.'

'Perhaps the story might seem "plausible", but there's a hell of a lot to suggest I killed Chuck and there are enough miscarriages of justice to make me not have much faith in our legal system. My only hope is that someone saw the real killer. Christ, he's still out there. For all I know that bastard has chucked the murder weapon into my garden just so the police can find it. He almost certainly knows where I live. But . . .'

My voice tailed off. What the fuck? My face was on the television! It was the photo from my work security card, the one on the office intranet. I ran to the TV and frantically pressed the volume button up. It was the London news programme.

'. . . Mr Johnson's body was discovered in a Notting Hill communal garden yesterday afternoon. Police are very keen to talk to Steve Jones, who was last seen leaving the scene of the crime. Police are appealing for any witnesses to come forward. And now the weather . . .'

Oh, sweet Jesus! I'm now the prime suspect in a high-profile murder case. How the hell was I going to explain this to my parents? What the fuck would all my friends and relations think when they saw my ugly mug on the box? The police might have contacted my parents already. In fact they almost certainly had. Christ, I'd done some pretty stupid things in my life but this really was the big one. I'd been in trouble with the cops before, but this, this was the pièce de résistance. Mum and Dad would be worried sick about their youngest son. The son who'd always caused problems. The black sheep of the family. The fuckwit. I should call them to tell them I'm OK. But I couldn't. Not before I'd come up with . . . a strategy.

'Fucking hell! This has just got even more fucked. Christ! *Shit!*' I couldn't contain my panic.

'I still think you should go to the police. Explain everything. You'll be all right. Just tell the truth.' There was a forced calmness in Gemma's voice.

I held my head in my hands and desperately tried to think. 'Look, there's no way I'm going to the police. Even if

I don't eventually get prosecuted, which, by the way, is a big fucking "if", I'd definitely be held in custody until the trial. And . . . and in the remand centre or prison or whatever I'd be sent to I'd be really fucking vulnerable. That's the easiest place to get offed. They'd know where I was and they're bound to have some vicious gangster mate inside who'd be willing to push me off a gantry or stick a sharpened toothbrush in my kidneys. No, I'm outta here. I've gotta go. I'm gonna go. Once I'm out of this country I can write a letter to the police explaining exactly what happened. But I'll do it on my terms from somewhere where I don't have to look over my shoulder every three seconds. I have to leave.'

'But you haven't got your passport, and even if you had you couldn't use it.'

'I know. But there's more than one way to skin a cat. I know someone who lives in Jersey and you can get there without a passport. It's only a few miles from the French coast, and—'

'Listen to yourself, Steve. This isn't a bloody film. You're not James Bond. You're a nice middle-class boy, a stockbroker. These kinds of things don't happen in real life.'

'No. Not true. I've met lots of people on the run in Goa. You get a false passport, the years go by, the police lose interest. I don't want to live in this fucking shithole anyway. I want sun and freedom, not greyness and bullshit. I want the sea, I want to ride motorbikes bare-chested. *I want life!*'

'Well, I think you've really got to think about this. For a start . . .'

My BlackBerry started vibrating on the kitchen table. Oh, God! Who was it? Probably the police . . . or my parents. I picked it up. There were seven missed calls and six messages – I'd left it in the kitchen last night and had obviously slept soundly through all the calls. I didn't recognise the number and let it ring out before listening to the messages. The first few were from yesterday and were a couple of mates inviting me to parties and a rather sweet call from Suzie asking how I was. Jane had also left a message asking me to ring her. She had clearly just seen a TV report featuring me as the main suspect in Chuck's murder and she sounded genuinely worried. She wanted to know where I was and suggested we should meet. She finished off by saying that the police had already contacted her and that I shouldn't give myself up to them as they appeared convinced I'd killed Chuck.

The next three were more worrying: two from the police urgently requiring me to contact them as soon as possible and one from my mum, clearly in tears, pleading with me to call her. My dad came on after she'd spoken and said in an unbelievably calm way that I should call them or, indeed, come round to their house where they'd be waiting.

It was the last message, the one I'd just received, that put the fear of God into me.

Twelve

'SEÑOR JONES. I AM STANDING outside the house of your parents. The police have left. I strongly suggest you call me back immediately.'

I stared at my BlackBerry. The man who had spoken had a strong South American accent. He didn't need to say anything else. Things had just got a whole lot nastier.

Gemma sensed that something was desperately wrong. 'What is it?'

'Some bastard's left a message which sounds pretty damn threatening about my folks. Apart from that everything's just fucking peachy.' My sarcasm shocked me more than it did Gemma.

'You're joking, right?'

'No, I'm not. I've got to call this bloke right now and find out what the score is. How do I know he's actually outside my parents' house? How did he get the address? Whatever, I've got to call him . . . I've got no fucking choice.'

Gemma said nothing but the look in her beautiful brown

eyes said she concurred. I steadied myself, located the last missed call and dialled it, my fingers trembling. Once again my heart was racing away. I was beginning to get used to feeling close to a nervous breakdown.

The same heavily accented voice answered the phone. 'Ah, Señor Jones. So pleased you called. Leesten to me. If you do not do what I say your parents will die and die very painfully. All I want ees the copies of the emails and files you took off your boss. Involve police and parents die. Cooperate and everyone fine.' There was something so menacing about the way he spoke that I had no doubt he meant business.

'I'm not going to the police. This is between you and me. Anyway, they're after me cos they think I killed Chuck when . . . when, of course, it was you.'

'I no know what you talk about. Señor Johnson is dead? *Mierda!* May he rest in peace.' Now, this was a joke. He had to be a total idiot if he thought that acting like an innocent man was going to mean I'd be happy to meet him down some dark alley. I supposed he might also have been worried that I was recording the conversation. He might have wanted to ensure that I had no way of proving my innocence. It was certainly to his advantage if I continued to be scared to contact the police.

'Look, what is it you want me to do?'

'Señor Jones. Come to the garages just behind your parents' house' – shit, he definitely was there – 'and give me all the evidence of the crimes you think you discovered. We will have a little talk . . . and thees will be finished . . . *y punto final*. The story ends.'

'No dice, mate. I'll meet you, but somewhere more open and more public.' I didn't know what I was going to do about the files. I didn't have any, but if his conviction that I had them gave me any kind of bargaining power in this situation I wasn't going to correct him. 'Listen, there's a park near my parents' house called Holland Park. Ask anyone you meet on the streets and they'll show you where it is. There's a café in the middle of the park. Again, ask anyone in the park and they'll direct you. There's a big flower garden by the café. Pick a bright flower and put it in your lapel or buttonhole so I know who you are. When I see you sitting down in the café I will come and join you.'

'Very clever, Señor Jones. I come to thees park, you see me and run off after you call your parents so they can escape too. Then I 'ave nothing.'

'Well, you'll just have to trust me.' Shit, this guy was no dummy. He'd seen through my hastily contrived plan in about two seconds.

'No, señor, I don't have to trust you. That is because I have a colleague with me outside your house. One of us can meet you and the other can stay here . . . just in case you are not an honest man.'

Christ! How do I get out of this one? Think.

'OK, OK . . . erm . . . look, you go to the café and I'll make myself known to you . . . but from a distance. Neither of us will move. You then call your colleague. When I see him arrive and see you shake his hand I'll know my parents are safe. Then I'll come to you and we will conduct our business in the open. All the time I will be visible to you so you'll see there's no way I could call my parents to warn them.'

My voice was hoarse and shaky. Somehow, I'd managed to come out with an impromptu plan that sounded almost plausible. I began to breathe again and released a huge sigh of relief. On realising how weak it made me sound I held the phone away from my mouth. At least there was no way this fucker could hear my heart pounding away. There was a considered pause.

'OK, Señor Jones. I will meet you at the café in one hour and my colleague will join us. For the sake of your parents, please do not try anything stupid.' The line went dead.

'Did you hear all that? He says if I go to the police he'll kill my folks. He says he wants the files I took from Chuck and that's all. Christ, this is just a fucking bad joke.'

'Well, that's all right, then. Just hand over the files and everything's cool, no?'

'No. This is obviously the bloke who croaked Chuck. If they killed him they won't have a second thought about offing me. He just wants me to go over there and then he's gonna kill me too. Anyway, I don't even have any fucking files – I was just blagging. All I've got is one incriminating email and a few print-outs of it. And they're back at the ranch.'

'Christ – this is unfuckingbelievable. Shit, this is totally and utterly fucked. What the hell are you gonna do?' Even Gemma's usually steely demeanour was faltering.

I thought for a minute. 'All right, darling, it's game on. Have you got a razor you use for your legs, and have you got any big shades and a beanie hat or something?'

'Yes. The razors are in the bathroom above the basin. I'll get the sunglasses and hat.'

I went into the bathroom, located the pink ladies' razors and proceeded to hack away at my goatee. Then I stopped shaving and stared into the mirror at my own hollow expression, letting my mind wander off. How the hell had it come to this? What the fuck was I doing? I just wanted to escape from everything – the killers, the police, Britain. I wanted to lie with Gemma on a deserted island listening to a warm sea lap on the shoreline. How could I have been so fucking idiotic? Despite my best efforts my eyes began to fill with tears but something in me resolved not to break down. I had to be strong. I had to show Gemma that I was a man. After a few deep, long breaths I wiped my eyes and resumed the shave. My shaking hands ensured that I cut myself several times, but after I'd towelled my face down it was clear that I'd dramatically changed the way I looked. I'd sported that goatee for the best part of five years and I felt my newly smooth chin with some bemusement.

Gemma entered the bathroom, amazed that I had the time or the inclination to stand there staring at a new, younger-looking me. With a quizzical look on her face, she said, 'Well, you can stop admiring yourself now. Here's a choice of sunglasses and hats. I'm afraid they're all pretty feminine.'

I picked out a huge pair of Coco Chanel shades that could be mistaken for trendy raver sunglasses. The hat was a bit more problematic, and I ended up choosing a chequered pink baseball cap, which was the best of a bad bunch.

'OK, you stay here. Before I get to the café I'm going to set up a text message to be sent to your mobile with the press of just one button. It will say . . . it will say "now". As soon as you get that you have to call my parents' house and tell them to leave immediately. Their number is . . . write this down . . . 020 7727 9109. Shit . . . I've just realised there could be three of them. Fuck it! I'll just have to assume there're two. Killers always come in twos, don't they? Yes, they do . . . that's it. OK . . . OK . . . I'll call my folks now to explain the plan.' I was gabbling. Gemma looked seriously concerned. This was going to be no fun at all.

'Hi, Mum, it's Steve. I—'

'Steve, what's going on? The police have been here. We're desperately worried. They seem to think you killed your boss. Your dad and I can't—'

'Mum, listen to me. There's been a huge misunderstanding and Chuck's real killers are chasing me. I can't go to the police quite yet for reasons I'll explain later.' I took a deep breath and enunciated each word clearly so there was no confusion. 'This is the simple fact. There are two killers outside your house now. One of them killed my boss. Gemma – you know, the girl who came to your seventieth birthday party – is going to call you as soon as they've gone and it's safe for you to leave. You've got to get out of there and go to the police yourselves and don't go back to the house until they say it's safe.'

'What? What? Are you on drugs? Killers waiting for me and Dad? Have you lost your mind?'

'I wish I had. I haven't got time now, but Gemma will explain. *Do not leave the house until she calls*. And please don't look out of the window or they might work out I'm talking to you. Please, just trust me. I am not joking. I love you both but I have to go now.' I clicked the phone off.

'OK, wish me luck. I'm outta here. Do I look OK?' I was wearing an old moth-eaten baggy sweatshirt I'd left around Gemma's months ago, the huge dark shades and the pink baseball cap.

'You look like someone desperately trying not to be recognised.'

'Story of my life.' It didn't matter that the comment didn't really make any sense; it was one of the inane phrases I frequently punctuated conversations with. We both laughed nervously and then hugged each other, squeezing each other hard. Without further ado I left Gemma's flat and walked towards my scooter.

Over the next hour I was going to find out what I was really made of.

Thirteen

THE MAN I NOW KNOW to be called Juan Rodriguez needn't have bothered wearing a flower in his jacket lapel. Even without it I could have recognised him as a contract killer from about ninety yards. He looked short, perhaps five foot five, but he had an immensely strong build and a bull-like neck which supported a large, square head. His low-hanging forehead almost covered his dark eyes, which even from this distance resembled those of a shark. He was sporting some kind of Beatles mop-top haircut circa 1964 which, together with a thick moustache, certainly made him stand out from the tourists. His skin was tanned and his whole being somehow exuded menace – helped by a deep scar on his right cheek. He wore what looked like an immensely cheap red Terylene shirt, an equally naff black leather jacket and a pair of faded jeans so tight you could tell his religion.

He was sitting outside the café on the Kensington High Street side of the park. It was a bright, clear September day.

There was a slight chill in the air. A gentle breeze ruffled the tops of the London plane trees that lined the path. Below me was a large area of open ground. Just over the other side of the wooden fence two well-built shirtless lads threw a rugby ball to one another. Below them a frantic football game was taking place between two groups of young black guys. The calm was occasionally broken by a desperate shout for the ball from one of the players. Everything looked so . . . normal.

Much to my satisfaction there were numerous people milling around the café – young mothers with prams, couples making out, an old man wearing thick NHS glasses. If this fucker wanted to kill me he'd have a job doing it without getting caught. I walked past him once in my oh so subtle disguise and he didn't seem to notice me. Good. I then checked to see if there were any police around and, on seeing none, stuffed the sunglasses and rolled-up baseball hat into my left pocket. I pulled my BlackBerry out, typed in the text 'now' and prepared it so that just a single push on one button would send it straight to Gemma. I put the BlackBerry back in my right pocket. I then walked back past Juan and, on reaching the furthest possible point where he could still see my face, turned round. I put my hands in my pockets and leant against a wall, my index finger hovering over the BlackBerry's send button. Juan just sat there staring into the middle distance.

After a while he swung his head to the left and eventually his eyes rested on mine. I returned his gaze and nodded my head. After a few seconds he recognised me and I nodded my head again to show him that I was aware I'd been spotted. He made to stand up as if he'd forgotten the terms of the agreement but sat back down just as I raised my outstretched left palm to stop him in his tracks. He stared at me with a faint smile on his face. It was as if he was trying to make me think he wasn't such a bad guy after all and that this whole thing had just been a little misunderstanding. In fact, his barracuda smile made him look even scarier. It was going to take a bit more than a false grin to calm me down after having seen Chuck's lifeless body.

Very deliberately Juan then picked up the mobile that had been resting on the table in front of him. He actually held it up and showed it to me, perhaps trying to prove to me that he was a reasonable chap who was abiding by all the rules. He pressed a few buttons and began a conversation, speaking very softly and frequently looking up at me whilst he was talking. This wasn't cool. Something was going on. My pulse began to quicken and I felt my forehead begin to bead with sweat. Finally, he put the phone down and again placed it very deliberately on the table in front of him. I nodded my head and kept my right hand in my pocket, the finger still poised over the send button. I waited, trying to look as nonchalant as possible. Juan just sat there staring at me. The man's shark eyes didn't seem to blink. The strange smile glued to his face just made my sweaty fear increase.

The walk from my parents' house to the café would take no more than ten minutes. As I stood there I knew these were going to be ten of the most nerve-racking minutes of my life. Every twenty seconds or so I looked to my right. Immediately behind me was a wall but there was an archway about fifteen feet to my right which housed an ice cream shop. I knew the archway led to another path and an alternative way of reaching my spot. I hadn't thought of that. If his pal decided to come from behind I'd only have seconds before he'd be on me.

Then I spotted two uniformed police officers walking in my direction along the path that lay between the café and the southernmost green: a tall, well-built male officer and a very short blonde female. They were deep in conversation, and about fifty feet away. Very deliberately, I pointed towards them with my left hand hoping Juan would spot them so that my next move wouldn't surprise him. Then, with the same hand, I reached into my left pocket, pulled out the sunglasses and put them on.

When the coppers were about thirty feet away I knelt down and started pretending to tie my shoelaces up. They passed me by and joined the small queue outside the ice cream shop. I stood up again, keeping the sunglasses on. I was in a terrible quandary. On the one hand the officers' presence ensured that the killers wouldn't try any-thing . . . nasty. On the other hand, there was every chance that the police in this area had specifically been warned to look out for me. I waited, occasionally glancing towards the shop. Eventually, the coppers bought their ice creams and walked through the archway away from us.

The minutes dragged by. How long was this going to take? Juan kept staring at me and I kept glacing around. I had to get my raging paranoia under control, but I couldn't shake the fear that these fuckers were up to something. Yes, there were lots of people around but the more I thought about it the surer I became that these guys wouldn't give two shits about witnesses. They probably killed people on crowded streets in broad daylight for kicks down Bogotá way and wouldn't change their habits just because they happened to be in Holland Park. They'd probably been flown in just for this one mission and wouldn't worry too much about being seen killing me because they'd be back home before any investigation could get started in earnest. I was becoming edgier with every passing second. My heart rate was steadily increasing.

I waited.

Suddenly I spotted him. His head was poking round the corner of the archway. He was tall and had a thick black moustache. His high cheekbones and Lee Van Cleef eyes might have made him look entirely different from Juan but he was still unmistakably South American. His moody, tasteless clothes merely confirmed my suspicions. As our eyes met I had to make a decision. It took approximately 0.3 seconds.

Run! Run for your fucking life!

As soon as I bolted away from Diego down the path between the café and the top green I saw Juan leap up and run to the gate in the railing outside the café. I would be past him before he'd get through but only just. Even before I'd started running I'd pressed the send button. Unless there were three of these wankers over here my parents should be safe within minutes.

I ran as fast as my legs could carry me. I've always been a strong runner and, more by chance than planning, happened to be wearing a pair of trainers for this particular 'meeting'. Both my potential killers were wearing black leather shoes and I had a few seconds' start on them. I also knew this park like the back of my hand, having mucked around in it endlessly as a kid. Still, these thoughts weren't giving me great comfort at that particular moment.

As I turned left at the end of the path I looked round and to my horror saw that both men were only about twenty feet behind me. Fuck! I needed to really step up a gear or I'd never lose them. I was now running full pelt and panting like an escaped loony. I turned left again behind Holland House and sprinted towards the adventure playground. My heart was already straining, my laboured breathing sounding like that of an asthmatic. I cursed the numerous cigarettes I'd been nervously smoking over the last few days.

My scooter was parked just over the railings in the car park that served the Belvedere restaurant. I remembered that you used to be able to get into the car park via the wooden fence at the back of the adventure playground. Not only was it not very high but also one of the big boys had broken several of the slats years ago. If I could get to the playground and run through it to the bushes by the broken fence I'd be home and dry. Even if the park keepers had got their shit together to fix it I'd be tall enough to climb over it now. Although I hadn't been to the playground for almost twenty years the fence was well hidden and if anything was probably in a worse state than when I'd last pushed through it.

I turned right down the path towards the playground, then quickly turned left and vaulted the low gate into it. There was every chance that the two killers hadn't seen me pull the manoeuvre, though if they were just coming round the corner they may well put two and two together and realise that was where I'd probably gone. I sprinted frantically past climbing frames and slides. The parents with the toddlers in the sandpit were looking at me as if I was some kind of nutter. A few of the bigger kids on the various climbing structures that were dotted around the playground were staring at me. The bushes on the far side of the playground were thicker than I remembered and branches and spines cut into my arms and face as I desperately scrambled through them to where the hole in the fence should be.

Shit! *Shit!* The old wooden fence had been replaced by a nine-foot-high smooth wall. *Fuck!* I turned my head left and right, looking for a tree that was easy to climb and had a thick branch overhanging the wall. There were none. I was completely trapped.

I was out of breath, and cut. My heart was banging. I had two choices: hide there and hope they didn't find me or try to work my way out by another route. If I stayed there and they did come and find me then I was in a perfect place to be killed – concealed and alone. If I went out they might well be waiting for me. At least no one could see me where I was. The dense undergrowth between me and the playground acted as perfect cover. I stood for a second trying to regain my breath. After a few more seconds I decided that I'd work my way along the wall to the other side of the playground. At least that way, I'd be hidden and somewhere different from where they'd expect if they'd seen me push into the thick foliage. After about two minutes I reached the far side of the playground. There was still no way over the wall, so I decided to creep to the outer edge of the bushes so that I could check out what was happening. It was risky but there was no way I was just going to sit there waiting to get carved up.

I came to the last big bush, crouched down and crawled on my hands and knees to a small hole in the foliage that I could peer out of. I was shaking like a leaf but would be difficult to spot unless one of them was staring at that particular shrub.

Juan was chatting away to one of the mothers. I couldn't hear what he was saying but suddenly she raised her arm and pointed forty feet to my right, to where I'd entered the bushes. What a bitch! Then I realised that he had probably bullshitted her that he was a copper and I was the criminal.

He began walking towards where she'd pointed, his eyes scanning the tree line. As he walked he dialled his mobile, spoke a few words and then terminated the conversation. He was probably calling the other guy. They'd do a pincer movement now, and I was totally trapped. Sure enough Lee Van Cleef appeared fifteen seconds later and calmly ambled towards my end of the bushes. Was it my imagination or was he fingering something in his pocket – something small and heavy? No, he definitely was. My heart rate went up another notch.

Two choices, one second to decide: run like buggery through the centre of the playground to the entrance, hoping they wouldn't dare shoot at me surrounded by so many kids and mothers, or back out of my little enclave and see if there was any way in hell I could get over the wall. I decided that these guys wouldn't give a shit if a couple of children copped a bullet or two and went for plan B. There simply had to be a way over that effing wall.

I backed out of my bush, the dry autumnal leaves rustling beneath me, and went back to the wall. It still looked completely insurmountable. A branch broke about thirty feet to my left. I heard movement to my right. I was almost crying with sheer panic. Then I saw a plank of wood about four feet long lying on the ground. It looked like one of the old fence's slats. Quickly, I placed it at an angle against the wall, giving myself a foothold from which I could reach the top. I could hear more branches breaking on both sides of me as the Colombians closed in. I had one chance at this.

I put my right foot up on the plank where it met the wall,

pushed off with my left foot and in one movement jumped up and grabbed the top. It was covered in some kind of sticky anti-intruder paint, but it didn't matter. I wouldn't have given a toss if there had been broken glass up there.

I heaved myself up and found myself on my belly on the top of the wall. As I swung myself down the other side I saw Juan's grimacing face emerge from the bushes to my right. I jumped the last few feet, almost managing to twist my ankle as I did so, and ran towards my scooter, my left foot giving me a pang of pain every time it hit the ground. I thanked God that it was the shorter man who had reached the plank first. I didn't think he'd manage the jump, though it would have been no problem for the tall one.

When I got to my scooter I even had the presence of mind to open the boot underneath the seat and put my helmet on. The bike started first go, and I zoomed off towards Holland Park Avenue with no sign of my assailants in either wing mirror.

I was free. I was alive.

Now I just had to work out what the fuck I was supposed to do.

Part Two

Part Two

- The International Monetary Fund estimate that between 2 and 5 per cent of the entire global economy is laundered every year – somewhere between $1.5 and $3 trillion.

- Whilst information is sparse, nearly all analysts agree that London is one of the largest conduits for 'money derived from criminal enterprises, corruption and tax evasion' in the world. Nearly all of the $1.6 billion alleged to be looted from Nigeria by the family of the former dictator Sani Abacha was found in reputable British banks.

- 'Around a third of banks . . . appeared willing to accept very high levels of money-laundering risk . . . Three quarters of the banks . . . failed to take adequate measures to establish the legitimacy of the source of wealth and source of funds to be used.' FSA report, June 2011.

Fourteen

'TOMÁS, THERE ARE THREE WAYS, three unmistakable ways which will tell you if a woman is good for sex. First, look at how she eats. A big appetite for food shows that she has a big appetite for . . .' Gabriel made an instantly recognisable gesture with his right hand. 'Second, you must watch her dance. The more graceful, the more rhythmic her dancing . . . the more powerfully she will move when in the bed.' Gabriel paused for dramatic effect, exuding the calm, experienced air of a man who understood women perfectly.

'Finally, and most importantly, observe how she laughs. The harder and stronger the laugh the more she can let go . . . the more she can allow the earth to move. *Comprende?* Have as much fun as you can with women but never forget these rules. If you bring home a woman to marry and I don't see these things I will not be happy. I want you to be happy and a man can only be happy with a wife who is like this.'

'*Si, Papa*, I understand,' said Tomás, who was only eleven, and had been listening intently to his dad's advice. It was a little mystifying but he relished the rare moments that he spent with his father. Gabriel had stopped talking and was now scanning his vast estate from the comfort of the terrace of his palatial hacienda. Usually this was the signal that the conversation was over, but Tomás had a question that had been plaguing him for several days.

'*Papa?*'

'*Si, hijo?*'

'My friend Carlos has been telling me about coca. He says that there is this powder that makes you feel . . . like Superman. He tells me that many of the *vaqueros* take this and they become powerful. He tells me—'

Gabriel cut him short. There was unmistakable anger in his voice. 'Enough! Your friend Carlos is a stupid little boy. Too many of my countrymen suffer because of this powder. Let me tell you about coca . . .' He took a deep breath as he thought of the precise message he needed to communicate.

'Coca is a curse from the devil but those who take it think it's a gift from God. When you first take it you feel powerful, like a jaguar, but that is just to trick you. Coca was developed by the devil himself to steal your soul, and to do that he must first make you think it makes you strong. It doesn't. It makes good men evil and strong men weak. It steals their *cojones*. They become slaves to it. Do you want to be a slave to the devil? No? I thought not. But coca can be used. It can be used to make money, but also as a weapon. The rich Yankees and their friends in Europe are stupid and weak and have not seen the devil's trick. They want this drug and we in Colombia sell it to them. It is perfect. It is not just business, it is war. We take their cash but we also make them weaker. They grow weaker every day. The politicians have realised this and they try to make it illegal, but it is their sons and daughters who want our product and whom we seduce. The gringos enslaved us many years ago. They raped and killed our ancestors. Now we take revenge. Moctezuma would be proud of us!'

Gabriel's voice became sterner and he stared directly into the eyes of his son. 'One final thing. If I ever catch you taking this devil powder I will cut your hand off. *Comprende?* I do not joke. I never joke. Now go to your mother. She has made you food and your father has many things to think about.' He kissed his son's forehead, and Tomás immediately stood up and ambled towards the house.

Ten minutes later one of Gabriel's bodyguards approached him with a phone in his hands. 'Don Llosa, *una llamada*. A call from Inglaterra. It is Juan.'

Gabriel accepted the phone. 'Juan, I hope very much this is good news. I hope everything is as it should be. I have been informed that one of our problems has been dealt with . . . I hope the other has now been dispatched too.'

'Don Llosa, I am so sorry. The second problem . . . he escaped us.'

Gabriel could hear the fear in Juan's voice, and spoke calmly but sternly. The menace translated itself across the Atlantic. If he had shouted in fury it would have been infinitely less scary. 'Juan, this is no good. Much depends on your success. My reputation requires that this problem is cleared up. I have contacts throughout Europe; they must know what happens to those who cross me. If this boy names us we will lose many millions. Also, the British police will tell the Yankee police and we will have problems in America too. Our operations will be investigated everywhere. We must end this as soon as possible. So, have you found his parents?'

'Si, Don Llosa, but Diego has been watching their house and they are no longer there. I think Señor Jones has warned them. We don't know what to do now.'

'He still runs from the police, yes?'

'Yes. The police think he killed Señor Johnson, so he hides from them too. This is good, no?'

'Yes, for many reasons. Keep watching his parents' house. This boy will slip up. They always do. When that happens you must get to him before the police. Do anything necessary to terminate this insect . . . this mosquito. Do not even think of returning before you see his last breath leave his body with your own eyes. My alligators are hungry and you, my dear Juan, would make a fine meal.'

He put down the phone.

Fifteen

I FOUND MYSELF HEADING BACK west, towards Shepherd's Bush. There was no logic in doing this but my natural instinct was to head towards my manor . . . my turf. I didn't go to my house, in case the coppers or some South American nutbags were staking it out awaiting my return, but instead continued up the Goldhawk Road and stopped outside the Goldhawk – a pub I'd been to many times.

I walked in holding my helmet under my arm, wearing the dark glasses but not the preposterous pink baseball cap Gemma had given me. I figured I was probably more visible with it than without it. I ordered a pint of Stella and then sat down at the most isolated table in the dingiest corner facing the entrance. Keep all the bases covered, that's the deal. The table was covered in newspapers. After a long satisfying gulp of lager I began to calm down a little. My heart rate began to return to normal. I picked up a newspaper in a vain attempt to look casual, and noticed my hands were still shaking.

Every newspaper contained an article about the high-flying banker who had been stabbed to death in Ladbroke Square and every single one of them had my work intranet photo attached to the story. I saw myself in the *Daily Mirror*, the *Telegraph* and *The Times*. I looked like a demented suited-up Nazi with a debilitating crystal meth habit and some pathetic, vain part of me wished they'd chosen a different photo. Each article confirmed that I was effectively the prime suspect and was wanted for questioning by the police; that no other murder suspects had been seen leaving the scene of the crime; and if I was seen by any member of the public I was not to be approached as I was possibly 'armed and dangerous'. Rather, they should call the police immediately.

My God! This was really happening! It was written in black and white in front of my very eyes. All my friends and family were probably thinking that I was a ruthless murderer . . . a cold-blooded killer! I nursed my pint and contemplated my fate, desperately trying to think of a way out of this heinous situation.

I looked around warily. Suddenly, the pub seemed a lot less friendly. *Look at that couple chatting over there. Didn't he just point at me and whisper something to her? Shit, that black dude over there who's talking on his mobile . . . why does he keep glancing over at me? Is he describing my every detail to the police? Fuck, the barman who served me. Now he's on the phone too, the old-fashioned white one suspended behind the bar.* Whilst he was gabbing away he actually turned round and smiled at me . . . but it was a false smile, the smile of a man who was shopping me to the pigs. I had to get out of there but I had to do it subtly. I needed to change my appearance, too. I'd go to Gemma's. I'd disguise myself around hers and then I'd start on my odyssey to Jersey.

I skolled the last third of my pint and calmly stood up, my eyes darting around, checking out all the police informers who had so obviously identified me. The clever bastards were all chatting away and pretending everything was normal but they'd have to up their game if they were going to pull the wool over my eyes. I could see right through them. I knew without a shadow of doubt that as soon as my back was turned they'd all be staring at me, noting down my appearance and what I was wearing. Those who hadn't already called the cops would then take their mobiles out and sing like canaries as soon as I was out of earshot. I tried my best to stroll towards the door in as nonchalant a fashion as possible. As I did so I could feel every single person's eyes boring into the back of my head. I was almost at the door and so far no one had stood up to stop me. *Yeah, that's right . . . cos I'm fucking 'armed and dangerous' so don't mess.* Hopefully, they weren't aware that I'd struggle to fight my way out of a paper bag. I left the pub, mounted my scooter, put my helmet on and without fastening the strap speeded off back towards Shepherd's Bush Green. A narrow escape if ever there was one.

Or maybe it was all in my head? How the fuck did I know?

The problem was I didn't know what was real and what wasn't any more.

When I reached the northern side of Shepherd's Bush Green, I slowed down and stopped outside a chemist's. It was a double yellow line but I needed to disguise myself ASAP. A quick glance around showed me that there was no sign of any traffic wardens. I ran in and bought some black hair dye and some scissors. As I paid for the items with a twenty-quid note I noticed that I only had forty pounds left in my battered leather wallet. This was not good. Next I drove to Portobello Road to buy some new clobber and a pair of glasses. What I needed was a pair of conventional specs that looked like prescription lenses but were actually just plain glass . . . the kind that thick-as-pigshit pop stars wear to make themselves look vaguely intellectual.

This time I parked my scooter legally in a bay and, on taking off my helmet, wore both the sunglasses and the baseball hat. A belt and braces operation. It was a reasonably sunny Saturday afternoon and Portobello Road was absolutely rammed. I prayed to God that I didn't bump into anyone I knew and headed off towards the covered area by the railway bridge. That's where they sold the kind of second-hand crap I was after.

Within minutes I'd located a stall selling old-fashioned glasses. I explained to the stall keeper what I was after and he showed me three pairs that fitted the bill. I chose the cheapest, put them on and checked myself out in the mirror. Excellent. I really did look quite different from the intranet photo now that I didn't sport a goatee and wore glasses. Once I'd dyed my hair I'd look like a complete stranger, and a spoddy one at that. I'd hardly recognise myself. I only had twenty-five quid left after the purchase of the glasses but I managed to buy a faded denim jacket and some nasty cords for twenty. Even with my notoriously piss-poor taste no one would expect me to be wearing that kind of clobber. I was now fully sorted. I just needed to disguise myself round Gemma's and then . . . and then go on the run, I suppose.

On the way back to the scooter I passed an HSBC bank, and decided that I'd take out as much cash as humanly possible. Without money I'd be in big trouble. Without money I might as well give up the ghost right now. The queue was long but I had no choice but to wait. After about ten minutes I reached the ATM, punched in my PIN and asked to withdraw four hundred pounds.

Transaction denied.

What the fuck? That couldn't be right. Maybe there wasn't any money left in the machine? Maybe my daily limit was lower than that? But I'd seen people take cash out just before me and four hundred pounds had been my daily limit for years. It dawned on me that something was up.

My suspicions were confirmed when the machine swallowed my card. OK, so the police had requested that my bank block my access to cash. Now I was really in trouble. No wedge, the coppers after me, my photo in all the press and, last but not least, some effing Colombian hitmen on my case. Fucking brilliant.

I left the queue cursing everyone I could think of to blame for my situation, especially myself. As I marched back to the scooter muttering obscenities I wondered whether I should just give up there and then. Should I just hand myself in to the cop shop on Ladbroke Grove and hope that the British justice system didn't fail me? But I knew I'd be done for – especially after I'd effectively done a runner. If the evidence wasn't totally damning before, the circumstantial case against me certainly looked concrete after I'd been on the run for over twenty-four hours. I had well and truly fucked myself. I needed to think. I needed to cry. I needed to calm down. I'd go to Gemma's. She'd sort everything out.

I parked the scooter round the corner from Gemma's gaff in the same place as before and stowed the helmet in the seat. I walked towards the house feeling happier with each step. I was approaching safety and I was getting closer to my girl. I was only about thirty feet away from the stairs leading to her basement flat when I felt my BlackBerry buzzing in my pocket. I took it out and checked the text message I'd just received.

Received from Gemma.

'Don't come here. Police around.'

Christ alive! How did they get to her? Shit, that phone call I'd made to her home phone number yesterday . . . or maybe the phone call she made to my parents? I didn't care what the reason was, I just knew I had to turn tail and leave immediately. Without looking to see if there were policemen sitting in cars outside her flat I simply spun round and headed back to the scooter, walking unnaturally quickly.

My head was filled with horror. Everywhere I looked there was trouble, every path I tried to take seemed to be blocked. I sat on my bike feeling nothing but despair. I needed to go to someone unconnected to all this. I pulled out my BlackBerry. Surely, there was some local mate who would put me up and help me. As I scrolled through the address book I saw a name . . . a name that made me happy for two major reasons. Nick was a great, trustworthy old friend who lived less than a mile away . . . and much, much more important, Nick was a dealer with the best Charlie this side of La Paz.

Sixteen

'AS THE NEWLY APPOINTED HEAD of the FSA I completely accept that the buck stops with me. When this body was set up in 1997 it had a simple remit – to keep the Square Mile clean whilst not reducing the City's competitive advantage through over-regulation. Many critics, unsurprisingly often from foreign financial centres vying for our privileged position, claimed that self-regulation would never work but we have proved them wrong. London has avoided the scandals of Wall Street – the Enrons and the Worldcoms of recent times – and it now stands as the financial capital of the world. Our foreign competitors look at our success with envious eyes!' Peter Saint virtually shouted these last words and then paused for dramatic effect. Certain journalists at the press conference couldn't resist a little laugh and there was even a light smattering of applause. Although they were a cynical, sceptical bunch they did feel some vague pride in the success of the City. On numerous counts it was now beating Wall Street and any victory over the Yanks was always appreciated.

The auditorium in the newly built London Stock Exchange in Paternoster Square was usually used by companies delivering their full-year results to analysts. It resembled an old-school tiered lecture hall. The journalists, scruffy and out of place, sat next to each other behind the long, thin desks that graced every level, occasionally taking notes but generally just looking bored. Attending this glorified self-promotion by the new City regulator was proving to be predictably dull. Peter Saint continued his speech.

'However, we must not be complacent. Our light-touch regulation does not stifle growth and it does encourage innovation . . . but we need to be tougher. Without in any way criticising my illustrious predecessors I must point out several worrying statistics. Our own research suggests that over a quarter of corporate merger announcements are preceded by suspicious share price movements, yet we have only sought insider trading fines six times since 2001. Likewise, we have not managed to convict anyone of market manipulation although we all know that the spreading of false rumours is becoming *de rigueur* in the City, with the finger often pointed at certain hedge funds. There is evidence too that money laundering is reaching epic proportions. Since the nine/eleven tragedy and our partnership with the National Criminal Intelligence Service we have taken this issue much more seriously, yet there are still some analysts out there who claim that the City launders more dirty money than any other financial centre in the world. Despite this, successful convictions can be counted on one hand. This will not do. Finally, the recent run on the Northern Rock Building Society, just before my appointment, suggests that our own monitoring systems may need to be improved.'

Again several journalists laughed, though this time it was Peter Saint's blatant understatement that they found amusing. The run on Northern Rock had confirmed everything they feared about the incompetence of the City regulator. The FSA's chief executive cast a steely eye over the assembled journalists, focusing on those who dared to bring levity to the proceedings. His imposing stature, perfectly coiffured greying hair and immaculate navy blue pinstriped suit lent him an air of authority – an officious headmaster, surrounded by errant schoolboys.

'I propose a crusade of sorts to clean up the City. I have spoken to the Treasury and I can announce that the FSA will receive an extra fifty-five million pounds of funding over the next three years specifically earmarked to combat financial wrongdoing. We propose increasing our workforce by thirty per cent with the majority of the new hires dedicated to investigating City crime. Rotten apples are giving the Square Mile a bad name and we need to make examples of them. Financial criminals must know that they will be found out and prosecuted.' The head of the FSA was doing everything in his power to suggest he meant business, finishing off each sentence with a menacing glare around the room. After pausing for what seemed like minutes, he concluded his speech, his voice a few decibels louder than necessary.

'The City of London is an organised, respectable place. It is not a wild west casino manned by ruthless gangsters intent on lining their own pockets by whatever illegal means they can find, as some of you have claimed. The new cash and increased workforce will mean that no City criminal will rest easy. I will take questions now.'

A flurry of hands shot up. Peter Saint pointed at an attractive female journalist sitting in the front row.

'Hi, Deborah McKenzie of *The Times* . . . It seems that Northern Rock was the victim of a tightening credit market and that its inability to borrow was the product of a rapidly spreading financial uncertainty related to toxic securities backed by poor-quality American mortgages. My question is this: if it can be proved that certain bankers have knowingly infected the global financial system with such loans, can they be held to account?'

'I think it's far too early to apportion blame. However, you can rest assured that if it can be proved that bankers have knowingly created and then sold on poor-quality assets using markets that we regulate, then we will strive to prosecute them. Of course, it will be difficult as they will be able to claim that these collateralised debt obligations appeared to be sound investments at the time and had rock-solid credit ratings, and that they are as flummoxed as the rest of us by recent developments. Still, if this drama develops into a crisis I say now that we will find out who is at fault and do everything in our power to bring them to justice.'

The strident reply received several murmurs of satisfaction from the audience. After a brief pause the questions resumed and Peter Saint continued to impress with his hard-hitting answers. The next day's newspaper headlines would focus on the 'new sheriff in town'. He looked as if he intended to clean up Dodge City come hell or high water.

After the Q&A had drawn to a close Peter Saint gathered his papers, grabbed his beige raincoat from the back of his chair and folded it over his arm. He was about to leave the back of the hall when he spied a familiar figure standing alone by the side of the front entrance, a concerned look on her face. It was his daughter Jane. He went over to her and she tiptoed up to kiss him on both cheeks, hugging him for what, to certain journalists who had yet to leave, seemed an unnaturally long time.

'Hello, darling. You look worried. Is anything wrong?'

'Daddy, I think something's going on at the bank . . . something you should be interested in.'

'Oh, really? Let's have coffee and discuss it. Whatever it is, I'm sure we can deal with it.'

Seventeen

NICK'S TOOT REALLY WAS AS good as he said. Within minutes of snorting a fat line my nose and the back of my throat were totally numb. My mouth soon followed after I wiped up the rest of the coke from the mirror with my finger and rubbed it into my gums. Then came the oh-so-familiar rush of euphoria, the dopamines exploding around my cranium giving me the unstoppable urge to talk total codshit extremely confidently. I sat back in Nick's armchair and for the first time since the whole shitstorm started began to feel pretty damn good. I would deal with this as I'd dealt with a thousand difficult situations in the past. OK, this was a shitload more serious than being caught in flagrante in the bogs at a party with my mate's girlfriend or having to do a presentation to two hundred people after having had no kip the night before, but it was . . . dealable with. I just needed to get my analyst brain on the case and I'd show these *tosspots* who the boss was. They'd rue the day they messed with me. *Oh yes!* The pigs, the Colombians and all those police informers out there better get their shit together because I was not going to take this *fucking bullshit* lying down. *Oh no!* They'd understand pretty damn soon the fucking meaning of the word 'power'. All those *snivelling* toerags are gonna look pretty stupid with no fucking teeth! They think they're big-time . . . they're gonna *fucking die big-time!* Oh yeah . . . *I'm gonna show these fucks what's going on! I'm gonna* . . .

'Blinding nozz-up, innit?' said Nick. I emerged from my seething power trip as if from a dream. Nick was a mate from school. Supersmart, but had got into pills at a very young age. He'd got expelled from school for smoking a joint, literally behind the bike sheds, and had subsequently not gone to university like the rest of us. He'd tried a few menial jobs but soon realised that was a mug's game. He'd assessed his situation quite logically and decided that being unemployed and dealing puff was a far smarter life-choice. More money, more free time, no income tax, no suit and no little jobsworth telling you what to do. Soon he realised there was a lot more cash to be made punting racket. By the time we'd all come back to London after our university days he'd become established as a discreet, sensible coke dealer. I'd continued seeing him during the university holidays, and after I came back to London our friendship grew even stronger. He had a shedload of posh clients and didn't need to take unnecessary risks. He made good money and lived in a perfectly decent flat in Harlesden, paid for partly by the taxpayer. He was tall, with an angular, intelligent face and long blond hair. He rarely spent the winter in London, preferring to chill in Thailand or Bali developing the kind of deep tan that takes years of committed sun-worship. Only the slight dark patches under his piercing blue eyes and the crows' feet that appeared whenever he laughed, which was often, betrayed the extreme partying that he'd crammed into his life. He was a man who knew himself and was seldom fazed. His flat was clean and tidy and reflected his sharp, ordered mind, although his hippy tendencies were revealed by the ethnic rugs and psychedelic posters that he'd accrued on his numerous travels. Despite, or maybe because of, the premature termination of his academic career he read voraciously and knew significantly more about politics, literature and art than most of my contemporaries from Cambridge. As far as I could see he lived the life of Riley.

'You are *not* wrong there, mate! This is the fucking *business* . . . the real deal on the wheels of steel! Straight off the block or via the Colombian poontang express or I'm a monkey's uncle.' Nick was a truly great mate and the fact that I often scored blow off him had not affected our relationship. He never ripped me off and I never screwed him around. This time I'd called him from a public telephone so as to not have any phone record connecting me to him. I'd even turned my BlackBerry off before I drove over to his pad, having remembered someone telling me once that the police could still locate you by triangulation from a mobile even if you weren't actually using it. I didn't know if that was paranoid bullshit or not but figured that it was better to be safe than sorry. My call had woken him up and the relaxed way he spoke to me suggested that he hadn't seen anything in the papers or on the TV regarding my predicament. Good. That way I might be able to get some help off him without letting him know just how serious the situation was. I had to play this cool, but in order to do that I also had to get over the initial, mind-bending rush from this damn fine yeyo. I sat there and contrived a vaguely plausible story.

'Listen, Nick . . . I'm in a bit of trouble. I'm suspected of insider trading and it looks pretty bad for me. I know this is going to sound really fucked up but I've done a runner. I want to prove my innocence but not whilst all these wankers are hassling me. I need you to help me, man. The fuckers have blocked my bank so I can't get any money out and all I want to do is chill somewhere whilst I think of how to deal with this. Listen, can you . . . can you lend us five grand? I know you've got shitloads of cash hanging around and you know I'm good for it. I'll give you six back in two weeks' time. I've just got to assess what the score is, formulate a plan and then deal with it. That's why I'm fucking off.' My mouth was gnashing away as I lied to my good friend. Frankly, it was a miracle I had any teeth left after my impassioned diatribe.

Nick looked at me with a degree of astonishment. I wondered whether he'd bought my top-grade horseshit. We were old friends and we didn't lie to each other, but this was perhaps a tad far-fetched. After a longish pause he started racking up another couple of fatties and said his piece. His voice was both mocking and angry. He was taking the piss, but he obviously meant what he said.

'You fucking Cityboys! You're all at it, aren't you? The City's just a fucking club designed to make its privileged members as much cash as possible. It makes me laugh that I'm supposed to be the real criminal here when what we do is exactly the same. I get a product and trade it with customers just like you guys. My trade is as vulnerable to market forces as yours is. Recessions hit my revenue hard and weak sterling always means the quality of my gear goes down. It just happens that the government deems my business to be dishonest whilst yours is apparently OK. In reality, I'm more honest than you. Half the time you lie to your clients about the virtues of the crappy financial products you're trying to punt and the other half you're giving your colleagues dodgy tips and inside information. Whilst I might occasionally tell the odd mug punter that my product's purer than it actually is, at least I don't use someone else's money to schmooze them over a Michelin-starred meal while I'm doing it. And I don't try to pretend that my business is legitimate. Yeah, and when I screw up, all that happens is I make less profit or get nicked. When you cheat or screw up we all suffer!' Nick was on a roll. He flicked back his long hair and stared at me for a few seconds, then snorted his line and handed me the CD case with mine on. As I felt about 0.2 grams of edgy granulated bliss sail up my nasal passage, leaving me with a burning sensation in my raw sinuses, Nick began to wax lyrical again.

'Anyway, Steve, I don't know if you're telling me everything but I'm your mate and I'll help you. You helped me that time when I was thinking of buying a gaff and needed some clean money for the deposit. I'll lend you that wedge and you can forget about any interest bullshit. You didn't charge me anything when you did me a favour. You also don't have to tell me what's really going on. Frankly, it's probably better if I don't know. But listen . . . if you're in big fucking trouble I'd prefer if you don't hang around here, though you can stay tonight no matter what.'

What a diamond geezer! He knew I wasn't giving the full story but he was rolling with my blag. Cool. Now we could sit down for a good old-fashioned coke session and deal with all this shit tomorrow.

We snorted line after line and Nick even went out for a six-pack when the wine ran out. It was when the skunk jays started making an unexpected appearance that my thoughts suddenly took a turn. A nasty turn.

What the fuck was I doing? Here I was wired like a bastard and I had threats from all sides. I had pigs desperate to make a name for themselves by nicking me for a high-profile case. I had contract killers desperate to end my life. I had the general public anxious to inform on me so they had a story for their grandchildren. Nowhere was safe. Everyone was after me.

When Nick went to the bog I got up stiffly and sidled up to the bay window in his living room. I peeked out. Nothing. They weren't here yet but they soon would be – no doubt about that. My heart was racing. My breathing was laboured. I had to calm down. I desperately wanted to call Gemma but I knew I couldn't. I sat back down. I stood up. Then I sat down again. I placed both my hands on the chair's arms but it felt awkward so I folded them instead. I unfolded them. Suddenly Nick came in, looking concerned. After a few quizzical seconds he spoke up.

'Mate, you're acting a little bit milly there. Are you cool?' He was moving slowly towards me and speaking in a strange, artificially calm manner, as if he was trying to placate a tetchy cat.

'No, man, I'm not *fucking* cool. I'm far from *fucking* cool. This whole situation is getting to me . . . and . . . and what's *fucking* "milly" mean anyway?' My throat was so parched that I kept having to swallow every couple of seconds.

'Steve, you've just smoked three biftas of proper date rape psycho skunk and hoofed a fair amount of ream sparkle. You're just in the grip of paranoia, OK? Now, there are five stages of paranoia. First is paro. Then super-paro. Then milly, i.e. militant. Then metric and then digital. When you're digital you're prepared to jump out of a four-storey building because you're convinced every fucker in the room wants you dead when in fact you're having Sunday roast with your ever-loving family. Now, I'm looking in your eyes and you're acting pretty fucking milly if you ask me.'

'Listen, Nick, have you got any vallies? I need to kip. I need to chill. This whole thing has been a real mind-fuck. Diazepam, twenty mils min – that's what I need. Have you got any?' My voice had the unmistakable jerkiness that coke paranoia can engender. I'd definitely over-egged this pudding of a brain.

'Yeah, I got some. I've actually got something even better. Temazepam. Two of these babies and you'll be sweet as a nut. You'll be kipping like a baby in twenty minutes, guaranteed or your money back.'

I took the pills and necked them using the can of Löwenbräu. Probably not the best mix in the world – few doctors would recommend combining coke, alcohol, weed and downers – but desperate times and all that. Soon, I felt everything go fuzzy. I asked Nick where I could kip and he directed me to the spare bedroom. I staggered to the room, took my clothes off and fell into bed. The last thing I remembered was hoping that the next day would prove a little less troublesome.

I couldn't have been more wrong.

Eighteen

I AWOKE WITH A START, and checked my watch. Christ! It was two in the afternoon. I hadn't dreamt and I didn't know where the hell I was. I looked around. Nothing was familiar. I wasn't at mine and I wasn't at Gemma's. I felt groggy and my brain was numb.

I eased myself out of bed. No sudden movements now – God knows if my half-awake heart could take it. I wandered into Nick's living room in my boxer shorts and found him watching the TV and smoking a reefer.

'Afternoon, son. You've been kipping for ten hours. Told you those pills would work.'

'Yeah. Not feeling too sensible though.' I needed to get with the programme ASAP. I made myself a strong, black coffee, then walked back into the living room. 'OK, here's the deal. I'm gonna dye my hair in your bathroom. I'm then gonna drive to Paddington and try and almost certainly fail to buy a ticket to Swansea with one of my credit cards. I'm then gonna fuck off somewhere else. You don't need to know where. If you could give me those five Gs now that would be a right result.'

'No probs, man. It's in that plastic bag on the coffee table. Now, you know and I know that this has got fuck all to do with insider trading. Don't tell me anything. Don't do anything that connects you with me. No phone calls. Nothing. I love you, and I'm helping you, but I can't have the rozzers round here looking for you. Is that cool?'

'That is cool. You've been a total star, mate. I won't forget this.'

And with that I took the packet of hair dye and went into Nick's bathroom. The instructions were fairly simple and after about half an hour my hair had changed from its usual mousy blond colour to extremely dark brown – almost black. Just to complete the image-change I cut it all over. It wasn't a great job but with a bit of Nick's hair wax it almost resembled a plausible spiky haircut, albeit one that hadn't been fashionable for about thirty years. It also looked somewhat incongruous with the specs and the dodgy denim jacket and cords I'd bought, but it would have to do.

I borrowed a small rucksack off Nick and put my old clothes inside it. I then put two grand in each of my new jacket's inside pockets and the last one in the rucksack, wrapped up in a plastic bag.

'OK, mate, wish me luck. One last thing. You might see some shit about me in the papers or on TV. None of it's true but until I can prove it ain't I've got to do what I've got to do. D'you understand?'

'Dude, no probs. Be careful. Don't trust anyone. Don't tell anyone who you are or what you're up to. Just be fucking smart. I'll see you when all this shit is sorted.'

We hugged each other somewhat awkwardly and I left.

I drove carefully to Paddington railway station, never going over thirty. I parked in the scooter bay just outside the station and put my helmet in the boot. I then walked into the concourse, went to the automated ticket machine and selected a ticket to Swansea. I did this because my parents were from Swansea and had a house there. I also had various uncles and aunts who lived around that area. For this blag to work, my destination needed to be plausible so that some thick flat-footed member of the Old Bill would think he was Albert Einstein when he saw where I was headed and worked out my family connection to it.

The credit card I used was predictably rejected. Every fucking card had clearly been cancelled by the bizzies. I then took some of Nick's wedge out and paid for the same ticket with cash. They'd have a record of me trying and failing to buy the ticket with a credit card. It was worth a bash, anyway, just to throw the fuckers off the scent. I made sure I had my pink baseball cap on for the whole mission so that if I was captured on CCTV my new dark hair wouldn't be revealed.

Then I decided to give the rozzers another piece of evidence that I'd left London. I put my BlackBerry on and called Mum's mobile. She answered after only one ring. She'd obviously been waiting for me to call.

'Mum, it's me. Are you OK? Are you out of London?' She told me that she and Dad were staying with her brother in Devizes and that apart from worrying about me, everything was fine. She wanted me to go to the police immediately. I interrupted her.

'Listen, I'm gonna leave London. I can't tell you where I'm going but just trust me that I'll be safe in familiar territory. I love you and Dad but if I stay in London I'm gonna get killed or the police are gonna nick me for something I didn't do.' Mum was trying to talk but I wouldn't let her. 'And Mum, one other thing. Don't even think of going back to the house. I'm not joking, you will get killed if you do. Please trust me. Just stay out of London and whatever you do don't go back to Ladbroke Road. Or you will be killed and I'll never forgive myself.'

And with that I ended the call, ignoring her desperate pleas for me to hand myself in. Hopefully, I'd been on the phone long enough for the police to get a fix on my position. Hopefully, they would come to Paddington and when they found my scooter outside my actions would be confirmed. It might take the heat off me for a bit. I really hated scaring Mum and Dad but they didn't understand what was going on. They had to trust me. Now there was one last person to contact whilst I was still able.

I was just about to call Gemma when I noticed there were three voicemails waiting. Seeing as I was still in the location that I wanted the police to believe I was in I thought there was no harm in picking them up. The first was another one from the cops. Some bloke called Sergeant Oliver was requesting that I hand myself in so that we could 'clear this mess up'. He left a phone number to call and I wrote down his number just in case. The second message was from Jane imploring me to call her immediately. She said something about 'beating this thing together'. I decided to call her.

Jane cut to the chase. 'Steve, I don't think you killed Chuck. I've been thinking about that email – I think Chuck *was* up to no good, money laundering to be precise. And there might be lots of others at the bank involved too so don't talk to a soul about this, OK? Anyway, I've been speaking to my dad about it and he's willing to talk to you without involving the police. You know, I really don't think you should go direct to the police. They seem absolutely convinced you did it and it'll take weeks before they understand the complexities of this type of crime. God knows what could happen to you in remand whilst they're faffing about trying to work out what layering is. But Dad knows exactly how laundering works and he wants to get a high-profile conviction. He knows that a conviction on this with all the publicity that Chuck's murder has generated could kick-start his clean-up of the City. Look, tell me where you are and I'll come and pick you up in a cab right now.'

'Listen, Jane, that's really kind but I've got my own plans. You're absolutely right about the laundering and it's the fuckers involved in that who killed Chuck and now are after me. I've got to get out of here or I'll be dead too. I'll contact you and your dad when I feel safer. I've got to go now, but you will hear from me again . . . soon, I promise.' I needed to get Jane off the phone. I could barely think straight and she was just making me even more confused. I needed to hole up somewhere and work out how I could get out of this mess. Maybe I'd take her offer up later, but first I desperately needed to sort my head out. If I dwelt on my situation for more than a few seconds now I'd feel physically sick. The only way to cope was through non-stop denial of the realities of my position.

Despite Jane's protestations I ended the conversation and listened to the third message.

It chilled me to the bone.

Nineteen

'SEÑOR JONES, IT IS ME . . . your *amigo* you met so briefly in the park. Why did you run? There was no reason. We had arrangement and you were not honest. We mean you no harm. Please call me as soon as you hear this . . . your girlfriend Gemma wants to talk to you. If we no hear from you within an hour we take her for a walk.' The message ended ominously abruptly.

Oh, God! Christ! For fuck's sake, when will this shit end? Now, not only was I potentially going to get killed, so was my beautiful girl. How the fuck did they get to her? Have they somehow got access to my phone calls? Have they got pals in the police? This was just getting worse and worse by the minute.

I stared into the distance. Juan was being very clever with his voicemails; he never left overt threats so I'd have nothing to replay to the police to point them in the direction of Chuck's real killers. I desperately needed some evidence if I was ever to get the pigs off my back, but these guys never gave me anything.

But first things first. I needed to call back immediately. The message had been left fifty-one minutes ago, so she should still be OK. I had less than nine minutes to get her out of this mess. OK, analyse and act. Analyse and act. Analyse and act . . .

I needed a weapon. I needed a gun. Whatever the situation was, we were both doomed if I was unarmed. But who would have a gun . . . or know how to get one? This wasn't fucking America and I couldn't just get a replica from some shop. That wouldn't be enough.

Suddenly a synapse in my panicking brain flicked on . . . Nick! He was a drug dealer – he was bound to have one or know some wannabe gangster mate who had one. I spied a public telephone without anyone by it and ran to it, keeping my head down to avoid the ubiquitous CCTV cameras. The blood was pumping through my veins. My temples felt as if they were going to explode. I had to keep it together, despite an unremitting urge to fall to my knees and plead with God for some respite.

I punched in Nick's number and breathlessly waited for him to answer. As I listened to his phone ring I pre-planned my phraseology. I had to communicate just how desperate I was without sounding as if I'd lost it. Each passing second meant Gemma was closer to being harmed. He answered and I steadied myself.

'Nick, listen, it's Steve. I know I said I'd be out of your

hair but there's been a . . . a development. No, don't worry, this is a public phone. OK, how do I put this . . . erm, I need . . . I need a gat.' I was aware of the fact I couldn't ask for a gun over the phone and so I whispered the last word. There was a small chance his mobile was bugged, and he'd be mad as hell if I spoke too blatantly. Somewhat bizarrely for a middle-class West London boy, I'd opted for a Los Angeles hip-hop term. I remembered hearing Niggaz with Attitude use the expression in their song 'Straight outta Compton' and I knew that Nick knew the song well because we'd listened to it religiously as teenagers.

'What? You need some gak?'

'No, no. I need a . . . a piece.'

'A piss?'

'No, for fuck's sake . . . a shooter.' Again, I whispered the last word as if any bug would somehow not pick it up because I'd said it quietly.

'Mate, you're not talking to fucking Al Capone here . . . and you ain't talking about shit like this on my phone. I think, whoever you are, you have the wrong number. Goodbye.'

'No! *No!* No, mate, please listen to me – I need something, something to stop them hurting Gemma. Please, I can't get the pigs involved. Anything . . . anything that can disable a man or two men from a short distance.' There was a long pause.

'Meet me in Finches on Portobello Road in thirty minutes.' The line went dead.

OK, now I had five minutes to decide what to say to Juan. My mind raced through the variables. A strategy formed in my desperate brain. My shaking fingers almost dropped the phone as I punched the BlackBerry's buttons.

'Hello, hello . . . it's me, Steve.'

'So pleased you called, Señor Jones. *Bonita Gemma* ees smiling. You hear her?'

I heard some muffled noises as the phone was passed over to someone and then Gemma's panic-stricken voice repeating my name over and over again.

'Darling, darling . . . can you hear me?' But it was too late. Juan was already back on the phone.

'So, Señor Jones, please come to meet us and give us the files.'

The next lie was going to test all my bullshitting skills – everything I'd learnt about deceiving clients during my ten years in the City. This had to be the *chef-d'oeuvre*, my finest hour, the amalgamation of everything I'd learnt as a conniving stockbroker. My voice had to not betray for an instant the fact that I was lying through my chattering teeth.

'OK. I have the files and I promise I will give them to you. There is a park bench in Kensington Gardens near Kensington Palace. The best way to get there is by taking the westernmost path from Bayswater Road which leads down through the park. The bench is about halfway down just outside the palace. I will wait until I see you there with Gemma and I will come and sit next to you and pass you the files. I know you would kill her without a second thought. I know I have to do what you say and I will, I promise you. I will meet you there at six p.m.' That meant it would still be light and it gave me an hour and ten minutes to meet Nick and get whatever it was he had for me.

'Señor Jones, you tricked us once before but I think you now know we mean business. I will have a knife at your girl's stomach and if I see one suspicious thing she die. If you one minute late she die. If I see one policeman looking at me too long she die. Goodbye, Señor Jones. Eet ees time to finish this business. Eet ees time for you to be . . . *inteligente*.'

I replaced the receiver and took several long, deep breaths. Before heading off to see Nick I popped into the WH Smith by the entrance to the station and bought a memory chip which I promptly took out of its packaging and placed inside my jacket pocket. I didn't think it would be necessary but it was better to have it and not need it than need it and not have it.

I then went outside and joined the queue for the black cabs. I kept the sunglasses on as well as the hat just to ensure that no taxi driver would be able to tell the police they'd seen me leave the station. There were various families in the queue who'd obviously just come back from holidays in Wales or the west country. They all looked so bloody normal – a bit frustrated, a bit bored perhaps, but normal. What I wouldn't give to feel normal. Shit, I'd donate all my wealth to the fucking Jesuits just to be able to feel mildly unhappy like everyone else.

In the taxi over to Finches I contemplated my predicament. I was dealing with two trained killers who probably had guns. I had no idea what weapon I was going to be given by Nick. I only had a vague plan about what Gemma and I would do on the very off chance we managed to escape. I had no access to cash. My situation, by even the most optimistic standards, was not looking great.

Nick was already sitting outside Finches at one of the wooden picnic tables when I rolled up. I'd asked the cab to drop me a block away just in case. Nick looked mildly annoyed and was nursing a pint of Guinness. He was wearing a beanie hat and a pair of large shades. He was clearly getting into this disguise thing too. I sat down opposite him and said nothing. He just looked me straight in the eye and shook his head. After a bit he broke the silence.

'Mate, I've seen your face in the papers. You certainly didn't tell me the whole story, did you?'

'Nick, you've got to understand. I did not kill my boss but the fuckers who did want me dead too. Not only that, they've kidnapped Gemma and said if I don't meet them she's brown bread. They say they want some files but they'll kill both of us the minute they have a chance. I can't get the pigs involved and I can't beat them without a weapon.'

'You really have got yourself in a right pickle, haven't you? OK, I'm not going to try to influence what you do but my recommendation is you go straight to the police. This Bruce Willis shit just doesn't suit you. Anyway, that's the end of my advice. What I'm about to hand you under the table is a canister of Mace. I bought it ages ago when I went on a trip to Paris but it should still do the business. It's what I have around the house in case a customer gets . . . difficult. This shit will disable any motherfucker from about six feet. Go for the eyes. That's all I can offer but it should do the trick.'

'Mate, you've done it again,' I said, reaching under the table and putting the small, black canister into my trouser pocket. 'I promise no more hassle now. The next time you hear from me is when all this is cleared up and I'm giving you back your dosh. Thanks. You are a true friend.' I shook his hand and left, walking back up Portobello Road towards Notting Hill Gate.

Twenty

THE PARK BENCH BY KENSINGTON Palace was well placed for my hastily contrived manoeuvre. The path was relatively wide and there was a constant throng of people walking up and down it. For me the main attraction was a narrow passageway that led from Kensington Church Street and emerged some seventy feet behind the bench. This minor entrance into Kensington Gardens was not used very often and, because there was a wall between the pathway and the bench, was also obscured from anyone sitting on the bench, who would be facing in the opposite direction anyway.

I'd arrived about twenty minutes before our allotted meeting time, hat and sunglasses hidden in my rucksack. I spent several minutes scanning the horizon trying to see if my would-be killers were hiding behind one of the many trees that lined the main path, but saw nothing. Then I approached the bench from behind, using the Kensington Church Street entrance. A mother and her child were sitting on it with their backs to me. I wondered how the Colombians were going to get rid of them. I decided that was their problem and suspected it would present no significant challenge. One look at the tall one's eyes should just about do it.

I wandered up and down the main thoroughfare. There was no sign of any Colombian killers. Just lots of people walking around – young lovers, mothers with kids, a few hoodies nervously smoking reefers . . . the usual suspects. After five minutes I retreated to the passageway behind the bench and concealed myself just behind the end of the wall. From here I could check out everything that was going on by the bench but not be seen myself. I sparked up a fag and leant against the wall so that I wouldn't look as if I was just loitering with intent.

After about ten minutes of failing to look remotely cool I spotted the short fat one walking down the main path towards the bench. His right arm was round Gemma, inside her jacket. I had no doubt he held a knife to her chest but to everyone else he just looked like some ugly bleeder who'd lucked out with a beautiful girl. I could imagine passers-by concluding that he was some nasty gangster who'd rented himself a high-class Russian brass. Gemma's face was extraordinarily calm considering her situation. That's my girl. Don't fuck this up by looking panic-stricken and attracting unnecessary attention.

They approached the bench – the woman and kid were still sitting on it – and sat down rather stiffly next to them,

Juan's hand never leaving its hiding place. After about three seconds Juan leant over and said a few words. The poor woman immediately stood up with a distraught look on her face and promptly left.

There was one problem. Where was the other one? What was Lee Van Cleef up to? These guys worked as a pair and the other one had to be somewhere. I scanned the tree line on the side of the main drag. I couldn't see him but I had no doubt he was there.

I looked at my watch. I had three minutes to act. My heart began racing in anticipation of what I was about to undertake. I'd never felt more scared. OK, get a grip. You and Gemma are in mortal danger. Grow some balls and act like a man. Forget your fear and take control. I played through in my mind exactly what I was about to do. I took a deep breath and started walking slowly towards the bench. Juan wouldn't see me until I'd passed it and turned round. Even then he might not recognise me immediately. If Lee Van Cleef was somewhere spying on the action then I hoped he too wouldn't clock me until I was right next to his mate.

I approached the bench. My stomach was tying itself in a thousand painful knots. I could see Gemma's long dark hair and the back of Juan's thick bull-like neck. His muscular arm was still round her. Juan sat on the left of the bench with Gemma on his right. There was just enough space for me to sit next to Gemma. Each step towards the bench made my heart pump even harder. I took the memory chip

I'd bought out of my pocket and held it in my fist. I held it so tightly my knuckles went white. I was about fifteen feet behind them and there was still no sign of Diego. My eyes darted around trying to locate him but wherever he was he was well hidden. I was now within five feet of the bench. Juan had still not turned round. I was sure I was in some kind of trance. The adrenalin coursing through my veins was making me shake. My walking was stiff and unnatural.

I reached the bench and sat down on its right side, as far away from Juan as possible. He immediately looked up. At first he clearly didn't recognise me. He looked as if he was about to tell me to fuck off. Then his eyes widened and a sly smile appeared on his face. I knew my own face had been drained of all its colour. I didn't have to pretend to be scared so as to give him the necessary feeling of superiority. I was absolutely shitting myself.

'Ah, Señor Jones . . . so pleased you could make it, and your pretty girlfriend 'ere ees even more pleased. Do you 'ave the files?'

So, he was playing along with the charade until the bitter end. He was probably just trying to drag it out so that Diego had time to run up behind me and stab me in the neck. I had to act fast to prevent that particular scenario from materialising.

'Yes. Here it is.' I showed him the memory stick nestling in the palm of my left hand. Then I moved that hand to where his right one would be underneath Gemma's jacket, all the time fingering the can of Mace with my free hand. I made sure he couldn't see what I was up to by holding the Mace low down on the other side of my legs.

Juan was faced with a quandary. My hand with the memory stick in it touched his. I could feel the knife digging into Gemma's ribs. There was a moment of hesitation. Then Juan carefully began to pull his right hand back whilst slowly bringing his left hand up to take its place. He clearly intended to transfer the knife from one hand to the other and then use his right hand to grab the memory chip. I had to time the next move perfectly or Gemma would die.

As soon as I felt a slight fumbling and sensed that the exchange was in progress I thrust the Mace to within six inches of Juan's square head and squeezed down on the nozzle. There was a look of shock on his face and even before the caustic spray hit his eyes both his hands automatically went to protect them. He still held the knife but it was no longer pressed into Gemma's torso. His eyes started weeping immediately and his mouth began gasping for air. His face turned completely puce.

But there was a problem. I hadn't been entirely accurate when spraying Juan. Some of the spray had hit Gemma on the side of her face. Her whole face was contorted and her eyes were clenched shut. She was coughing and spluttering as if she'd just been saved from drowning. It was clear that she couldn't see a damn thing. I pulled her up, put my arm round her and began a quick march towards Kensington Church Street. Gemma was stumbling and I had to hold her close to me just to keep her standing up. Where was Lee

Van Cleef? I glanced back and saw Juan desperately trying to rub his eyes and stand up. He fell over. There were a few bemused spectators but no Diego. It looked as if we might reach the wall without hindrance.

And then I saw Diego emerge from behind a tree and start sprinting towards us.

Twenty-One

THERE WAS SIMPLY NO WAY we'd be able to escape. He was running at full pelt and was already within sixty feet of us. We, on the other hand, were staggering around like a couple of demented pissheads who'd been on the sauce all day. There was no choice but to stand and fight. But what chance did I have against a trained killer? He almost certainly had a gun on him, whilst all I had was a half-used can of Mace that would only be effective at close range.

By now I'd dragged Gemma to within ten feet of the wall that lay to the side of the pathway that led to Kensington Church Street. Gemma's breathing was horribly laboured. She was wheezing, her nose was running and her eyes were streaming. She was gasping like a severe asthmatic desperate for air. Even her legs didn't seem to be working properly. She tried to drop to her knees but I forced her to keep standing up. I had to carry her the last few yards to the wall. Her feet dragged uselessly along the tarmac path. Her eyes were shut and her cheeks were bright red. I mustered one last effort and, despite feeling out of breath myself, managed to pull us both behind the wall. From Diego's angle of approach he wouldn't see us until he turned the corner.

As carefully as I could I stood Gemma against the wall. She instinctively placed both hands by her sides to give her balance. I had about two seconds to prepare myself for Diego.

I took the can of Mace from my pocket and held it where I estimated Diego's face would appear. I was only a few feet away from the beginning of the wall so my reactions would have to be super-sharp. I could hear him coming, his shoes slapping the ground. He was close. Just feet away. I could hear his breath. It was now or never.

Diego's sweaty face suddenly appeared. Fuck! He had a gun with a silencer on it in his right hand. I pressed down on the nozzle with all my might. The spray caught him full in the face: it was a direct hit. He instinctively raised his hands to his eyes, still holding the gun, and charged into me, his momentum carrying him forward. We both fell to the ground, where he rolled into a foetal position, holding his face with both hands.

After what seemed like an eternity I managed to get back on to my feet. I then did something that shocked even myself. I began to kick the motherfucker as hard as I possibly could, releasing all the anger and hatred that had been building up in me over the previous days. He tried to protect his face and, in so doing, dropped the gun. I instinctively picked it up and put it in the waist of my trousers, covering it with my jacket. Without further ado I grabbed Gemma and pulled her towards the exit. One glance back confirmed that Diego was prostrate on the floor. Shit, I might even have knocked him out.

It didn't matter. All that mattered was that we were both alive, both unharmed. Now, we just needed to reach safety. But where was safe? These arseholes were going to be up and about within minutes, probably. Gemma looked in slightly less trouble than before but she still couldn't see properly. We needed to find somewhere to lie low until she recovered, but where? In a few moments we emerged on to the road, which was full of shoppers going about their business.

I looked up and saw a black cab approaching us on our side of the street. I held Gemma close to me and stuck my arm out. The driver stopped and despite the difficulty involved in opening the door whilst supporting Gemma I just about managed it. I manoeuvred her into the back of the cab, followed her in, shut the door behind us and shouted, '*Drive!*'

'Where exactly are we headed?' asked the cabby, bemused.

'Just get out of here . . . erm, Shepherd's Bush.' I wasn't thinking too carefully at that point and had slurred those words to a thousand late-night cabbies in the past.

'Looks like you've had a few sherbets, my son. Is she all right? I don't want any puking in my cab.' He still hadn't actually set off. I was frantically looking over my shoulder.

'Look, she's fine! She's just having an asthma attack. She's left her inhaler at home so I'd really appreciate it if you got us there quickly, OK?'

At last he drove off. I looked out of the rear window. Nothing. No one. Fucking brilliant. We'd made it . . . at least for now.

Twenty-Two

GEMMA HAD RECOVERED A LITTLE more by the time we reached the Havelock, a cosy gastro pub hidden away south of Shepherd's Bush Green. I used to go there all the time when my mate Angus had been the head chef. As was now becoming my custom I'd asked the cabby to drop us a couple of streets away. Once in I guided Gemma to the ladies and told her to splash tap water in her eyes and not to come out until she could at least walk unaided. Then I ordered a pint of wifebeater and a glass of Coke for Gemma and sat down. I could virtually feel the adrenalin seeping out of my system. I was shaking, but not half as badly as I had been in the cab. As I waited for Gemma I played through the spiel I was going to lay on her as soon as practically possible. I considered the main arguments that I would propose and anticipated the counter-arguments she would inevitably raise. It was going to be like a presentation to an obstreperous client. All that was missing was the PowerPoint flip chart. I had to be on killer form if I was going to pull this one off and a lot more depended on it than merely bringing in a bit of commission to my bank.

Eventually, Gemma emerged from the bogs and sat down next to me. Her eyes looked unbelievably sore and her nose was red and still streaming. God, that shit really works.

'I am so sorry about all this. I had no idea they'd be able to get to you. If anything had happened to you I would . . . I would never have forgiven myself. Can you forgive me?' I held my breath.

'Steve, this is all your fucking fault. You got me into this, you fucking wanker!' Gemma's voice was trembling with emotion. 'You have no *fucking* idea what I've been through. Those fuckers came to my flat and said they were from the police. As soon as I opened the door they pushed in and grabbed me. I tell you, I thought they were fucking gonna *rape* me at one point. I . . . I can't believe this is happening. This isn't real. It can't be real . . .' Her voice tailed off as tears welled up. This time it wasn't the Mace that was making her cry.

'Gemma, it *is* fucking real. I wish with all my heart that it wasn't but it is.' I took a deep breath, held her in my arms and said in as calm a way as possible: 'Listen, I've been thinking about our predicament. I want to run something by you. I know what I'm about to say might sound crazy but it's the only thing to do . . . the only thing we can do.' There was another long pause as I composed the main points of my argument in my head.

'Look . . . you've got to come with me. You have no choice. These cunts now know you and where you live. They probably suspect I've told you what this is all about and so they probably feel they have to . . . they have to . . . silence you too.'

Gemma opened her mouth to respond but I continued before she could get a word in.

'Look, I know we can get to Europe via Jersey. We ain't got our passports but we'll find a clever way of getting out. My mate Paul DeGruchy will help us. I know we'll be safe once we're out of the country. We can go and chill somewhere and let this blow over. Eventually the police are gonna understand our story, and then we can come back. We'll be protected. Shit, maybe they'll give us new identities. You and I won't be safe until we've got them on side and we'll never be safe here. Please come with me . . . we can do this. It ain't exactly like you've got a job that's gonna miss you . . . it ain't like you've got obligations here. We might even have a good time . . . living on some beach until this shitstorm blows itself out.'

'Are you serious? What are we . . . fucking Bonnie and Clyde? Steve, I do love you – or at least I did – but . . . I just don't think this is feasible. It's sheer fucking madness.'

'It's not. We've outsmarted these fuckers twice and we can do it again. Anyway, what's the alternative?' I was looking directly into her eyes, praying for a positive response.

'Let's say you're right that I'm now on their hit list too . . . I could go to the police, or hide out in the country for a bit, or something.'

'No way. You'll never be safe here. If they can't find me they'll go to the next person who they know can get to me . . . and that, I'm afraid, is you. Shit, you should even tell your folks to go undercover for a bit. I wish this wasn't the only way, but trust me, it is.'

I could see my argument was being considered. I really did believe what I was saying and my conviction was helping my case . . . I could tell that she realised it made sense.

Eventually she looked up. I could feel her softening a little. Was it my imagination or was there begrudging affection in her eyes? I thought I even saw the faintest of smiles on her face.

'You got me into this hole, but . . . but I suppose you did save me. You risked your life for me. I do want to be with you . . . but come on, do you really think we can get away? Do you really think we can do it?'

'Definitely. No doubt. You need to change your appearance – new hair, that kind of thing. We need as much cash as possible . . . I can't get any out but you will still be able to. Come on . . . let's do this. We'll be together. It's just you and me now.' My voice was pleading.

Gemma looked at me quizzically for what seemed like an eternity, then dropped her head and held it in her hands. Eventually, with tears in her eyes, she looked up and said it.

She fucking said it! 'OK, let's do it. Let's get away from these bastards.'

I took her in my arms and hugged her with all my strength. There was some begrudging reciprocation. Now all I had to do was to convince myself that my plan might work.

Twenty-Three

THE BOARD MEETING WAS NOT going very well. The finance director was complaining that whilst global demand for the company's product had been growing at a compound annual rate averaging 22 per cent for the last ten years, competition was keeping prices lower on a real basis. It was a result of a supply/demand imbalance mainly caused by greedy rival exporters increasing their production with little concern that their actions were flooding the market. However, he was happy to inform the board that there was every indication that the overall demand growth would actually expand over the next two decades and outstrip current supply. He used a series of PowerPoint charts and an overhead projector to show the largest potential growth regions, which were mainly located in Western Europe, and produced some bar charts showing the percentage of national GDP spent on the product, revealing that Germany and France were definitely lagging behind Britain and Spain.

The FD went on to discuss the developing sub-prime mortgage issue and the potentially damaging effect any upcoming recession would have on consumer spending. He complained that certain competitors were gaining the upper hand in the core US market and debated whether it was worth pursuing either a merger or a hostile takeover of various rival companies. He also argued that their own company had numerous inefficiencies that needed to be ironed out if profit margins were to be expanded, including transportation costs and the price of the raw materials necessary for their product. Finally, he did a SWOT analysis of their company – analysing the Strengths, Weaknesses, Opportunities and Threats.

Gabriel listened to his subordinate with a degree of disdain. He longed for the old days when drug trafficking was a simple business. Now, like any chief executive of a multi-national corporation, he had so much to think about . . . so many issues to consider. He hated to delegate, but the operation had become so enormous since the old days when he was just a Bogotá gangster that he had no choice but to form a committee of people he vaguely trusted. Nevertheless, he knew that each and every one of his executives could try to stage a boardroom coup at any moment. The time had come to remind them who was boss.

'Enough,' he said. The FD immediately stopped his presentation and stood awkwardly silent. The regional representatives shifted uneasily in their high-backed leather chairs. Some had been looking out of the vast windows at the lush forests stretching out below them in the midday sun. Others had been examining the classic pieces of Colombian art that adorned the walls of the large, panelled boardroom – oil paintings by past masters like Fernando Botero and Enrique Grau. They too had been bored by the FD's speech, but now that Gabriel had spoken they desperately tried to appear interested. Two of the younger attendees picked up pens and started pretending to take notes.

'Sit down, Lopez. Before we go into further detail regarding our plans for international expansion there is a small matter that needs to be dealt with.' He turned to one of the two bodyguards standing directly behind him, who handed him a stiletto knife, holding it with care as he passed it to Gabriel. Its thin, razor-sharp blade was solely designed to enter the human body with as little resistance as possible.

Gabriel then slowly stood up and began calmly circling the group of ten men seated around the large, circular mahogany table at which all the board meetings were held, tapping the flat of the knife's blade leisurely and rhythmically on the upturned palm of his left hand. Each of his subordinates tried desperately not to look round or show fear as he passed behind them. Gabriel started to speak in a slow, almost hypnotic voice, as if he were telling a bedtime story to his son.

'My father was a very poor man. He mended shoes in Bogotá and earned less than a dollar a day. When I began to realise the poverty we lived in, the cheap clothes my mother wore, I vowed never to be like him. We lived on rice and beans, with the occasional stringy chicken on Sundays. I saw the wealth of the men who sold coca and saw the cars they drove and the women they fucked. At the age of nine I became a runner for the local *jefe*. I worked my way up his organisation and into his affection. Soon he was like a father to me. He taught me how to thrive in this trade. But when the time was right I killed him. I stabbed him in the neck with this very knife and took over his organisation.' Gabriel had now done a full circuit of the table and started on another measured tour. The fear and tension in each of his men's faces grew with each passing step. It was like some sick game of musical chairs.

'Perhaps some of you in this room have had that very thought. I hope not, for your sake. The main lesson my former *jefe* taught me was that there is only one way to treat a rat . . . only one way to remind ambitious men of the rightful order of things.'

And on that final word he stopped. The fat, sweaty man in front of him dared not turn round but his face betrayed to the others the fact that he knew his death was imminent. Gabriel waited. The man was shaking uncontrollably, his hands flat on the table before him. Suddenly he broke, and was just about to turn round and protest his innocence when with one swift movement Gabriel plunged the knife into the base of his neck. He slumped on to the table. A pool of thick, dark blood began to form around his head, covering the papers in front of him. The other men tried to look as emotionless as possible but each and every one felt a palpable sense of relief. Gabriel withdrew the knife and wiped its blade on his victim's shoulders.

'Ignacio was a foolish man. He had been speaking to the Fernandez cartel in the south without asking me. This is not a democracy. If I find any one of you has done anything without first asking my permission I shall take you to my zoo and introduce you to my animals. I have spies everywhere. I am judge and jury and in my court you are guilty until proved innocent. Justice, as you can see, is swift. We all make good money and there is no need for this . . . this silliness.' He waved his hand dismissively towards the corpse and the ever expanding pool of blood. 'This is the end of business for today. Go to your rooms and come to me in four hours with ideas that will increase the profitability of your divisions. The meeting is adjourned.'

The men filed out of the room, averting their eyes from the lifeless body of their former colleague. Gabriel sat back down in his seat and stared out of the window, a smile on his face. He loved his job.

There was a knock on the door. One of Gabriel's bodyguards opened it slightly, had a short, quiet conversation, and then allowed the butler into the boardroom. The butler tried his best not to stare at the body at the table and walked reverentially towards Gabriel, holding a portable telephone on a silver tray.

'Don Llosa, Juan is calling from Inglaterra.'

Gabriel took the phone. 'I hope for your sake this is good news, Juan.'

'Don Llosa. So sorry. Please forgive. The boy . . . he's not stupid. We took his woman but he attacked us with an acid spray and they have escaped us. He has coloured his hair and shaved his beard. We don't know where he is but he is still scared of the police, we think.'

There was a pause. To Juan, nervously awaiting his boss's response, it was worryingly long.

'This, Juan, is totally unacceptable. This is unforgivable. You and Diego must ask for Santa Maria's blessing now, for she is more forgiving than I. You have disappointed me very much. The more this boy humiliates me the more I want him dead. It is time to call the Panther.'

'Are you sure, Don Llosa? Diego and I . . . we can handle this. Your police informants and friends in the secret service will give us information, I think. There are now two of them – more easy to find, no? Please don't give up on us.'

'Juan, never question anything I say again. You will continue hunting this vermin until you or he is dead. But we need a professional, someone with contacts in Europe . . . an expert. Call me in three hours and I will help you redeem yourself.'

Gabriel put down the phone. He had to put himself in the shoes of a frightened British stockbroker on the run with his girlfriend. What would he do if he was wanted by the British police, had seen his photo splashed across the British media and knew two killers had come to London to murder him? Very quickly, for Gabriel's brain was sharp as a razor, he decided that he would leave Britain as soon as he could. There would be no way they could leave via any means that required the use of a passport, which meant that they would probably try to make their way illegally to the nearest country, France. The boy was not a gangster, but he was intelligent. Gabriel would send the Panther to France and then he'd call Pedro in London to see if he had heard anything. He'd also call his contacts in France and Spain. He had many in the latter country because much of his cocaine entered Europe via Spain.

Gabriel picked up the phone.

Twenty-Four

THE BED AND BREAKFAST ON Queensway was pretty damn grotty but we had nowhere else to stay and we didn't have the cash to blow on somewhere flash. We had considered staying with a friend but had decided over my third pint that we didn't want to involve anyone else in this hideous shit. From now on it was just going to be Gemma and me. In a strange fucked-up kind of way I wouldn't have wanted it any other way. It was this disaster that had brought us back together and as we lay on our bed in our drab room nothing else mattered. For a brief moment 'Mr and Mrs Smith', as we'd called ourselves on checking in, felt OK . . . or at least I did.

Of course, I desperately wanted to make love to Gemma to confirm that we were officially back on, but she had taken a shower with the bathroom door closed and had come out draped in two fluffy white towels. She borrowed my T-shirt and only removed the towels and got into bed after I'd gone into the bathroom. When I came back I started playing with her beautiful dark hair but she had stopped that sharpish by kissing my forehead quickly, turning her back and saying authoritatively, 'Come on, it's time to sleep.' I lay awake wondering if I should give it another bash until I began to hear gentle snoring. I'd crashed and burnt again. Still, at least we were together . . . or at least we were in bed together.

As soon as I woke up I rolled over, put my arms round her and began spooning her. She held my hand for a moment. She made small circles on my palm with her thumb. My heart began to pound. It was probably sensing my ardour that made her jump up and go to the bathroom. I heard her turn on the shower and get in. I lay on my back wondering if I should join her. The little head was definitely keen on the idea but the big head kept telling me to be patient. I listened to the water drumming on the shower floor, cursing my indecision. I couldn't move.

Eventually I reached under the bed and pulled out the gun I'd taken off Diego. I had hidden it there the previous evening and had been thinking about it all night. I'd decided just before falling asleep that I would keep it. It seemed like a crazy thing to do but I felt so completely defenceless. I'd also decided not to tell Gemma that I had it. She'd been blind when I'd picked it up and I knew that she would just freak if she saw it. I had no idea what I'd do with it but as I felt its heaviness while Gemma showered I immediately felt more . . . powerful. My hands were shaking as I moved it around, targeting a vase and then a picture on the wall. I could hardly believe I was in possession of a real, working firearm. I hid it back under the bed as soon as I heard Gemma turn the shower off and looked as nonchalant as possible when she re-entered the room.

We discussed what we needed to do over our hotel's greasy full English breakfast. But as we planned our day Gemma began to get a faraway look in her eyes. She began to move her food aimlessly around the plate with her fork. Something was wrong. Eventually, she spoke up.

'Steve, I just don't know if I can do this.'

'Gemma, please . . . we have no choice. Trust me, if I didn't think you were a target now I wouldn't take you with me. Leaving this city . . . this country . . . is the best way to make sure you stay alive.'

I spoke with as much manufactured authority as I could muster. My hand moved across the table and gripped hers. I could see she was close to tears. I had to make her understand that we were doing the smart thing.

Eventually, after a heart-stopping few minutes, she nodded her head. I wiped away a tear rolling down her cheek and said, 'Look, I love you. I really love you. Please trust me – we're gonna be OK.'

This time she nodded her head more forcibly and, after another few seconds, simply said, 'OK.' I couldn't hide the smile of relief that spread across my face. I just wished she didn't look so goddamn glum.

We spent the next few hours putting into practice the various plans that we'd formulated over breakfast. First, Gemma popped into the nearest chemist's and bought some blond hair dye and a pair of scissors. Ensuring we weren't identified was still the main priority. When she returned I cut her hair into some crude approximation of a bob. Gemma then began to dye her hair and since my assistance wasn't required and it was approaching check-out time, I left to buy her a small rucksack from one of the local tourist shops. Using Gemma's purse, I bought another change of clothes for me, including a more masculine plain black baseball hat and a sensible pair of fake Ray-Bans, and a map of Europe. Finally, I went to the post office near the Kensington Gardens end of the road, bought an A5 Jiffy bag and wrote a note.

Dear Nick, I seem to keep on saying this is the last time I hassle you but this time it definitely is. You'll find my BlackBerry in here. It's turned off and has been since I last used it in Paddington. Gemma and I are gonna head off for a bit. It might be the stupidest thing I've ever done, who the fuck knows? All I know is that you'd help keep the rozzers off our trail if every day or so when you're far away from your gaff on one of your errands you'd turn the phone on and make a single call with it. Call things like the information line for First Great Western or maybe one of my mates in America like Razzall or one of my pals in Swansea – you'll find them in the address book. Don't bother chatting to them, just cut them off if they answer. Also, turn the phone off as soon as you've done with the call. I know it's a big ask but it would really help out if you could do this most days for the next week or two. Of course, destroy this note as soon as you've read it. You've been a star and I owe you big-time. Your reward, of course, will be in heaven! Lots of love, Steve.

I folded up the note, put it in with the BlackBerry and waited in the queue to pay. By the time I returned Gemma was almost platinum blond. I felt sad; I'd always loved her flowing dark hair but chose not to reveal my feelings. I changed into my new nondescript clothes, and we gathered our shit together and left. I'd carefully placed the gun at the bottom of my rucksack, wrapped in a stolen pillow case. Gemma was now wearing her pink hat and the Chanel sunglasses she'd lent me three days before. Christ . . . it might have been only three days but it felt like an eternity.

There were three more things to check off the list before heading out of town. First, we bought Gemma a complete change of clothes. Again we opted for the least recognisable combo possible – a pair of jeans, some cheap trainers, a beige jacket and a wide-brimmed hat. We then went to the Barclays bank on the corner of the road and I loitered outside whilst Gemma went in to extract as much cash as possible. I knew that this would give the police, and possibly our Colombian friends, a big clue as to where we'd been but we needed wedge if we were to get anywhere. I waited and Gemma came out beaming. She'd managed to take out all her savings – £6,237. We now had over ten grand between us.

The final thing was to phone Gemma's parents. We found a phone box in Queensway tube station and I gave her all the change in my pocket. I waited a few feet away from the booth. I didn't want to be within earshot because I knew it was not going to be an easy conversation for her.

After ten minutes Gemma returned from the booth and came and stood next to me. Her face betrayed the fact that the conversation had not been a pleasant one. It looked as if she was holding back the tears.

'How was it?'

'Not good. They've seen all the press reports. They're worried about me. I think they bought my story about going up North but they sensed something was wrong. When I started telling them they should take a holiday they got really concerned. I'm not sure they're gonna do it. Shit, I hope those fuckers don't try to get to them. We've just got to hope and pray we're doing the right thing . . . we *are* doing the right thing, aren't we?'

'We are, honey. I've no doubt. Come on, let's get a cab to Victoria. I ain't using the tube . . . way too many people.'

Twenty-Five

'YOU HAVE TO FIND THIS lad immediately.' Peter Saint took a sip of his fine malt whisky, leaning towards his guest to emphasise his point. The luxurious dining room of the City of London Club was full and the noise was irritating him immensely. This place simply wasn't what it used to be. It seemed they were allowing any Tom, Dick and Harry nowadays into what was once the finest gentlemen's club in the Square Mile. Peter Saint despaired at how standards in so many walks of life had been allowed to deteriorate. So few things had any class these days. So few people understood that you never had butter with brie . . . that it was white wine that was drunk with pork. The world had become a place of ignorance, bad manners and crudeness.

'We need to find him before anyone else can get to him. There are some nasty bastards out there who would love to get their hands on him before us. You need to use all your resources to track him down. If my daughter's right, then this is genuinely very important.' He leant back in his chair and surveyed the walls of the grand dining room. Impressive nineteenth-century paintings of English landscapes were positioned every few feet, reminding the diner of wonderful times forever gone.

The second in command at MI5 sat in his armchair and continued to listen, his stiff, upright posture betraying his military background. Rupert Montague had known Peter since their school days at Harrow. He was quite used to his forceful manner.

Peter continued, 'He's on the run now and he's scared. He knows that people who will stop at nothing are tracking him down and he knows the police are after him too. He hasn't gone directly to the police himself, which means either he really is guilty or he's worried they think he is. He's with his girlfriend and they're probably trying to get out of England. I want you to do everything you can to make sure we get him. This could be a real feather in my cap. Some very powerful people will be extremely happy with me if we sort this out.'

'Peter, of course we'll do everything we can to find him. I'll double the number of my people who are looking for him and we'll keep up the pressure on the police to pull their finger out. They'll find them. It shouldn't take long. It's all going to be just fine.' Rupert smiled reassuringly. He was beginning to get a little tired of his old friend's worries. The whole lunch had been focused on Peter's endless concerns about this little nobody. Rupert hadn't traipsed across half of London just to sit there being bombarded by tiresome demands for action. Peter sensed his friend's boredom. His eyes narrowed and he pointed aggressively at Rupert.

'Look, what's important is that we get to question them before some little jobsworth bobby does. I think he knows a lot, this lad, and we want to make sure we're there when he starts dishing the dirt. I cannot emphasise enough how important this could be for me. If we get him, my position will be cemented.'

'OK, Peter, I get the message.' Rupert's voice betrayed his irritation. 'Now let's forget about all that and enjoy this remarkably fine malt.'

'Rupert, it ought to be "remarkably fine" . . . it's costing me forty-five pounds a fucking shot!'

Both men laughed before simultaneously raising their glasses to their lips.

Twenty-Six

'SO TELL ME ABOUT THIS Paul DeGruchy bloke. What's his story?' Gemma whispered. The bus journey from Victoria station had been stuffy and unpleasant. The wheezing, tracksuit-sporting degenerate who'd been sitting in front of us consuming anything he could lay his pudgy hands on had clearly not washed for several days, possibly months. We'd been breathing in his rancid fragrance for the entire journey.

'Well, I knew him at Cambridge. Proper inbred autistic weirdo from the Channel Islands . . . gran was probably shagged by some genetically modified Nazi during the war. Webbed feet, cross-eyed, the full shebang but smart as fuck. We've gone our separate paths and I only see him now and again but we're still mates. Anyway, he's back over in Jersey now, living with his missus and three kids. I don't even need to ring him. He doesn't ever leave the place . . . just breeds and does his lawyer shit. The main thing is that he's got a sailing boat. We went to Sark on it once two years ago and almost karked it the weather was so horrific.'

Just as I finished saying my piece the bus stopped at Poole Harbour. I swear some of the passengers had been looking at us strangely during the two-hour journey but it had probably all been in my mind. In fact, it was almost certainly all in my mind, but it was getting harder and harder to disentangle my strident paranoia from reality. We gathered our stuff together, put our sunglasses-and-hat disguises on and exited along with the rest of the fat, sweaty British tourists. Apart from the fat sweaty bit we fitted right in. Just another couple off on our late summer hols.

We followed the signs to the boat to St Helier, bought our tickets at the booth and were ushered towards the exit to the gangplank. We were marching towards the gate to freedom when suddenly I saw them – two policemen checking passengers' documents at the front of the queue to get on the boat. One of them was armed with an effing machine gun! *What? This can't be right!* I grabbed Gemma by the arm and said, 'One minute. Let's get something from the newsagent's over there.' She hadn't seen the coppers. My mind went into overdrive.

'OK, Gemma, don't panic and don't look now, but I just saw a couple of radicks over there checking people's ID.'

'Oh, shit! We're fucked now. I thought you said . . .'

'Yeah, it usually is cool. Something's going on. Maybe some terrorist scare or something . . .' I lied. I knew they were probably looking for us. 'Let's just sit down here for a sec. I've got to think.'

The boat was going to sail in twenty-five minutes and the gate would close before then. I didn't have long.

We needed a distraction . . . something that would take the police away from their post. That would do it. But what? I racked my brain. Then I remembered something I'd read on the internet. A particularly confused weirdo I'd met in Goa had sent me a link to a site dedicated to anarchism. I remember shitting myself when I checked it out because I'd opened it at work and it was clearly totally illegal. An idea began forming in my head. After about two minutes I said, 'Look, I've got a plan. Don't worry about it. I'm gonna sort this out. Just wait here and read a paper. I'm going to the shop.'

'But—'

I was already on my way.

I went into the newsagent's and bought a pack of cigarettes, a pack of bubble gum, a lighter and a can of lighter fuel. Then I went into the toilets and constructed what can only be described as a homemade bomb. I pulled four pieces of bubble gum out of their wrappings and began chewing them into a large sticky ball. Meanwhile I wrenched the plastic top off the lighter fuel and opened the pack of cigarettes. I removed a cigarette and broke off its filter, then dipped two-thirds of the cigarette into the lighter fuel and left it sticking out of the open can. I stuck it in place with the big ball of bubble gum, being sure to not squeeze it in too tightly. The timing had to be right. I was working on the basis that a cigarette takes about seven minutes to smoke – I'd heard that once but frankly had no idea if it was true.

I went back to Gemma. She was standing around trying to look as casual as possible – examining her fingernails and pretending to read the small print of the posters advertising various different hair products.

'OK, here's the deal. We're gonna join the queue as soon as I've put this in that bin over there,' I said, furtively showing her the primitive device that lay at the top of my rucksack. 'There should still be a few people between us and the cops by the time this thing goes off. If it doesn't we'll suddenly drop out of the queue as if we've forgotten something.'

'Christ, Steve! Are you sure? This is fucking dodgy.'

'Let's just hope my GCSE physics is shaping up,' I said lightly. I actually hadn't even done GCSE physics. Brownian motion was all that I remembered from my third form studies and I was undoubtedly experiencing it at that precise moment. I hardly dared think through what I was doing because that would cause my fluttering heart to beat even more erratically. I could also feel my right eye blinking involuntarily – a nervous tic I hadn't exhibited since my school days. It had always been an embarrassment then and now of all times it chose to reappear. I turned my face away from Gemma, ostensibly to motion towards the bin that would hopefully soon become our saviour but, in reality, to hide my newly reacquired facial spasm. I couldn't let Gemma see the sheer panic that was rising from my acidic stomach.

'OK, but for God's sake be careful,' she said after a surprisingly short pause. I gave her a reassuring look as if it was going to be easy. I had to seem as if I knew what I was talking about . . . Fortunately, I'd spent my entire career doing that.

I walked over to the bin, which was one of those cylindrical ones with an ashtray on top and two five-inch holes opposite each other three-quarters of the way up. I lit the cigarette and then, whilst kneeling down and pretending to tie up my shoelace, placed the can carefully in the bin, ensuring it was still standing upright. Then I quickly stood up and went back to Gemma, and we both joined the queue.

There were about fourteen people in front of us. The police were looking at either their passports or their driving licences and checking out each passenger's face.

Two more people went through. The queue was getting shorter. Another couple passed by the coppers and walked to the guy checking the tickets. Shit, another tourist was allowed past. There were now only nine people between us and the cops. My heart rate began to soar.

We took another step forward. Fuck! Still no boom. A drop of sweat dripped down my forehead, and I wiped my brow. An elderly couple walked slowly past the police and towards the ticket inspector. The cops weren't looking up at what remained of the queue, which was good. They were engrossed in their checking procedure. My breathing became uncontrollably fast and shallow. A young man was allowed through. OK, we were gonna have to turn tail. The plan hadn't worked. Another tourist was let by. Gemma's hand squeezed my own so hard it hurt my knuckles. Something had gone wrong. The cigarette must have burnt out. Maybe I'd used too much bubble gum? A young mother holding a baby was allowed to go past.

'Steve, let's go! We've got to go now!' Gemma's strained voice revealed her desperation as she tugged on my arm.

But there were now only four people between us and the pigs. If we left at this stage we'd draw attention to ourselves. If they saw us beat a hasty retreat they'd probably come after us and ask for ID. We were done for either way. Shit, we'd come so far, and now we were going to get caught trying to leave the mainland. This wasn't going to look good when it came to my trial. Shit, I had a fucking gun in my rucksack! Christ, even Gemma might be in trouble. They might—

Suddenly there was a loud but muffled explosion from the bin. Everything stopped. The policemen and everyone else looked round with startled expressions on their faces. The one with the gun actually flicked the safety catch off. I noticed he kept his finger hovering above the trigger rather than wrapped around it. Everyone was staring at the bin. Some people just ran away – probably expecting another bigger blast to go off at any time. A young kid began crying, and his mother took him in her arms. The bin's top had been blown off, and the bin was now lying on its side. Pleasingly, the newspapers and rubbish inside were alight.

The cops moved impressively quickly. They must have

thought it was some kind of terrorist attempt. I remembered those bombs two weeks after the 7/7 tube bombings in London in 2005 that made a bit of a noise but failed to go off. They probably thought this was the same deal. They left their post and ran to within about fifteen feet of the bin, both talking in an extremely animated fashion into their radios. The one with the gun was holding it ready for action with his free hand.

Without further ado I pulled Gemma as quickly as possible towards the ticket inspector. We had to move fast but we didn't want to draw attention to ourselves either.

'What's going on over there?' the guy said when we reached him. He seemed somewhat surprised at our arrival when everyone else was checking out the bin.

'Fuck knows! Probably just some kids having a laugh,' I said, handing over our two tickets. He took them, punched them and let us through.

We were leaving the mainland.

Twenty-Seven

'YES, STEVE, BUT IT IS a little bit different, is it not? When you helped me out back then it was simply a question of you taking all the blame for possession of approximately a sixteenth of an ounce of black hash when the porter caught us smoking marijuana in my room.' Paul DeGruchy's voice and his manner of delivery hadn't changed since I'd first met him seventeen years before when we were both undergraduates at Queens' College, Cambridge. He spoke like some kind of robot with little change in intonation no matter what he was discussing. You wouldn't notice the difference if he was talking about the best way to boil an egg or how his whole family had just been cut to pieces and sold as dog food. What he said was not just monotone, it was also consistently logical and difficult to argue against.

'However, what you are now asking me to do is to smuggle a suspected murderer and his girlfriend abroad. There has been sufficient press coverage regarding the unfortunate demise of your boss to mean that the police are unlikely to believe that I had no prior knowledge of your wanted status. Hence, were I to be caught with you in my boat sailing to France or indeed here right now, there would be a chance that I would face a custodial sentence for aiding and abetting a known fugitive. This would prove most distressing for myself, my wife and children and, of course, our respective families. At the very least my legal career would be over.'

I was about to interject and plead my case. Barrister DeGruchy here had only stated the prosecution's position and I'd formulated a pretty damn strong defence. Although my main point – that he owed me, due to a sacrifice I'd made almost two decades before – had quite rightly been decimated in front of my eyes, I had some other aces up my sleeve. Before I could bring out the big guns, however, Paul continued.

'Nevertheless, you are an old friend and friendship is important in an increasingly atomised society. Also, were we to be caught, I could easily plead that I had never seen any footage of you and the alleged crime. Whilst this may be theoretically unlikely any prosecuting barrister would require a witness who had actually seen me watch a specific news programme or read a specific newspaper article regarding your predicament. Since I rarely leave this house only my wife is likely to be in that position, and since I doubt she would testify against me the chances of being prosecuted seem slim. I can simply claim that you are an old friend who arrived unexpectedly and was keen to have a day trip to

France. I could then claim that you simply ran off once we had landed. These are the two principal reasons why I am going to take you and your girlfriend to a landing point on the French coast two miles south of a town called Carteret only twenty-two miles from the harbour my boat is currently moored in. I have been there many times, there are no customs requirements and I have never seen any police or officials in that area. I believe it would fit your purposes perfectly.'

I squeezed Gemma's hand. A huge smile spread across each of our faces.

After three nervous hours on the boat from Poole Gemma and I had landed at St Helier, where much to our relief there were no officials checking identification. We then took the bus to a town called Gorey. From there it was just a short walk to Paul's house, which lay only fifty feet or so from the sea. As soon as we arrived we knew that both he and his wife had seen my face in the newspapers. Paul's wife Mary had looked extremely nervous and her eyes kept trying to connect with those of her husband. He was taking everything in his usual measured way, and they'd had a brief chat on their own in the kitchen whilst Gemma and I enjoyed a glass of good-quality French red wine. The spiel that Paul had just laid on me was clearly the product of that conversation and it wasn't over.

'Whilst I enjoy your company and it is indeed a pleasure to meet your delightful girlfriend, my wife and I have concluded that you should undertake this journey as soon as practically possible. We mean no offence by this but feel that the less time you spend here the better for all concerned. The tide happens to be advantageous in approximately forty-five minutes. If we catch it and are efficient in our sailing then we should arrive on French soil just after it turns dark. Again, this I think will be a benefit regarding all our requirements. If you have some sterling I will exchange euros for said amount with you in order to facilitate your initial interaction with our French cousins.'

'Mate, we are at your disposal. We've got nothing to pack, nothing to stay for and no one to call. We've got a few hundred quid for euros and I'll let you decide the exchange rate. Please just ask Mary not to tell a soul about our being here and we'll be on our merry way.' I downed my wine with a flourish and signalled that Gemma should do the same.

'I can vouch for it that Mary will not say a word. However, if the police do turn up we will both recount the story that we have agreed upon. An old friend turned up unexpectedly and was insistent on taking a quick trip to France. We had no idea of his . . . predicament. I took him over since he was quite adamant. I think I'll claim you had indicated you were keen to buy some good-value French wine.'

I exchanged a glance with Gemma and we both allowed ourselves another smile. I felt a nervous excitement at the adventure that lay ahead. There'd soon be no going back for either of us. I prayed that we were making the right decision. I put on my bravest face, stood up and addressed no one in particular.

'Come on, then. Enough faffing around. Let's get this show on the road.' Three bemused pairs of eyes watched me march out of the door.

Twenty-Eight

I'D FELT SEASICK BEFORE BUT nothing like what I experienced on that poxy little boat. The wind was blowing a wicked gale and the waves were horribly choppy. Within five minutes of leaving the harbour I was green to the gills. After fifteen I was chundering into the chemical-smelling toilet like it was going out of fashion. I puked and I puked and I puked again until I was just dry-retching. There was nothing more to come out.

Somehow, throughout what must have been the most horrific conditions since the Spanish Armada tried to invade England back in 1588, Gemma looked as cool as a cucumber. She'd always claimed to be the man in our relationship anyway so this was particularly irritating. Once again I was proving to be a total Wendy.

From the cramped confines of the yacht's tiny bog I could actually hear her and Paul having a perfectly normal conversation, occasionally interspersed with the odd exclamation from Gemma about how the sea was 'a bit rough'. Was she taking the piss? It wasn't just rough, it was tsunami central out there. We were all doomed and they were banging on about some shit to do with shipping lanes! *We're all gonna die, you crazy fucks!* Certainly, the greasy Cornish pasty I'd eaten on the way over from Blighty had done its worst. I raised my head and pumped the handle that released some horrific blue chemical shit down into the cistern to flush away the grisly remains. I felt like retching again but my throbbing brain had worked out that there was no more food to evacuate from my body. Slowly, I gathered myself up and climbed the three steps back on to the deck.

'Looking a little seasick there, Steve? How are we feeling?' Gemma actually laughed as Paul said this. Christ, she was nursing a glass of red wine. I was never going to live this down.

'Look, man, I don't know what's going on but this ain't right. This can't be right.' I burped slightly as I uttered the last words. I thought I was going to vom again.

'Dear boy, this is the English Channel – the most dangerous shipping lane in the world. If I'd known we had a landlubber on board I would have called the whole thing off.' Shit, even Paul was laughing now. I had to get a grip.

'No . . . it's all cool. I don't think I've got anything else to puke up. God almighty, you're drinking . . . are you mad? I feel fucking rotten.'

'Oh, poor me, poor me, pour me another drink. Ahh, bless! Feeling a bit peaky, are we? Well, that will learn you. You shouldn't go around getting framed for murders and taking poor defenceless girls on the run with you.' I think she was actually a bit pissed. She was cracking up about our horrific predicament. What was going on here?

'Listen, you, I'm gonna be absolutely fine. I've had a lot to deal with recently. I shouldn't have had that bloody pasty. Usually, I'd be sweet as a nut. Anyway, I'm better now . . . are we there yet?' I was sure my voice was betraying the fact that I was desperate for this hideous journey to end.

' "Are we there yet?" I didn't realise we had one of my boys on board.' This was beginning to hack me off. Even humourless Paul was finding my sorry state a source of amusement.

'All right, you two. Without any piss-taking, how long are we gonna be?'

'We should be there in approximately half an hour. We've been making good progress and your wonderful girlfriend has been great company. Better than certain other members of the crew, I may add.'

'You two can stop flirting. Don't forget I'm armed and dangerous, according to the press. You don't wanna be found washed up in Normandy with a knife in your back.'

'Yes . . . well, let's hope that doesn't happen. It seems to me, Gemma, that your boyfriend has lost his sense of humour. Such a shame. Believe it or not, he was quite well known for it at Cambridge. What a terrible tragedy! What a shame that ten years in the City have turned a once amusing fellow into such a bore. I'm sure comedians across the land are crying with joy knowing that a potential competitor had been rendered harmless by his soul-destroying job, as he called it so often in his articles. Oh yes, Steve, I knew you were "Cityboy" even before the press mentioned it.'

'What the fuck? The press have worked it out? How the . . .' My voice tailed off. I don't know why I was even concerned about such a development, taking into account all the other stuff that was going on, but this was a bit weird.

'Steve, there was an article in *The Times* yesterday exposing the fact that the Steve Jones wanted for the murder of his boss and the notorious columnist Cityboy who exposed the squalid workings of the Square Mile were one and the same. Apparently, your secretary spilt the beans. I, of course, had worked it out some time ago. Your phraseology, your jokes and your attitudes haven't changed since Cambridge. Since I found your website I've been watching your career with some interest. Let me tell you that you can occasionally be quite amusing. Let me also tell you that you're running out of things to say and are not half as funny as you used to be.'

'Cheers for that, Paul. Join the back of the fucking queue. I've had dickheads emailing me those thoughts for the last six months. I'd like to see you try to write something funny and interesting week in week out.'

'Well, there's the thing, isn't it? I don't have to and I don't want to. I'm just expressing my view, that's all. Now, here comes land, so I suggest you two go below deck and I'll steer us in.'

Gemma stood up somewhat unsteadily and we both went down to the tiny cabin. I still felt rough but was determined not to show it. After about five minutes Paul turned the engine off and I felt the boat come to a halt. When we went back on deck, I could see we were only about seventy feet from a small, pebbly beach. Paul was lowering the dinghy suspended on the side of the boat into the water.

'OK, you two. I'm going to take you to the shore in this and then bid you adieu. No point in my coming with you. If you walk inland you'll hit a road on top of that raised ground. Turn left and after about two miles you'll come to a small town called Carteret. I suggest you tell them you're backpackers who've come from Flamanville or something. Gemma should get away with it though you, dear boy, look a bit old for all that, eh? Anyway, from there you can get a bus to Caen or another major conurbation.'

The rowing boat's bottom touched the pebbly sea bed and I immediately stood up, almost falling over in the process. Paul then shook my hand very formally and said, with a wry smile on his face, '*Au revoir, et bon chance.*' He kissed Gemma on both cheeks and we jumped off on to the beach with our bags. I relished the feeling of solid ground beneath my feet. Nothing at that moment could have felt sweeter. Gemma and I pushed the boat off and waved before turning and heading into the twilight to the rhythmic sound of Paul's oars breaking the water's surface. We began walking east along a narrow coastal path and within forty minutes we'd arrived at Carteret. After a brief exploration of the quaint seaside town we soon found a cosy, traditional guesthouse on the high street.

As we tried to settle down to sleep I ruminated about our situation. We had made it abroad. We had no passports but things could be worse. I could be lying dead in a bush in Holland Park or on a park bench in Kensington Gardens . . . or in prison. I felt so alive that I found it difficult to sleep. Gemma's deep breathing reminded me that I was also with my girl . . . though, once again, she'd been remarkably coy when getting undressed in front of me. This time I made no effort to break down her resistance. I simply resigned myself to another night of sexual frustration.

Anyway, tomorrow was going to be a big day. Tomorrow, I'd have to explain my plan to Gemma in a little more detail. She might not take too kindly to it.

Twenty-Nine

WE AWOKE WITH A START. It was early, barely past dawn. A golden light seeped through the crack in the curtains. Birds were singing just outside the window. Slowly, I began to remember what was going on. *We're at a guesthouse in some village in Normandy*.

I thought maybe I'd run the next part of the plan by Gemma over a *pain au chocolat* at breakfast. Unfortunately, she was not quite as patient as I was. As usual, her brain was working super-fast. So there was no need for me to raise the subject – she saved me the bother.

Whilst I was dressing, Gemma got out of bed and nonchalantly removed her T-shirt and knickers. I tried, and failed, not to stare at her tanned, beautiful body. My God, this was amazing . . . this was progress! She walked into the bathroom and started the shower. I could barely contain myself. She must have known what she was doing to me but she gave nothing away. After a minute or so she felt the water with her hand, adjusted the temperature and tentatively stepped in.

'So, Steve,' she said, after having allowed the water to wash over her for several minutes, 'you've dragged me to France . . . and now what's the big idea? Have you got a plan or are we doomed to be always looking over our shoulder?' Gemma had always shown an admirable ability to cut through the bullshit.

'Ah . . . well, I was coming to that, actually. Erm, I think we should go to the very south of Spain – you know, close to Gibraltar sort of thing – and I think from there we should consider hitting North Africa.' It was hard keeping my mind focused, when I was trying to focus on not getting hard.

'So that's the genius plan, is it? Hit Casablanca and set up Rick's Bar?'

'Well, it may not seem so, but I've actually put a lot of thought into this,' I lied.

'Yes, OK . . . I'm listening. Do fill me in on our . . . strategy.' She didn't sound too convinced.

'Well, d'you remember when I went climbing in the Atlas mountains this January just gone? You know, Toubkal? "Morocco's highest mountain"?'

'Yeah, I remember you doing that. You said it was a piece of piss.' I'd actually found it gruelling but felt at that early stage in our relationship that it would pay dividends to pretend to be some kind of macho Grizzly Adams type.

'Yeah, well anyway . . . when I was in Marrakech after the

climb I bought you a carpet as a present. You know the one you've got in your lounge now?'

'Yes?' Gemma was showing the patience of a saint but the word was steeped in suspicion. I had to pretend to her that I knew what I was doing. She still seemed unsure about everything. I was desperate for her to believe that running away was the sensible option. I had to convince her to trust me.

'Well, the geezer I got the carpet off wanted to buy my passport off me. He offered me five hundred dollars and said that I could just report it stolen and we'd all be laughing. Obviously I didn't go for it since that was about two hours' work back then. But I remember exactly where that bloke's shop is in the Medina. I went there twice and it's not far from the main west entrance.'

'Yes?' Gemma seemed to be enjoying my discomfort. Each 'yes' was accompanied by raised eyebrows as if she was a sceptical mother listening to her four-year-old son's cock-and-bull story about how some ornament had come to be smashed to pieces.

'Well, this geezer who buys passports obviously punts them too, or at least knows some other bloke who does.' I took a deep breath. 'We go to southern Spain and see if it's cool down there. Maybe chillax for a wee bit . . . Costa del Crime and all that. If we feel the heat is on we hit Marrakech and buy a passport off this dodgy bloke and then go somewhere sensible. I . . . I was thinking about Goa.'

'What, cos that's where Matt Damon goes in *The Bourne*

Supremacy when he's on the run? You actually think you're in a film, don't you?' She jabbed her finger at me as she asked the last question. I couldn't tell if she was angry or joking.

'No. Bollocks. I've been there twelve times, most years since I was eighteen. I know the lie of the land. I've got mates there. One of my best pals, Alex, lives out there. It's a wicked place. Cheap. Nice beaches. Good puff. Lovely tucker. Lots of crims on the run. What's not to like?'

There was a long considered pause. As always, I had no idea what was going on in her head.

'Steve, you managed to get us this far. You keep this up and I'm gonna start believing you actually know what you're doing . . . and if I start doing that I'll follow you all the way to Baghdad . . . or Bognor Regis!'

'Shit, even fucking Bognor Regis? You must really love me!' I felt a wave of relief wash over me. She had told me all I needed to know. I took her in my arms and we kissed. I was fully dressed, she was naked and wet. My clothes were getting soap suds all over them but I didn't give a tinker's cuss. After a few seconds she gently pushed me away and took a towel and began drying herself. My hands involuntarily reached out for her but I stopped myself. So desperate was I to prove that my plan to travel to the very southern tip of Spain was entirely logical that I reined in my natural urges and began another presentation – despite the fact that Gemma didn't appear to require any more persuasion. She continued drying herself off as I said my piece.

'There are four principal reasons why I believe that

heading for the southern bit of Spain is an extremely sensible move. First, the further we are from Britain the better. I think that the British police and Interpol are now our biggest worry cos they've obviously got greater resources to track us down than our Colombian friends. And if the pigs do find us I'll go to jail and you can bet your bottom dollar I'll be dead within days – so the police are almost as dangerous as the hitmen. I reckon the cops will realise pretty damn soon that we've left Blighty and they'll look in France first, knowing we lack passports and hence couldn't have left by air. Southern Spain is geographically one of the furthest places you can be from Britain whilst still in Western Europe. Second, I believe that there are no border controls between France and Spain. I may be making this up but I think they're Schengen countries or some such shit which means we can easily get into Spain without any document-ation.'

'Oh, this is great stuff,' said Gemma with mock seriousness. 'I feel privileged to be in the presence of such a tremendously powerful intellect. Your extraordinary ability to rapidly ascend the City hierarchy is being demonstrated before my very eyes.' I tried to ignore her.

'The third reason why Spain suits our needs is that for some inexplicable reason those crazy dagos don't like extraditing people to Blighty. Ronnie Knight, Freddie Foreman, Howard Marks . . . every well-known wanted crim in town used to hang out at the Costa del Crime. My international law is a little rusty but I'm pretty sure that we can chill there safe in the knowledge that any attempt to force us back to Mother England can easily be headed off at the pass. We could tie those boys up in legal red tape until at least 2076 if we felt like it.' Now, I had no idea if that was still the case but, as usual, it was all about feigning confidence and knowing a little bit more about a subject than the person I was lying to. She would surely be taken in by my nonsense bearing in mind the PhD in bullshitting I'd obtained on entering the Square Mile. She'd be no match for my grade A horseshit. I was running circles—

'No, Steve. I think you'll find that all those old rules don't apply any more. Spain is a member of the EU and there are numerous recent examples of criminals being extradited back to the United Kingdom from there. All the examples you've given were about thirty years ago. Please give me the name of a recent well-known criminal who has resided in Spain safe in the knowledge that some arcane legal complexity will allow him to keep supping sangria for the next few decades.'

'Well ... that's unfair. The point is that now, for ... erm ... obvious reasons, the police like to suppress discussion of this legal loophole and hence we never hear about all the bad boys who relax down there. Yes ... absolutely ... it's still going on, but we just don't hear about it these days.' I sounded as though I was trying to convince myself more than anyone else.

'Whatever. Anyway, what's the fourth point in your oh-so-credible argument?'

'My fourth killer point is that the south of Spain is the point in Europe closest to Morocco. So, if for some reason we do feel the need to chip over to North Africa, it will be a piece of piss. And here endeth the lesson for today.'

'Just a minute. Why would we want to go to North Africa when you've just explained so clearly that we will be as safe as houses in Spain?'

'Look, I don't know . . . something might happen. Maybe we'll decide we need to eat a goat's brain or suddenly feel an irresistible urge to buy a carpet or . . . something like that.'

'OK, Steve. Spain it is, but please, please don't try to bullshit me. I know you like the back of my hand and there's literally no point you trying it on. You are so ridiculously transparent it's embarrassing . . . but also kind of sweet.'

'Well, that's just fandabadozy. But let me tell you, my plan doesn't just stop there. Oh, no! There's also one last genius part to my devious scheming. Once we're nestled in somewhere safe, miles away from our killers, I'm gonna write a detailed letter to the pigs back home explaining exactly what's been going on. I'm also going to send the same letter to the editor of *thelondonpaper* and give them the exclusive on what happened to their Cityboy columnist. They'll jump at the chance to tell my side of the story. I'm gonna send these letters to dealer Nick in another envelope and he'll post them on. That way, no one will be able to trace where they came from and the postmarks will suggest we're still in London, which might throw everyone off the scent a little. I'm gonna explain everything about the money laundering and those two nasty fucks who are trying to kill us. We're gonna show them what really happened and then we'll be free as birds.'

'Now, that is probably the first sensible thing you've said for about five days. But let's get to Spain first and then you can start writing your letter.'

'Brilliant. You're on board, yeah? Well, that's made my fucking day! Let's pack our shit, go downstairs, have a croissant and be on our way.'

And that's exactly what we did.

Thirty

THE MAN SAT IN THE lotus position on the floor of his vast hotel room. He wore nothing but a pair of white silk boxer shorts. His hands rested gently on his knees, his back was perfectly straight and he was totally motionless. His eyes were closed and his clenched jaw and slow, deep breathing betrayed his unwavering concentration. He sat there for several minutes. There was no sound in the room other than that of air being exhaled and inhaled in long, calm breaths through his strong, Roman nose. His head was totally bald and his skin was tanned. His ethnic origin was indiscernible and his age could have been anywhere between thirty and forty-five. His broad shoulders and toned physique suggested he could unleash tremendous power with perfect accuracy in a millisecond were it required. His body had an impressive covering of large muscles but not the sort that vain bodybuilders strived to achieve by pushing weights. These were long and not bunched up, more like the muscles a swimmer or a martial artist developed after many years of hard training.

In front of the man lay a white, embossed hotel towel. Carefully placed on top of it were the five main removable working parts that together form a Glock 17 9mm semi-automatic pistol. Each of the dark heavy metal pieces had been placed in a very specific position by the Panther precisely ten minutes before he had begun his meditation. He had previously spent almost fifteen minutes cleaning them. The only other object within reach was an old-school chess clock which lay six inches from the Panther's left knee.

Suddenly, the bell in the neighbouring church emitted its first chime. There would be six more chimes as it had just turned seven o'clock. There would be a gap of about two seconds between each chime, which gave the Panther a maximum of twelve seconds to reassemble his pistol, though he hoped to beat that time convincingly. Of course, as always, he would not open his eyes at any point during the complicated procedure.

The speed with which the Panther started the chess clock and leapt into action was beautiful to behold, incredibly fast but also totally controlled. There was no unnecessary movement and no fumbling. The slightly stiff, almost robotic manner in which he moved was like that of a machine on a car assembly line, but there was a balletic grace too. First, he inserted the barrel of the gun into the slide. He then placed the rod and spring in the barrel, which was always tricky as the required tension in the spring made even the Panther's finger shake slightly. He then pulled the slide along the grooves on to the pistol's main body and attached the firing pin, which secured the slide in place: a fiddly operation even with open eyes. Finally, he firmly but gently pushed the magazine into the pistol's handle with the palm of his left hand and moved a bullet into the chamber by shifting the slide back and forth once. As he pulled back the hammer with his right thumb he straightened his arm and raised the pistol to eye level, simultaneously pushing down the button on the chess clock with his left index finger. Then, very slowly, he opened his eyes. When he looked down and saw that he'd completed the whole procedure in exactly eight seconds his face didn't betray the slightest whiff of satisfaction or pleasure despite the fact that he'd just beaten his best time by a whole two seconds. After a brief pause, he began to carefully disassemble the pistol again. He would carry out the same ritual another three times before the night was out.

Suddenly his mobile phone began to vibrate on the bedside table where it lay. The Panther never had his phone on anything other than vibrate because in his line of work an unexpected ring could cost his life were it to occur at the wrong time. He lifted himself off the floor using his powerful arms and uncurled his legs in mid-air. He extended them out in front of him parallel to the floor and then pulled his knees close to his chest. With one graceful movement he lowered himself slightly and then pushed himself off the floor with such force that he could stand up. He walked slowly to his mobile, saw a number that he recognised and pressed answer. As always, he said nothing. He just waited for instructions.

'Señor Panther, it is Gabriel here.' Gabriel spoke in his native Spanish – one of the seven languages the Panther was fluent in.

'*Si.*'

'We have a situation that needs resolution.' Gabriel awaited a response but there was none. The Panther was probably the only man in the world who could get away with this . . . this unspeakable rudeness. Gabriel continued, pretending that the silence had not annoyed him in the slightest.

'There is an English couple who need to disappear. Within an hour you will receive photos of them at your hotel. The photo of the girl is a little blurred because it comes from a bank's camera. The photo of the boy is from the papers. We know the boy has shaved off the little beard and has dyed his hair a dark colour. Likewise, the girl has had her hair cut and dyed blond. This couple are smart but they are also predictable. The envelope you receive will explain what they were last seen wearing and some background information, which may help your hunt for the quarry. Remember, they are not just wanted by us. They are also on the run . . . wanted for murder by the British police, who have so far been very helpful to us, as the envelope will show. The police suspect very strongly that they are now in France. This assignment shouldn't be too difficult for a man . . . with your skills. Payment will be double the usual rate . . . not because there are two but because this job is very important to me. There, that is it. I would wish you good luck but I know you don't need it.'

The Panther placed the phone back on the bedside table. He lived for the hunt. For the first time in many days a slight smile crossed his face. He now had a purpose – a purpose that gave his life meaning. It was the only purpose that had ever given his life meaning. He'd ceased to feel anything about other human beings as a small child. When he was five years old he had watched his parents being hacked to pieces by uniformed animals claiming to protect democracy during the civil war in El Salvador. They had laughed as their machetes had chopped into the bodies of his beloved mother and father, and had spat on their corpses as they left. The Panther, viewing everything from a crack in a cupboard door, had actually seen the life slowly leave his mother's eyes as she lay on the floor. He didn't climb out of the safety of his hiding place for six hours. By the time he'd mustered the courage to move, a rat was already feasting on his father's tongue.

The Panther had seen what men were capable of then and had gone on to witness much more bloodshed during that thirteen-year conflict. By the time he was eighteen he viewed humans as such brutal, ugly things that killing them seemed to be God's work and not that of the devil.

They were just useless pieces of flesh.

Thirty-One

THE THREE-HOUR COACH JOURNEY FROM Carteret to Paris was blissfully uneventful. We got what I initially thought were a few suspicious glances from some of our fellow passengers but this time I was able to dismiss my fears as the putrid imaginings of my scrambled mind. This was definitely just my old friend paranoia coming back to haunt me. My previous healthy appetite for drugs had always meant she'd been a passing acquaintance of mine but since this whole shitstorm had kicked off paranoia had become a constant companion, an undesired live-in lover. Nowadays rarely a moment went by when I couldn't hear her twisted whisperings, her seductive calls.

The bus alighted at the Galliéni coach station and we immediately took a cab to the Gare de Lyon. There was a beautiful old clock tower that read 4.20 in the square outside the station. Even before we stepped out of the cab we could see that the place was absolutely crawling with rozzers and these fuckers had guns too. As we entered the vast concourse and without any prompting Gemma put on her shades and baseball hat. I followed suit. Once inside I instinctively looked round the walls for CCTV cameras. They were everywhere and they all seemed to be trained on me. I told Gemma to keep her head down. She raised her eyebrows with a 'no shit Sherlock' look. I then left her at a café nursing an espresso whilst I went off to organise the tickets. I figured that we'd be more conspicuous as a couple and so should try to stay apart whenever we were in well-policed public places. I queued up impatiently. We were in luck – the next express train down to Montpellier on the south coast of France was leaving in thirty-five minutes. It would only take six hours. I bought a couple of second-class tickets and meandered back to Gemma, studiously keeping my eyes on the floor and avoiding any pigs that happened to be bowling around. Before you could say '*tout est bien qui finit bien*' we were sitting on a spotless French train heading down to 'freedom' at about two hundred miles an hour. We removed our jackets, settled into our comfortable seats and watched the flat, featureless countryside fly by. Our carriage was relatively empty and the hypnotic noise of the train's rumbling passage was broken only by an animated mobile phone conversation from the French businessman sitting opposite us.

It was after about an hour that I decided to go and get some wine from the buffet car with the last of the euros I had left. We'd just passed Orléans and Gemma and I were beginning to feel marginally less stressed. We were chatting away to each other and it was clear we were both almost looking forward to the life that lay ahead for us. With each passing second we were getting further and further away from killers, cops and prying do-gooders. I gave Gemma a quick kiss on the cheek, stood up and began strolling through the carriages towards the middle of the train, feeling almost calm for the first time in days.

I was just about to enter the buffet car when I saw them. My finger was poised over the red lit-up button that would open the connecting door when through the door's window I spied two *gendarmes* hassling some poor Algerian bloke. He was fumbling around in his inside pocket. They'd clearly asked him for identification. I stood there like a rabbit in the headlights, completely transfixed. My heart rate immediately doubled.

I instinctively took a step to the side of the door and pushed my back against the wall. Nervously, I observed the two cops though the window, keeping most of my face and body obscured from view. This could just be a specific crim they were after and maybe they'd found him. They'd obviously just got on at Orléans and had been doing a sweep of the train from the rear carriage. Unfortunately, after the Algerian chap had shown the policemen his ID they moved on and asked a fat, red-faced old man sitting at the bar for his papers. Shit! These guys were clearly asking everyone on the train for ID. Maybe this is how they rolled in France. Maybe they were on high alert due to some recent terrorist bullshit. But maybe they were after me and Gemma. *Fuck!* Neither of us had our passports and I don't think these boys would be satisfied with a British driving licence. I cursed whichever Tory wanker it was who'd decided that we weren't to be part of the Schengen agreement or whatever it was. Anyway, if they were actually after us any form of ID would condemn us to being transported back to Britain – to either imprisonment or execution. I turned round and began to walk back to Gemma as briskly as possible without raising suspicion. I hoped I'd come up with a plan on the way.

As I went, failing dismally to look untroubled, I racked my brain for a way out of this hellish situation. The next station was at least another hour away so a quick march to the front of the train in the hope that the rozzers wouldn't get to us by the time we stopped again was a pointless strategy. What to do? What to fucking do?

An obvious trick sprang to mind. It was something I'd pulled myself as a poverty-stricken student a few times when avoiding ticket inspectors. You simply locked yourself in the toilets and waited until they passed. In the absence of a better plan it would have to do.

I arrived at our table. Gemma was looking out of the window, where the countryside seemed to be rushing by at a thousand miles an hour. I was mildly breathless and sweating a little. Before I'd even opened my mouth she looked up and asked, 'What's wrong?'

'What's wrong is that we've got two fucking cops going through the fucking train checking everyone's fucking ID. That's what's fucking wrong.' I had lowered my head close to hers and was spitting the words out through gritted teeth just in case one of our neighbours could understand English. 'We need to move up the train right now and hide somewhere – probably the bogs.' I grabbed her upper arm and virtually tried to lift her out of the seat. Her face twisted into a grimace and she shrugged me off angrily.

'Stop that! That hurts. Don't be so fucking forceful.' Worse still, her raised voice and angry expression had drawn attention to us. Our fellow passengers probably thought I was some kind of demented sex pest hassling this poor defenceless beauty.

'OK. I'm sorry. I didn't mean to hurt you . . . but you must come with me now.' My eyes were pleading with hers. I desperately wanted to communicate the seriousness of our new predicament.

'All right, but you don't need to grab me like that. It really fucking hurt.' She stood up and grabbed her rucksack from the luggage rack above her. There was an irritating lack of urgency in her every movement. I grabbed my bag and lifted it on to my shoulder. Then I held my hand out behind me for her to take so that I could lead her towards the front of the train at a pace I dictated. She refused to take it. I marched down the aisle, anger replacing the fear I'd recently been feeling.

I came to the door at the end of our carriage and pressed the button to open it. We entered the interconnecting section that partitioned our carriage from the next one. I saw the door to a toilet on our right. I pushed the button to open it but nothing happened. I frantically pushed again and again but still nothing. I looked round desperately and saw a red light on above the door. Oh, shit, it was occupied. We were going to have to try another one.

After a fast march through the next carriage we found ourselves at another toilet. This time the light above the door was green. We both bundled in and I pressed the close button. At last the door slid shut and I locked it. We were 'safe'. Gemma still looked really pissed off. When I attempted to apologise again she simply raised her finger to her mouth. She would have said she was doing it to avoid raising the suspicions of anyone who happened to be outside, but in reality she was just doing it to wind me up.

After about forty horrible, quiet, nervous seconds she suddenly spoke up. 'Listen, Steve,' she whispered, 'we've got to leave. We've got to go somewhere else.'

'What?' I spat out the word.

'If the police find us in here we're in big trouble. We need to move out.'

'No fucking way! We don't even know if they're outside right now. We've got to stay here and wait.'

'No, honey, that is simply not happening.' She ended the argument by pushing the open button.

The door slid open and we crept outside and looked back into the carriage we'd just come through. The two policemen were at the far end, still checking everyone's documentation. They were so engrossed in their activity that I doubted they'd seen us through the door's window.

Gemma grabbed my hand and led me through the door

to the next carriage. Somewhat against my wishes we continued our brisk walk away from the police. When we reached the next partition I pulled her back and said angrily, 'So what are we going to do now, smartarse?'

She appeared to have no answer. I began frantically looking round for a solution to our problems but there was none.

Then I focused on the exterior doors. Obviously, they would only open when the train was at a complete standstill, but above them were two slide-down windows that, if they were pulled down completely, you could just about fit through. They were only about a foot wide but if you went sideways you could manage it.

I pulled down the window on the door nearest me. The air rushed in and the noise of the train, which had seemed muted before, was now deafeningly loud. I pushed my head out. The wind immediately made my eyes stream and blew my hair in all directions. I looked down. There was a step about four feet below the bottom of the open window. It was just about big enough for someone to crouch on. You'd have to be damn careful but there was a bar on either side that you could hold on to for stability.

I turned round to Gemma. She could see what I was about to suggest.

'No fucking way! You have *got* to be joking! You want me to jump?' She had to shout to be heard over the roaring wind.

'No, no . . . listen, this is definitely doable. Check it out.

I'll help lower you down on to the step outside this one and then I'll go and do the same on the one opposite. Please, it's our only hope.'

Gemma tentatively poked her head outside and saw what she was supposed to make her home for the next five or ten minutes – a six-inch step, three feet above ground that was rushing by at approximately two hundred miles an hour.

'Steve, I cannot do this. Why don't you try it and I'll go in the toilet?'

'No way. You can do it. If you're caught they'll ask for your ID and then we'll both be done for. Please, I'll lower you down. It'll be fine.'

The two cops were about halfway down the carriage we'd just left. We had about three minutes to execute our plan or it was game over.

'Look, the cops are nearly here. Please, please do this.'

Gemma gazed despairingly at me but a certain look told me that I'd managed to win her over. I pulled the window right down. She tentatively pushed her right leg through it, using my shoulder to support her as she did so. She then put both arms on my shoulders and lifted her other leg through. My legs were shaking from the strain as well as from the adrenalin that was coursing through my body. Gemma's platinum blond hair was blowing everywhere and her face looked absolutely panic-stricken. Her little rucksack was catching the wind and making it hard for her to stay close to the side. Slowly but surely she lowered herself down on to the step. She grabbed the bars on either side of the door and flattened herself against the train. Her cheek was planted on the outside of the door. I took one look out of the window at her and shouted, 'Stay there until I come and get you.' Whether she heard me over the wind it was impossible to say. I tried to slam her window shut but it bounced back a little, leaving a tiny gap. Time was too precious to care about that.

As I turned to the opposite exit I glanced to my left and saw that the cops were now merely ten feet from the door leading into our section and that there were only about four people left to question. I grabbed the top of the window and pulled down. It moved about three inches. Fuck! I pulled down with all my might. It budged slightly but only another few inches. Shit! I glanced around desperately. I contemplated entering the next carriage but there was every chance the cops would see me through the connecting door's window if I tried that. I'd have one last go at pulling the window down before I gave up. This time I grabbed the top and brought my knees up to my chest so that all my body weight was hanging from it. Suddenly, the panel slid down. It was now about three-quarters open.

I virtually threw my left leg through the window. Then I manoeuvred my head out too. I felt like some kind of Chinese contortionist. I began squeezing my body into the rushing wind.

Suddenly, I saw a tunnel up ahead. I was stuck half in and half out. I had about five seconds to sort myself out. Oh,

Christ! Of all the ways to die this wasn't the one I'd envisaged.

I frantically pulled my right leg through the window and lowered myself on to the step. I flattened myself as much as possible to the door but still had one more thing to do, tunnel or no tunnel. An open window would be a dead giveaway to the cops so I had to close it. I began pushing up with my right hand. My hand kept slipping and sliding on the greasy surface, leaving telltale smear marks. The glass was only moving in tiny increments.

Then the tunnel was on me and there was a roaring noise like nothing I'd heard before. My cheeks were being sucked inwards as the breath was forced out of me, and I gripped the two bars on either side of the door with such force that my knuckles turned white. Despite turning my head away from the front of the train my eyes were streaming with tears. Some light came out through the train's windows but it only succeeded in creating a horrifying strobe effect on the walls of the tunnel. I squeezed my eyes shut and prayed that Gemma was OK. I desperately wanted to close the final few inches of the window. But there was no way in hell I could do anything other than cling on for dear life. Besides, there was every chance that the cops were now in our section so I couldn't do anything that would draw attention to my whereabouts.

We emerged from the tunnel after about thirty seconds of sheer, unremitting hell. I was shaking with cold and fear. The rucksack on my back had been catching the wind and I had constantly thought that it might catch on some rock and pull me off. Still, I was alive and in one piece, but was Gemma? I wouldn't find out for another five minutes or so because I had to wait some time to ensure that the cops had passed through to the next carriage.

Suddenly I heard a muffled noise above me. Two men were talking in French just above my head. It was the cops. They were probably wondering why the hell the window was a few inches open. I flattened myself to the door even more, praying they didn't look outside and down. Fortunately, they weren't that conscientious. Unfortunately, they completely closed the stubborn window with a few firm upward pushes.

After an uncomfortable wait of three or four windswept minutes I decided it would be safe to re-enter the train. I carefully raised myself up on my step and peeped through the bottom of the window. No sign of the police. Good. I released my right hand from the bar it had been gripping for dear life and tried to pull the window down. But it was impossible. The burly policeman had clearly wedged it in so hard that there was simply no way a ten-stone weakling like myself was ever going to pull it down with one hand whilst suspended on the outside of a fast-moving train. Christ, we were in trouble now. Gemma and I would probably have to stay on our little steps hurtling through the French country-side until we reached the next stop. We were disastrously fucked now. I waited for a few minutes, racking my brain for a solution, but none appeared. I felt completely powerless and despaired at my stupidity. It would be a total miracle if—

'Steve, Steve . . . I'm here.' Gemma was shouting with all her might but I only just heard her over the incessant roar. One side of her face was entirely covered in grime, making her look like some kind of half-hearted Al Jolson wannabe. But fuck me . . . she'd managed to pull her window down, climb back in and open mine a couple of inches too. What a girl!

I lifted one hand over the top of the window and tried to pull it down further. She was desperately doing the same but we couldn't budge it. Realising we needed to do something a little more radical I simply lifted my other hand from its comforting bar and curled it round the top of the window as well. I then took a deep breath and carefully removed my feet from the step so that my whole body weight was forcing the panel downwards.

Of course, I'd over-egged it. The window came crashing down and had I not raised my feet up instinctively they would have hit the ground and that would have been it. Shaking like a leaf, I lifted myself back on to my step. After a few more deep breaths I clambered through the window to safety.

'Fucking hell, am I glad to see you!' I was virtually laughing, such was my relief.

'Christ, Steve, I thought I was a goner when we hit that tunnel.' Sweat beaded Gemma's forehead and there were little white lines round her eyes where she'd been squeezing them tight. I hugged her and felt her heart racing next to mine. Her deep breathing slowly returned to normal. I felt my tense body begin to relax. Relief entered every pore of my skin. Eventually I broke the silence.

'Let's clean off all this shite and head for the buffet. I need a fucking beer!'

Thirty-Two

W E ARRIVED AT THE TOWN of Tarifa, on the southernmost tip of Spain just below Gibraltar, two days after alighting from the train in Montpellier. Having learnt our lesson we'd taken a bus from Montpellier to Barcelona, arriving there at around ten o'clock at night. Much to Gemma's surprise, our passports weren't demanded as we crossed to Spanish soil – amazingly, the crap I'd been spinning about the Schengen agreement had actually proved to be true. We stayed the night in Barcelona and even managed a few glasses of sangria and some tapas on Las Ramblas. The next morning we took another coach to Marbella. From there we travelled to a town called Algeciras and, finally, used a local bus to take us to Tarifa.

It was three in the afternoon when we arrived in Tarifa. There was a terrifically strong wind blowing in from the sea. I took Gemma by the hand and we walked towards the port area. It was a small town and after about four minutes we arrived at the dock. We looked out over the numerous moored yachts to the sea beyond. My God, you could actually see Africa from here! It looked so close you could touch it. I'd grabbed a tourist map of Tarifa from the bus station, and using my thumb I measured out the distance between us and the coast of Africa. Freedom and happiness lay just ten miles away! I didn't tell Gemma but I decided there and then that we wouldn't be sticking around here for long. Our destiny lay in Morocco and beyond.

After a couple of glasses of white Rioja at a dockside bar I asked the youthful, mustachioed owner in my piss-poor Spanish – which was essentially the same as my French except I added o's and a's to the end of all the words – whether there was somewhere inexpensive to stay nearby. Fortunately, he spoke a little English and, even more fortunately, he told us that there were a few spare rooms above his bar that he rented out to tourists. Since it was no longer high season the rate was a measly thirty euros a night and there was no one else staying there. Fantastic.

That night we drank more white Rioja under a starry sky whilst watching the fishing boats return to shore. The sound of the gulls and the smell of the salty air helped us to pretend that we were in a normal situation. But I began to feel uneasy. I desperately wanted to know what was happening back in England. Questions kept plaguing me: were we still making headlines? Had the police begun pursuing anyone else? Had there been any sightings of us since we'd left Britain? I wanted answers but I knew I couldn't call my parents or brothers or anyone immediately connected to me because the police would be expecting that. It was then that I thought of Jane. We weren't so close that calls to her phone would be traced or bugged by anyone looking for me. She also knew more about my situation than anyone else and had even broached the subject with her father. I decided to call her, but for obvious reasons declined to mention it to Gemma. If she knew that I was calling the girl I'd 'betrayed' her for then my life wouldn't be worth living.

When Gemma returned from the ladies I announced that I was going to the shop round the corner to buy some fags, stood up and marched off. I had seen a call box just in front of the shop and had enough change in my pocket for a few minutes of chat.

I took out of my wallet the credit-card sized laminate that had all the members of the Geldlust utilities team's contact details printed on it. I had asked the team secretary to make several copies soon after I had become team leader and had insisted that everyone on the team kept it on them at all times. I inserted a few euros and nervously punched in Jane's mobile number. After six pips she answered her phone. I tried to sound as calm as possible but was sure my false bravado came over as just that. She sounded nervous and upset.

'Steve, where are you? You've got to come and talk to me and Dad. I've told him a bit about your situation. He thinks you should come and see him. He won't pursue anything before you do, but he's willing to listen to your story.'

'Look, I can't tell you where I am, OK? Just rest assured

I'm not in Britain any more. Listen, can you tell me what's going on back home? Are they still after us? Are we still in the papers?'

'Well, you're not exactly Lord Lucan, but there's still the odd article about you. There seems to be a general assumption that you're guilty, but I know you're not. I believe your story. Seriously, where are you? What are you going to do?'

'I'm gonna hole up somewhere safe and write down everything I know about Geldlust's involvement in this money laundering and exactly what's happened to me over the last week. Then I'm gonna send copies to the police, my newspaper . . . and your dad.'

'Steve, I strongly recommend you send it to me first and I'll show Dad. You need to get him on side and then the police are going to *have* to listen to you. He's a man of considerable influence. Please don't do anything rash.'

'Well, maybe. Look, I better go . . . my missus is going to be getting suspicious.' I'd decided to make sure I mentioned Gemma – it somehow meant that what I was doing wasn't a betrayal and that there'd be no misunderstanding.

'Oh, so the reports are right . . . you're back with her, are you? Well, that's a bit of a shame. I thought that once this was all over you and I could maybe hang out . . .'

I couldn't help feeling flattered, but Jane no longer held any interest for me. 'Jane, you've got to understand that I love Gemma. She's forgiven me now and I'm not going to allow anything else to fuck this up.' I don't know why I felt the need to explain my feelings to Jane. Maybe I just wanted to hear myself confirm the way I felt.

'Oh, I see.'

There was an awkward silence and I decided to terminate the conversation, but Jane kept talking to me every time I tried to say goodbye, until I ran out of coins and couldn't have carried on chatting even if I'd wanted to. I returned to our café and immediately ordered another bottle of Rioja. Gemma looked at me suspiciously but I ignored it and we soon settled back into a chat about 'the plan'.

Jane looked at her telephone for several seconds, then checked the small electronic device that she'd recently been given. The LED screen on the tracer displayed the number 0034 956 695854. She knew that the initial code 0034 meant it was Spain but it would take checking the internet to discover which Spanish town the code 956 denoted. Her first investigation suggested that the call was from Algeciras or Cadiz, but then she found that because the next group of numbers began with 69 Steve had been calling from somewhere called Tarifa. She typed 'Tarifa, Spain' into Google and immediately a map of the southern tip of Europe flashed up. Jane studied it for a while and then opened the drawer by the side of her bed, took out a pay-as-you-go mobile and punched in the number she'd been given two days before. Her fingers were shaking slightly. She felt a degree of pride that she'd managed to achieve what she'd been asked to do but she was also a little scared about how deeply involved she had become. She knew that if her father found out about what she was doing she'd be in very big trouble.

After three rings the call was answered and a low voice simply said, '*Si.*' It was impossible to tell anything about the man on the other end of the phone from that one word. That was probably what he wanted, Jane thought.

'Oh, hello. Erm, I'm a friend of Juan and Don Llosa. I was told to tell you that I was *amiga de Claudio.*' Jane didn't understand the significance of the code but it was what Juan had told her to say.

There was a long pause. The Panther enjoyed allowing those who called him to do all the talking.

'Erm . . . I have some information that may help you. The man you want to . . . talk to . . . called me ten minutes ago. The phone call was made from a small town on the southern tip of Spain called Tarifa. I do not know the precise location of the call but Tarifa only has a population of around fifteen thousand so it shouldn't be too hard to . . . meet them.'

Another long pause.

'Erm . . . that's all I have. I think—'

But the line was already dead. The Panther was calling an associate with a private jet before Jane had even realised he'd hung up.

Thirty-Three

RULE NUMBER ONE WHEN YOU start a stay of any decent length of time at a guesthouse is to make friends with the owner. If you do that he'll tell you everything you want to know about the local fun spots. He'll tell you where to get the best calamari (admittedly usually at his brother's restaurant) and, if he's a bit naughty, he'll be able to tell you where to procure the best puff or sniff. If you're very naughty he may well be able to point you to the most accommodating brasses and the most revealing strip joints. A friendly owner will also make sure your room doesn't get broken into and that you're warned in good time if for some reason the police come a-calling. It was this last potential service that was of particular interest to me and explains why I spent our first night in Tarifa getting absolutely wankered with Alejandro.

Gemma and I had been quite tetchy with each other since Montpellier. The constant travelling had been getting on our tits and I couldn't help but feel that she was wondering if this whole 'adventure' thing she'd recklessly set forth on was a major mistake. Despite feeling that she'd had no choice back in London, she had begun to question our escape plan since arriving in Spain. I'd caught her deep in thought on several occasions and she'd suggested a few times that maybe we, or more specifically she, had made the wrong decision. Perhaps we should just have gone to the police and chanced our luck. Our conversations had been stilted and awkward. For a couple of days I hadn't felt the connection with her that had previously been so strong. We hadn't been laughing much and there'd been a noticeable absence of meaningful glances into each other's eyes. We also hadn't had sex since we'd 'got back together' which was totally unacceptable in anyone's book. My nuts felt ready to explode and I was desperate to seal the deal. I had to know that Gemma and I were back on. I decided there was only one adult solution to our problem – we'd get totally bladdered and see what happened.

We ate our dinner at one of the tables outside Alejandro's café overlooking the docks. The chicken and chips I ordered wasn't perhaps the best meal in the world – in fact I suspect it wasn't in the top thousand consumed in Tarifa that night. Gemma's paella didn't look much better and some of the grotty prawns covering it looked like veritable health hazards. However, if it took eating some greasy chicken and a potentially lethal paella to ingratiate our man then that's what we'd have to do. After we'd consumed our tasteless swill we went and sat on the tall stools at the bar and began chatting to Alejandro. There was no one else around and soon we both started to relax. Gemma kept smiling at me and I kept smiling back at her. I ordered brandy after brandy for the three of us and by about midnight was chatting away in Spanish like a native . . . or at least it seemed like that to me. Every new drink made Gemma and me gaze longer into each other's eyes.

It was when everyone was so arseholed we were virtually frothing at the mouth that I decided to try to achieve the two goals that were playing on my mind. Gemma was kipping with her head resting on her crossed arms on the bar, and whilst her unconsciousness was likely to scupper my nocturnal plans it was also a Brucie bonus because her involvement in these particular discussions was not required. By this stage I was so lashed that I'd reverted to English because the effort required to speak even pidgin Spanish was getting a little too much for my addled brain.

'So Alejandro, tell me . . . if I wanted to talk to someone about goin' 'cross to Morocco by boat for a quick day trip . . . who would the best person be?' My words were slurred and would only just be comprehensible to an English linguistic genius. Somehow Alejandro seemed to understand everything I said, which, as far as I was concerned, ranked his command of English up there with that of William Shakespeare.

'Steve, there ees a boat three times a day every day from Algeciras to Tangiers. Eet only costs maybe thirty euros one way and takes just one hour.'

'But the thing is . . . it looks like I'm gonna have a friend coming over here soon. Now . . . this poor geezer has mislaid his passport and he can't be arsed going through official channels so he'd like to get to Morocco without any of that customs bullshit. To cut a long story short, do you know anyone who'd be happy to take us – I mean my friend – across the ten miles to Morocco in a boat for good money and no questions asked?'

God knows how much of my slurred drivel he took in but one thing he definitely understood was that I wasn't actually talking about a friend.

'Well, Steve . . . your "friend"' – you could virtually see the inverted commas as he mouthed the word – ''e ees gonna find eet difficult to find any *hombre* to do thees. The man you – your friend – would ask to do thees may be suspicious that thees person no want 'ave 'is passport checked because 'e criminal. Eet would cost your friend very much. I could ask people I know but I do not know eef thees will be easy. Eet may take a few days.'

'No problem, Alejandro. Please ask around and come back to me and I'll talk to my friend.' By this stage we both knew who we were talking about but it was best left unspoken. 'One other thing . . . you see Gemma here?' I pointed at my comatose girlfriend.

'Yes?'

'She has a nasty ex-boyfriend after her. He's very angry with me and he's been chasing us for a few days now. She met this guy in South America and he's one mean son of a bitch. He could get violent. Very violent. Now, if this guy, or in fact there're likely to be two of them, come round here looking for us I'd really appreciate it if you didn't tell them we're here. It would be really good if you'd say you've never seen us. Oh, and if these guys do come round they're likely to pretend they're police and start bullshitting you. Do you understand? *Comprende?*'

'*Si*, Steve, I understand completely. Please do not worry, I will say nothing to no one. You seem like nice people and I will be very, 'ow you say, deescreet.'

After I'd got my two key points across I decided it was time to hit the sack. Before I did so I made sure I paid for the meal and all the booze. I also gave a big tip. Although our resources were limited this was surely the best use of twenty euros that I could make.

I shook Gemma awake. She looked dazed and confused. I pushed her up the stairs at the back of the bar to our room and helped her into bed face down. She fell asleep immediately and after struggling for a few minutes to remove her clothes I gave up, turned the light off, removed my own clothes and lay down next to her. I put my arms round her and received a muted sigh of recognition.

I didn't know it then but that twenty-euro tip would prove to be a lifesaver . . . literally.

Thirty-Four

I WOKE UP SLOWLY. GEMMA was snoring next to me, now on her back but still fully clothed. I sat up and immediately regretted it. That cheap Spanish brandy had been a major error – especially the ninth one. I needed to get my shit together and start enquiring about how to get to Morocco but my head felt as if some large mammal had shat in it. Possibly a rhino or an elephant. Christ! I'd had some hideous hangovers in my time but they all paled in comparison to this. This was the one and only original bad boy – the gauge by which all hangovers henceforth would be judged. The *absolute* hangover.

The cold shower I forced myself into had the desired effect. At least when I got out I could focus my eyes and just about recognise my face in the mirror. I looked hideous. I'd aged about thirty years and I wouldn't want anyone under the age of twelve to see those scary eyes. They'd have nightmares for years to come.

Gemma remained sleeping. Cool. I'd have some breakfast and begin my mission. I staggered down the steps to find Alejandro looking absolutely fine behind the bar.

'Good morning, Steve. Oh, no, eet ees afternoon!' I must have looked disgustingly gruesome, because he was laughing.

'Hello, Alejandro. Not feeling a hundred per cent . . . for some reason. Can't think what that is . . . maybe the chicken, eh?' I said with a half-smile on my face.

'Possibly . . . but I think not. Would you like a little brandy . . . 'ow you say, "the 'air of the dog that bit me", no?'

I couldn't believe it. Alejandro was already nursing a large glass of brandy. He wasn't mucking about. This lad meant business.

'Er . . . that's very kind of you but I think I'll pass this time. I've got things to do.'

'Ah . . . try to find boat for your . . . *amigo* who is chased by the nasty South Americans, yes?'

'No . . . he's just lost his passport. It's me and Gemma the nasty ex-boyfriend's after. Yeah . . . that's it.' I was so unconvincing I didn't even convince myself.

'Of course! Do not worry. I remember all that ees said. If you want to find your friend a boat across the water then I suggest to ask the fishermen on the far side of the docks. They may help. Be careful, though. Their English not so good as me.' He was cracking up at the absurdity of us both keeping up our preposterous charade. I gave him a weak smile and shuffled towards the door.

I left the bar and stumbled towards the far side of the docks like a zombie on ketamine. The midday sun was hideously bright and I'd predictably forgotten my sunglasses. Each step was painful and I wished I'd been able to follow my usual hangover cure of washing down four Nurofen with a bacon sarnie and a can of Coke – something that had been standard practice back in London. If I'd had the option, I wouldn't have done anything at all for about forty-eight hours, but time was of the essence and we needed to get to Morocco ASAP. There was every chance some CCTV image of us at the Gare de Lyon had been seen by the cops or that someone on the train to Montpellier had clocked us evading the police and squealed. We were definitely not in the clear yet.

I passed a small beach on my right. There were a bunch of people renting out kitesurfers, windsurfers and jet skis. So that's what they did for kicks around here. There didn't seem to be many people using their services, though. I suppose it was end of season so tourists were thin on the ground. A couple of chaps offered to rent me out a windsurfer but I waved them away, feeling too dreadful to even try to confuse them with my bullshit Spanish.

I walked up the pier and tentatively approached a group of about five fishermen who were sitting around smoking tabs and fixing nets at its far end. Their grizzled faces, frayed clothes and gnarled hands conformed to all the stereotypes of Spanish fishermen. As I got to within about twenty feet they all turned round and stopped chatting. A couple began laughing to themselves. Shit, I must have looked bad. Come on, Steve, you can handle this.

'Buenos dias, señors. Uno momento por favor. Yo voudrais voyager a Morocco mañana si possible. Mucho dinare si necesario.'

They literally all cracked up as one. I flushed crimson. I knew that my hybrid Spanish wasn't perfect but I thought at least they'd get the gist of what I was trying to say. It might have merely been a bastardised version of French but I seemed to be perfectly understood last night at around midnight . . . well, after the seventh brandy.

'Señor, no entiendo,' said one of them finally, after he'd got his giggles under control.

After about five dreadful minutes of failing to explain what it was I was after I decided to give up. This was clearly a total waste of everyone's time. What I needed to do was go back and grab Alejandro and bring him here so that he could explain what the deal was.

I made my excuses and began to meander back towards our bar/guesthouse. I decided to stop off at a restaurant before I got back, not wishing to risk eating any more of the dubious nosh that Alejandro had on offer. After a reasonably pleasant Spanish omelette I almost began to feel vaguely human again, and it was nearly at a normal pace that I tottered back to the ranch. Alejandro wasn't there, which was weird. In fact, no one was there. There is something eerie about a totally empty bar. Still, I thought no more of it, and began the daunting climb up the one flight of stairs to our room. As I struggled to find the key to our door I heard someone coming up the stairs I had just scaled. There seemed to be an unnatural speed to the way he was bounding up the steps. I found the pair of keys and tried to push one of them into the lock.

The first key I chose was the wrong one. I tried to remove it from the lock but I'd jammed it in, and somehow I managed to drop them both when I finally pulled it out. It was whilst I was crouching down to pick them up that a tall figure emerged from the stairwell at the far end of the corridor. He stood motionless for a minute, then began slowly walking towards me. Now his pace was unnaturally slow.

At first I couldn't make him out in the shadows. He was panting. Something was definitely wrong.

'Alejandro?' There was no reply. The figure continued walking towards me.

'*Si*, Steve, eet ees me.' He was out of breath and, now that he was out of the shadows and his face was visible, I could see that he looked genuinely worried. 'Steve, a man . . . 'e come looking for you five minutes ago. 'E show me photo of you – but you had little beard and your 'air was different colour. Eet looked like eet was taken from a newspaper.'

'Oh, shit!' I couldn't stop myself. 'What did he say?'

''E said 'e was a policeman and that you were a criminal . . . that you had killed a man. But I don't believe him. He don't look like policeman and 'is Spanish . . . 'is Spanish was South American. 'E was strong, bald man and 'e looked . . . 'ow you say . . . 'e looked very, very mean.'

Christ! If he wasn't a policeman and it wasn't one of the two wankers who'd been chasing us in London, who was this new feller? An appalling situation had somehow just got even more hideous. My scrambled brain tried to assimilate the new information.

'Alejandro, what did you say to him?'

'I told 'im I never seen you. But I don't think eet will take long for 'im to find you. Tarifa ees only small. There are only maybe five or six guest'ouses open now – most of them on the sea front. If you've been anywhere round 'ere they'll say they've seen you and 'e will come back.'

Oh, God! Now that Spanish omelette didn't look like quite such a smart move.

'Steve, I really think you must go. I no want no trouble 'ere. Please, take your girlfriend and liv.' I was pretty sure he meant 'leave', but what it sounded like might have been more appropriate.

I had to think up a solution right now. I was beginning to sober up extremely quickly. I probably had twenty minutes at most before this fucker worked out where we were. For all I knew he had already spoken to someone who'd seen me come in here. He could speak Spanish, unlike me, so that was going to help him. He could be coming here right now. Or maybe he was waiting by the docks perusing the esplanade.

'OK, Alejandro, is there a back door to this place?'

'No.'

Suddenly, I knew that I only had one option. It was high

risk but my befuddled brain could see no other. At that moment it seemed like my only choice. With hindsight I wasn't thinking straight.

'OK, Alejandro, this is what we're gonna do. We're gonna put Gemma in another room and you're gonna go downstairs behind the bar and act like everything's normal. Now, when this guy comes back I want you to say that I just came in and took a room upstairs. Tell him exactly which room I'm in and tell him how to get there. I'll be waiting.'

'But Steve, thees guy does not look very . . . nice. I mean no disrespect, but eef thees gets . . . physical, I don' think you 'ave good chance.'

'Listen, don't worry about that. This is just that South American ex-boyfriend of my missus I was telling you about. I'll reason with him and everything will be fine. I'll tell him Gemma left hours ago for Madrid or some shit. Whatever you do, don't call the police, OK? This is between me and him.'

'OK. I wait downstairs at the bar. Here is the key to the room upstairs.'

'Cool. Don't send anyone up for five minutes, but after that go for it. One other thing . . . do you have some rope downstairs?'

'*Si*. I'll leave it on your bed.'

The next part of my mission was perhaps going to be the toughest: manoeuvring a near-comatose tetchy hungover girlfriend up a flight of stairs to a different room in under five minutes without explaining the reason for my urgency. It was a big ask in anyone's book.

'Darling, darling, darling,' I repeated, shaking Gemma's shoulder. Eventually she stirred, and at once started coughing violently. We'd both smoked about twenty fags the night before and neither of us was really a committed smoker. She opened her eyes. They were bloodshot and full of sleep.

'Wha' the fuck? Wha's going on? Where . . . wha'? I feel awful.'

'Honey, everything's cool. Alejandro has just remembered that he's promised this room to a cousin of his. So we gotta go to another room. I'm just gonna move you into another room.' My voice was so artificially gentle and calm that had Gemma not still been half cut she would have seen right through my crap immediately.

'Really? Fuck . . . all right, then.' Christ, I'd never seen her this compliant. I should get her hideously hungover more often, I thought.

As quickly as possible I pulled her out of bed and manoeuvred her to the door.

'Just a minute . . . I've gotta put my clothes on.'

'No, love, you're already wearing them . . . don't worry about that.'

She was still clearly half asleep. I opened the door and pushed her through, then took her hand and, trying not to seem in a total panic, pulled her up the stairs.

'Oi! What's the fucking hurry?'

'Honey, the cousin's downstairs already and he's bound to get moody with Alejandro if he sees someone else in his room. I'll sort out our things and join you in about an hour or so, OK?'

I found the upstairs room, opened the door and made Gemma take her trousers and shirt off before she got into bed. I waited for about one minute and she was asleep again. I stroked her hair for a bit. I remember thinking this could well be the last time I ever touched her beautiful hair.

I gathered up her clothes and closed the door behind me. This way, there'd be less chance that she'd just wander downstairs if she happened to wake up. I went back down to our room, made sure the door was locked and dumped her clothes in the corner. I put the rope Alejandro had left me on top of the pile.

Then I reached into the bottom of my rucksack and removed the pistol I'd grabbed in Kensington Gardens. It was much heavier than I'd remembered. The silencer made it longer and it somehow seemed more deadly than I imagine it would have been without. I knew virtually nothing about guns but one thing I had heard was that they had safety catches. Sure enough, there was a little lever on the side. I had no fucking idea what was on and what was off, but I had to know and there was only one way of finding out. I opened the window to my room about nine inches and then lifted the barrel up so that it pointed at a small cloud lazily floating by. I felt myself tense as I pulled the trigger.

Nothing. OK, now it was time to try with the catch turned the other way.

This time when I pulled the trigger I knew about it. The gun kicked back much more strongly than I'd expected and I almost dropped it. The noise it made was also louder than I'd expected considering it had a silencer on. Still, it was unlikely anyone would have heard it a storey below.

OK, we were in business. I sat down on the only chair in the room, facing the door. The gun lay on my knees. Now all I could do was wait.

Thirty-Five

I WAITED. THEN I WAITED some more. Nothing. God knows how many minutes passed. It felt like hours. My foot was tapping uncontrollably on the floor. I didn't dare move. But I had to. I couldn't just sit there pretending to myself that this wasn't a big deal. I stood up and went to the window. I crouched down and peered out, my eyes barely above the sill. The world was going on as if nothing was out of the ordinary. The odd tourist walked by the docks. The crusty fishermen were still at the end of the pier fixing their nets. The gulls were still calling out.

I became a bit braver and raised my head a little. I looked to my right, towards the café I'd eaten at. Nobody, apart from an elderly couple enjoying a glass of early afternoon wine.

I was about to go back to my chair when suddenly I saw him, coming out of the café. He was tall. Even from here and despite the fact that he wore a loose cotton sports jacket I could tell he was an extremely powerful man. His head was completely bald, and he carried a black holdall in his right hand. He began to walk slowly towards our guesthouse. He walked in a graceful, measured way that somehow belied his muscular body. He walked like a cat.

I checked him out as he got nearer. His face betrayed nothing: neither excitement nor boredom, nothing. There was a steely determination in the way he walked, but no urgency. He seemed to me to be some kind of cyborg terminator sent to this town specifically to end my sorry life. There was little about him that suggested he was human. He was a machine and I was his quarry.

He arrived at our bar. I couldn't see him any more but I tried to listen to the conversation he was having with Alejandro. I couldn't hear anything. The noise from the sea, the sound of the gulls and the odd passing car was all I heard. Shit. This was it. Now the stakes were really high. Now, I really was going to find out what I was made of.

I sat down and waited, my heart rate quickening with every passing second. Then, suddenly, sitting in the chair waiting for him just didn't feel right.

I ran into the bathroom and picked up the cheap, plastic mirror above the sink. I placed it on the chair I'd been sitting in and angled it so that I could see the door from inside the bathroom without being seen myself. Then I ran to the door and unlocked it. He'd be able to walk in now with a mere twist of the handle. I dashed back to the bathroom, put my back against the wall just to the right of the door and lowered myself to a crouching position. I turned my head so that I could see the mirror. I held the gun in both hands at my chest, my finger poised over the trigger. I could feel my heart pounding. I was sweating uncontrollably. This was going to be all about timing. I had to rely on the fact that he had no idea I knew he was coming or that I had a gun. My heart was racing away. I prayed he'd fall into my trap. I prayed Gemma wouldn't turn up. I prayed I'd be alive in two minutes' time.

A knock on the door. This was it. No turning back now.

'Señor Jones, I have a message for you.' His voice was deep and his accent hardly betrayed his South American origins.

'Oh, hi. Sorry . . . erm . . . I'm in the bathroom. Just come in and drop it on the bed.' My voice was so faltering that it must surely have roused his suspicions.

The handle on the door turned slowly. The door opened just as slowly. The man looked round and carefully stepped in. He turned his head and surveyed the room. His hand was already moving towards the bump under his jacket. I could see all this through the mirror. I tried to keep my frantic breathing under control. I had to act, but my legs were frozen.

It was now or never.

I leapt out of the bathroom, the pistol raised in front of me, pointing directly at the man's head. The gun was shaking uncontrollably. I was trying to keep it steady and show no fear but I simply couldn't do it. He was caught with his hand perhaps eight inches from where I knew he hid his own pistol. His eyes widened with shock. He stood motionless, like a waxwork. Not a sinew moved. He looked like a statue. There was total silence.

'OK, this is the fucking deal. You're gonna lie down on your front right now or I'm gonna shoot you in the fucking head. *OK, mister?*' I was absolutely petrified but something, some urge to survive, was making me function. I shouted the last words.

There was a long pause. He was clearly thinking about what he should do. He had most definitely not envisaged this. Finally, he spoke.

'Señor Jones, I am from the Spanish police. We wish to take you in for questioning regarding the murder of your boss – Señor Charles Johnson.'

His voice was completely calm. There was an air of authority about it. Suddenly, things weren't as clear-cut as they had been. Shit, he might actually be telling the truth! Perhaps he was some Spanish cop who'd been sent by Interpol to intercept me. How did I know who the fuck he was? There was every chance I was dealing with a legitimate cop here and not a trained killer.

'Bullshit! Why should I believe you? You don't look like a fucking cop to me.'

'Señor Jones, I have my ID in my breast pocket. Let me show it to you.'

'Don't you move a fucking finger. I'll shoot you in the brain if you fucking move a *fucking* finger!' The pistol was trained at his head. The tip of the barrel was shaking violently. Any attempt to appear cool was being completely discredited.

'Señor Jones, let me show you my identification. We can clear this up very quickly.'

His right hand was inching its way towards the bulge under his jacket. I couldn't believe his hand kept moving upwards. I couldn't believe that my gun wasn't scaring him. Why didn't he stop moving? Why didn't he just obey me? I wanted to run away. I wanted to cry. I couldn't do either.

'Stop right there, motherfucker! I don't give two shits who you say you are. It doesn't matter. Stop moving and no one gets hurt.'

'Señor, you have mistaken me for someone else. Please, don't do something you regret for the rest of your life.'

'No. I don't give a fuck if you're a cop or a gangster now. One more move and I will blow you away. Don't make me fucking do this!'

'Señor Jones, we know who you are. We just want you for questioning. Why should you shoot me?' His hand was moving slowly but surely towards that ominous bulge. It was now about an inch from his lapel and would soon be within the jacket. My voice was becoming more and more frantic.

'*Look! I am not fucking joking! I am gonna shoot you if your hand is not by your side in one fucking second!*'

'Steve, I know you're not a bad man. I know you never killed anyone in your life. I know you don't have the *cojones* to shoot me. Anyway, your safety is on.'

Now, when I look back at what happened over the next

seconds, I can see that the last words ever spoken by the man I later knew as the Panther condemned him. When he said he knew that I'd never killed anyone I realised for sure he wasn't a cop. Only the gangsters knew I hadn't murdered Chuck, because they'd done it themselves. He said my safety was on simply to distract me.

Just as this thought entered my panic-stricken mind the Panther acted. Like a striking snake, he suddenly made a grab for his pistol. Everything went into slow motion. In fact, time seemed to stand still. His hand was inside his jacket. He began pulling the pistol from its shoulder holster. It was a huge chrome pearl-handled motherfucker. I had about ten milliseconds to act. I had no time to think.

I lowered the gun so that the barrel was aimed directly at his chest. I squeezed my eyes shut tight. I instinctively moved my head to the left. I pulled the trigger. My world exploded.

Part Three

- 'Globalization opens many opportunities for crime, and crime is rapidly becoming global, outpacing international cooperation to fight it . . . it is estimated to gross $1.5 trillion a year – a major economic power rivalling multi-national corporations' UN Human Development report, 1999

- In 2000 the White House estimated that illegal narcotics sales in the United States had reached $160 billion. In that year it is estimated that Americans consumed 260 metric tonnes of cocaine. Those numbers have increased steadily since then.

- At least thirty-two thousand drug-related murders took place in Mexico in the four years following President Calderón's declaration of war on the drug cartels in December 2006. It is estimated that a drug-related homicide takes place every four minutes on our planet.

Thirty-Six

I HARDLY DARED OPEN MY eyes. The muted sound of the gun had immediately been followed by the thud of a body hitting the floor. I had just shot a man. How had this come about? These kinds of things were not supposed to happen to people like me. Nothing made sense any more. I stood motionless for an eternity. A hideous, stomach-churning nausea enveloped me. I thought I was going to vomit. I gagged, but just managed to keep my food down. Finally, I opened my eyes.

The Panther's body lay sprawled just inside the room. His head was in the doorway. The force of the bullet had pushed him backwards so that he lay face up. His legs were crumpled beneath him in an unnatural way. There was a large, rapidly growing red stain on the left side of his chest. He didn't appear to be breathing. I couldn't believe it. I must have hit him straight in the heart.

I tentatively approached his body, still pointing the gun

at him. The barrel was shaking more violently than ever. His own pistol lay inches away from his right hand. I wasn't taking any chances. I kicked his ankle hard. Nothing. I kicked it again, even harder this time. Still nothing. Finally, I stamped on it. He didn't budge. Either this guy was dead or he didn't feel pain.

I looked at his face. He was most definitely dead. No movement whatsoever and a hideous grimace that I will take to my deathbed. I could barely look at him. I had taken away everything he had, everything he was going to be. It dawned on me that I was now officially a murderer. I had taken another man's life. But it was either him or me. I had acted in self-defence. Surely anyone would have done the same? After a few seconds of horrified introspection my survival instinct kicked in. I had to act or my life really would be totally ruined.

I crouched down, snatched his gun and pushed it into the waistband of my trousers. My heart was racing faster than ever. I needed to get all of his body into the room before Alejandro or someone else saw it. I picked up one foot with my free hand, still training the gun at his face. I tried to pull him in one-handed but I just wasn't strong enough, so I dropped the gun, grabbed both ankles and dragged him a few feet across the floor.

Then I rushed to the door, put my head out and looked around. No one. The Panther's black holdall lay in the corridor to my left. I grabbed it and hauled it into the room. It was heavy and foreboding. I closed the door and let out an audible sigh of relief. The simple act of closing the door made me feel safer.

OK, what to do? *Think*. We had one dead hitman, one gangster's tool bag, a comatose girl upstairs and a concerned barman downstairs. My panic-stricken mind went into overdrive.

First thing to do was make sure Alejandro didn't hear anything suspicious. We might have had a good knees-up the previous night but he didn't owe me anything. If he had heard or seen anything dodgy he could call the police. Then I'd be really fucked.

I tried to compose myself but my breathing was still short and nervous. I closed my eyes and took some long, deep breaths. I replaced the bathroom mirror on the wall and made sure I had no blood on me or anything else that might raise suspicions. I wiped my sweaty brow with the cheap hotel towel, straightened my clothes and placed the two pistols under my pillow. Then I opened the door, locked it behind me and walked down the corridor, down the stairs and into the bar.

'Steve, ees everything OK? I thought I heard a noise.'

'Everything's cool. The guy was angry but I've managed to calm him down. Believe it or not, he wants to have a drink with me. He's given me a hundred-euro note to get the most expensive bottle of wine the town has to offer. I really hate to ask this but ... could you pop out and get one from the off licence at the end of the dock? I know it's a piss-take but I think it would really cool the situation down. You can keep the change.'

'OK . . . so everything ees cool. Strange, 'e come all thees way to see thees girl and now all OK.'

'Mate, you underestimate my charm! Anyway, I think he took one look at these arms of mine and realised I'd whup his sorry arse if things got physical!' I was trying to laugh but what came out was an unnatural giggle.

'Perhaps. OK, I get wine. I be five minutes.'

'No probs. See you in five.'

Great. Alejandro was now out of the equation for a bit. It was essential that he wasn't around for a little while if the next part of my blag was to succeed.

I ran upstairs back to the room. First thing was to pack both our bags. This took about thirty seconds because fortunately we had fuck all. I stuffed the two guns into my rucksack, had one final look around and was about to leave when I saw the holdall. I simply had to check out what was inside.

Apart from the usual crap someone takes when travelling there were two things of interest. First, an envelope which contained photos of me, a blurry picture of Gemma and various documents and newspaper articles about me. The second was a bundle of about fifty high-denomination dollar and euro notes wrapped up with a rubber band. I decided to take the envelope . . . I didn't want any police investigation to know immediately who had killed this man. However, I also wanted them to know he was a hitman so I could later protest self-defence. So I took out his pistol from my bag and, after having wiped it down with a towel, placed it in his hand. I decided to leave everything else except, of course, the cash. Before leaving I checked all his pockets and took out his wallet, which contained another five hundred or so euros but no ID. I also removed from his trouser pocket the photo of me he'd been parading around town.

After a final hurried check I left the room, locked the door and broke the key off in the lock so that entering it would take a little time and effort.

I then ran upstairs to Gemma's room and began shaking her awake. It took almost ten seconds before her eyes opened, despite the forceful shakes I was giving her. Thankfully, she looked slightly more together now.

'What's going on?' She yawned.

'Oh, nothing. Everything's totally cool. But . . . erm . . . look, I think we should probably head out of here right now. Alejandro seems to think some coppers were sniffing around.'

'You're lying to me. I can tell.' Fucking hell, even when half asleep she could read me like a book.

'OK. Look, something really fucked-up just happened. I can't tell you right now . . . but I got in a fight with some bastard and we've got to leave now or we're in big trouble. He's unconscious in our room and he'll be waking up fairly soon.'

'What? You knocked someone out? Bullshit. You can't fight for toffee.'

'Yeah . . . but I knew he was coming and hit him on the head with a lampshade when he entered our room.'

'What? Erm . . . not sure I believe you.'

'Look, it doesn't matter. Just trust me that we've got to go . . . right now. Put your clothes on and let's fuck off.'

'OK, chill out.' My panicky face must have convinced her of the seriousness of our predicament.

Five minutes later we were both fully dressed, with our bags, down at the bar. Alejandro looked confused when I told him that our South American buddy had buggered off. Luckily, Gemma stayed silent, despite clearly not knowing what I was talking about.

'So, thees man, he gone? Where?'

'Yeah . . . I thought it was weird too. As soon as I got back to the room he just got up and said he had to do something and that he'd come back in a few hours. Listen, I think he's going to get his mate and come back and fuck us up. He's just been pretending to be cool about everything. I don't trust him. So we're gonna have to head off for a couple of days, but we'll be back. I want you to keep our room for us, OK? Don't go inside . . . it's a mess and we'll deal with it when we get back. Look, here's two hundred euros. That's for last night and a down payment on the week we're gonna spend here in a few days' time, OK?'

'OK, Steve.' There was definitely a hesitation. I'm not sure if he bought my bullshit but perhaps he wouldn't go into the room for a day or two.

'Cheers, Alejandro. Look, we'll see you in two or three days. Bye.'

'Steve, you forgot your wine.'

'Oh, don't worry about that. Keep it and we'll all drink it when we get back.'

'OK. Goodbye, Steve, Gemma. See you soon.'

Gemma kissed Alejandro goodbye and we departed. Now all we had to do was figure out how to get to Morocco.

Thirty-Seven

WE LEFT THE BAR AND walked towards the pier at the far end of the docks. I hadn't got the slightest idea what we should do but putting as much distance between the dead assassin and us seemed a fairly smart move. After about three minutes we were by the beach and my pace slowed a bit.

Gemma sensed my fear. Eventually, she spoke.

'OK, what the fuck is going on?'

'What's going on is that we're gonna go to Morocco right now.'

'How? Explain to me how and I may consider coming too.'

'We're gonna . . . erm, we're gonna . . .'

At that precise moment one of the guys on the beach shouted out, '*Amigo*, you want to take windsurf?'

I stopped dead in my tracks. Gemma could see the cogs whirring in my brain. A look of utter disbelief crossed her face.

'Oh . . . that's your genius plan, is it? Fucking windsurf to Morocco?' She was almost laughing at the absurdity of it.

'No . . . not windsurf. Jet ski. This geezer rents them too.'

'Jesus motherfucking Christ! You've lost it! You're joking, yeah?'

'Look, it's only about ten miles between here and Morocco. Your mate Pablo went from Barcelona to Beirut on one of these things, d'you remember? He told me that they can go about fifteen, twenty miles on a single tank. Look, they might be serious on this coastline about stopping punters coming here from Africa but it ain't the same over there cos Europeans don't tend to illegally emigrate to Africa. And if we're caught we'll just say we rented it out over there. Come on . . . I know this can work!'

'You are fucking mental. What the fuck happened this morning? I do remember Pablo doing that trip . . . but do we really have to leave right now? I mean, can't we get a boat?'

'No way. We have to leave right now. That fuckwit will be waking up real soon. Look, grab my bag and meet me at the other side of the dock. I'll strip down to my boxer shorts – they're black cotton and look like trunks anyway. We can do this.'

'Oh, Christ. You're serious. I must be mad but . . . OK, if you're sure it's the only way . . . it is the only way, isn't it?' I reassured her that we had no choice and I could see that she was on board.

I took my clothes off, placed them in my rucksack and

gave it to Gemma, who headed off. Then I signalled to the chap that I was up for a jet ski. He looked a bit confused . . . almost as if he hadn't expected me to actually take him up on his offer.

'How much is it?' I asked.

'Forty euros for one hour.'

'OK. Well, they look a lot of fun, so here's two hundred for five hours. I wanna have a real laugh.'

'Have you done jet ski before?'

Obviously I'd never ridden one in my life. 'Oh, yeah, all the time. Presents no challenge.'

'OK, señor.' He gave me a life vest and walked me to the machine.

'So, out of interest, how far does one of these go on a full tank?'

'Señor, perhaps thirty kilometres.'

'Great. I want to have a real ride, so how much petrol is in this one?'

'It is almost full, but please don't go too far out. The waves very big out there, dangerous, no?' I thought I'd keep that information to myself. No use worrying Gemma about little details like that.

'Oh, don't be daft, I'll stick to the coast. So how does it go . . . erm, this is a different model from the ones I've used before.'

'So simple, señor. Press button in front of you to start and twist handle on right to go.'

Cool. It worked just like a normal motorbike. Around

five minutes had passed since Gemma had left and she should have arrived at the rendezvous. I said goodbye to my new *amigo* whose jet ski I was about to steal and started it up. I tentatively pulled back the throttle. Fuck me, it was powerful. I jerkily left the shore like a learner driver on his first lesson, to the obvious bemusement of the locals on the beach. It didn't matter; I was just about in control.

After no more than thirty seconds I reached Gemma. I looked round to make sure no one was watching and she got on the back. She passed me my rucksack, which I put face forward on my chest, and I gave her the life jacket. She put it on, then slung her rucksack on her back.

Now all I had to do was pilot a craft I had never touched before across ten miles of open, choppy sea to Africa without being seen by any coastguards on either continent. I gritted my teeth, twisted the throttle and set off.

My God . . . I thought the waves in the Channel were bad but these were truly horrific. On reflection, they probably weren't as big as those we'd endured on Paul DeGruchy's boat, but they felt fucking massive on our tiny little craft. The first mile or so had been relatively cool. The wind was rushing in our hair, Africa was getting closer and closer and the body of the Panther was getting further and further away. Every now and again I'd shout back asking Gemma if she was OK and each time she yelled that she was fine and gave me a reassuring little squeeze. She'd always told me that she wanted more adventure in her life and on that front at least I think I was fully delivering . . . possibly to a fault.

But after a bit we started rocking up and down like the proverbial cork in a storm. I almost lost control a few times and my muscles began to seize up. A combination of the cold water and my obvious stress were causing my legs to get painful cramps. I was gripping the handles so tightly that I wasn't sure I could actually open my frozen hands even if I tried.

At about halfway I was really beginning to doubt whether we were going to get across. The waves were even bigger, and sometimes came in sideways which made staying upright particularly tricky. Then things began to calm down a bit. I thought we were through the worst of it when suddenly a huge wave came from the right and smacked us straight on the side. I couldn't control the jet ski. Over it went, and Gemma and I suddenly found ourselves underwater. I was held under for what seemed like minutes until my lungs felt like they might burst. I thought the end had come there and then.

As soon as I emerged spluttering above the surface I began shouting for Gemma, but she was nowhere to be seen. I twisted my head around, panicking, trying to locate her. The rucksack on my chest was totally soaked and was dragging me down, the heavy gun pulling me under. I should never have brought it with me. I had thought of dumping it at sea but I hadn't wanted Gemma to see me do so. I couldn't see her anywhere. I prayed she hadn't hit her head.

I was about to start diving when I heard her voice.

'I'm behind you. I'm fucking behind you!'

I looked round and thanked God. She looked angry and upset but she was alive. The life jacket was doing its job. Now all we had to do was retrieve the jet ski, which was a good ten metres away and upside down.

'Honey, honey . . . grab this bag. Stay there. I'll swim and get the jet ski and come back to you, OK?'

'Steve . . . don't fucking leave me!' We were both bobbing up and down with the waves and water was getting in our eyes and mouths, causing us both to splutter at regular intervals.

'Honey, it's the only sensible thing to do . . . unless you wanna swim the rest. Don't talk, just wait.' And with that, to end any possible argument, I passed her my bag and began a front crawl towards the jet ski.

I've always been a strong swimmer but the waves and the cramp in my legs were making this short journey extremely tiring. Eventually I reached the jet ski, but then realised I had no idea what to do. The boy on the beach hadn't divulged the solution to this particular problem.

I tried pushing it upright but just succeeded in pushing myself underwater. I was on the wrong side of it, too, so waves kept on bashing me into it. One wave smashed my head into it and blood began to pour from my chin. I inevitably started wondering if there were any sharks around. I quickly dismissed those fears but still didn't know what the hell to do.

I looked round at Gemma. She was still there, bobbing

away, but she was struggling. This was not cool, not cool at all.

Then I had an idea. I could see that when the waves came the jet ski tilted quite violently to the left. All I needed to do was time as strong a downward push as I could manage so that it coincided with a wave. Together, there might be enough force to right it.

I waited. A big wave was coming towards me. I grabbed hold of the black rubber rim on the jet ski's side and steadied myself. When the wave was a few feet away I lifted myself up with my weary arms and pushed down with all my might. My head smashed into the jet ski again and I went underwater. I must have been under for perhaps five seconds. I was slightly concussed and didn't know which was up and which was down. Eventually, I saw which way the air bubbles were heading and followed them.

I emerged from the water and took a huge breath only to get a lungful of brine courtesy of another wave. I was spluttering away. I could hear Gemma's desperate cries.

Eventually, I gathered myself together. I looked around. *The jet ski was fucking upright!*

Still dazed and confused, I swam up to it and tried to figure out how best to get on without flipping it over again. I had no idea. I figured the best way was from the back but on inspection it was way too tall to be climbed. I'd just have to pull my stomach up on to the area where the driver's feet should be and pray that another big wave didn't come.

I put my hands on the black rim and on the count of

three carefully lifted myself up. The jet ski started rocking a bit but it stayed upright. Once my stomach was on I felt secure. Now all I had to do was use the handles to lift myself up and we'd all be OK. I did so and let out a huge sigh of relief. I sat upright. I took another deep breath. I closed my eyes for a brief moment to calm myself down. I felt the blood that had been furiously pumping around my system begin to slow down. I felt the adrenalin rush begin to subside. Then I started it, pulling the throttle back slightly whilst turning as sharply as possible. I made a half-circle and returned to Gemma, being sure to go slowly and release the throttle some distance before I got to her so as not to overshoot. I strained to see her expression. I had no idea what to expect.

Gemma's face was a curious mix of anger, panic and relief. She passed me up my rucksack and I pulled her on board. I couldn't help but feel that there was a potential hissy fit about to be thrown. I needed to think of a witty quip fast to try to deflate the tension ASAP.

'That was a giggle . . . shall we do it again?'

'Don't even think about it. I thought you'd died just then. *Just get us there now!*'

'OK . . . sorry.' I turned back round and resumed our course. I reckoned that we'd be on African soil within about thirty minutes. Now we just had to pray that this stretch of shore wasn't frequented by too many coastguards . . . that there were no police around . . . and that we didn't end up in the middle of a desert. That was all.

Thirty-Eight

AFTER ABOUT FORTY MINUTES WE were within a few hundred yards of the African coast. The waves had died down and dusk was approaching. Good fortune, more than careful planning, meant that we would be hitting the African continent at pretty much the perfect time. Light enough for me to see any rocks in the water but dark enough to mean we weren't highly visible to any diligent Moroccan coastguards out there.

For the last mile of the cold and painful journey I had been scanning the shoreline for any signs of life. We needed to land as far away from any buildings as possible. We also obviously needed to find a beach rather than rocks or cliffs. As I approached the coastline I could see a few houses with lights on to my left and so I headed right, out towards the Atlantic. The coast here looked deserted apart from the odd building set back inland. The problem was that there was no obvious safe place to land. As we motored along parallel to the coast all I could see were rocks being pounded by waves.

I looked down at the petrol gauge and saw that we had about a tenth of a tank left at best. This was not cool.

We kept on heading west about fifty yards or so away from the shoreline. The light was fading. I was tired, cold and wet. I couldn't see any safe way past the rocks and waves. Suddenly Gemma began to squeeze my waist. She freed up her left hand and began frantically pointing at the coast, shouting in my ear.

'Over there. There's a way in over there.' I could just about hear her over the sound of the engine and the sea.

'Where? What, there? You've got to be kidding me! Are you out of your fucking mind?'

Gemma was pointing at a small opening in the rocks that was being pounded by the surf. There was a way in but it was only about one and a half times the width of our jet ski and every five seconds or so a wave crashed into it making any attempt to drive through horribly dangerous. There were rocks jutting out of the water around the entrance, and it was impossible to see exactly what the lie of the land was once you'd passed through the gap.

'There is no fucking way we can make it through there!' I shouted. It looked like suicide. Then I looked again at the petrol gauge, something I'd been carefully shielding from Gemma's eyes by leaning forward more than was natural. The tank was virtually empty. We had no choice. It looked as if, at the very best, we'd get wet and cut up. At worst we'd be slammed against the rocks and drown.

'You know what? It actually looks OK. I reckon we can

do this.' I had to lie. I had to make a virtue out of the fact that we had no option but to attempt to land within the next two minutes. Gemma might not have been fully convinced by my sudden change of mind and false bravado but at least she didn't know just how desperate our situation was.

I turned the jet ski round and headed straight for the gap in the rocks. When we were about twenty yards away I slowed down to a virtual standstill. Now I could see that if we got through the gap we'd be in a fairly calm bay that had a small, pebbly beach at its far side. This was definitely the place to go for but it would be no walk in the park. The waves were actually a bit fiercer than they'd looked from fifty yards out and the opening through the rocks looked smaller.

I pulled the throttle back a little. The jet ski spluttered slightly as we tentatively approached the hole. Timing was everything. I had to wait for a break in the waves and then boost through the gap to avoid being thrown against the rocks. However, I couldn't just wait ten feet away and then perform the manoeuvre because the water close to the opening was far too choppy thanks to the funnelling effect of the surrounding rocks. I had to wait about twenty-five feet away, choose my moment and then go hell for leather. But I also had to release the throttle completely at least five feet before the gap otherwise I risked smashing into the rocks beyond it. I decided to aim to the right of the break in the rocks because even without being hit by major waves we were bound to be pushed slightly to the left by the movement of the ocean. I was tensing up with fear and cold. The cramps in my legs were worse than ever. Gemma gripped my waist so hard it hurt.

Suddenly, I saw a break in the waves and pulled back the throttle. We picked up speed and were heading just to the right of the opening. It looked as though I'd overestimated the pushing effect of the sea. We were going to hit the rock wall. I had to turn to the left but couldn't overdo it or we wouldn't approach the gap face on which would mean we wouldn't fit through. Gemma tensed up and squeezed my waist in panic. We were both screaming uncontrollably. About eight feet from the hole I released the throttle entirely but it still looked as if we weren't going to squeeze through. I'd hoofed it. We were going to clip the right lip of the opening.

And then a wave nudged us to the left just a few feet before we hit the rock. It gave us the perfect little push and we passed through the opening faultlessly. We both had to lean to the left and the rucksack on Gemma's back scraped along the rocks but it didn't matter. Our rapidly slowing jet ski entered the calm pool beyond the gap and, after about ten feet, ran aground on the pebbly beach.

My God! We'd made it! I was still trembling with cold and fear but we'd done it! I got off the jet ski and relished the firm ground beneath me. My legs still felt wobbly. It was as if the waves had somehow followed me on to dry land. I put my bag down and helped Gemma off. She immediately leapt on me and we hugged for minutes.

After a bit Gemma released me. I looked at her with astonishment in my eyes. '*We made it. We've fucking made it!*' Gemma was grinning insanely as she shouted the words.

'Of course we did. It was never in doubt. You should have more faith in me.' I wasn't sure whether once again she would see through my horse crap. I suspected my own astonishment was etched all over my face.

'God, I didn't think you were gonna go for it. I thought you were going to bottle it.'

'Nah . . . it was fine. Anyway, if I'd had any doubts we'd just have gone further up the coast.'

'Sorry? Oh . . . you think I didn't know about the petrol situation? Honey, I realised you were trying to hide the gauge from me about twenty minutes ago.' She was laughing.

'Oh, you knew? Cool . . . well, yes, I have to admit that did somewhat help make up my mind about whether to go for it or not.' I don't know why I ever bothered trying to lie to that girl. It was completely pointless.

'Anyway, you did it. Now we've just got to find our way to the road and then to Tangiers without bumping into any soldiers or policemen and we'll be fine.' There was some sarcasm in her voice but I ignored it.

'Yep . . . just gonna take a quick slash and then let's get with it.'

I took my bag with me and went behind a rock. I opened my rucksack, reached to the bottom and pulled out the gun. I used this to kill a man, I thought. I saw a freeze frame of the Panther's final grimace. I couldn't dwell on it for long or I'd go insane. I held the pistol by the silencer, swung my arm back and lobbed it as far as I could into the sea. It landed about twenty yards away with a satisfying plop.

Being caught with the gun would have given us big problems. Without it we could always claim to be lost tourists who'd had our passports stolen. Anyway, we were safe now. We wouldn't need it ever again. Or at least that's what I thought at the time.

Thirty-Nine

TANGIERS WAS A TYPICAL AFRICAN city. Car horns hooted non-stop, dust and exhaust fumes hovered in the air and the odour of spicy food emanated from every roadside café. I loved the hustle and bustle, the dry heat, the constant noise, the pungent smells. Most of all I loved the anonymity. Admittedly, Gemma and I received our fair share of unwanted attention from toothless beggars and persistent hawkers on our first morning in Africa, but that was just because we were honkies and our skin colour was a near-perfect indicator that we probably had more cash on our persons than some of these people would ever see in their lives.

The journey from our landing place to Tangiers had been relatively uneventful. When we arrived on the rocky shoreline we were both wet and cold, so the first priority was to find some shelter and try to dry off a little. We scrambled up the rocks and soon hit a small dirt track. There were no buildings around. We followed the track inland and eventually met a road running parallel to the coast. By that time it was dark and both of us were beginning to shiver. It wasn't particularly cold but there was a strong wind that was making our wet clothes feel chilly. We sat in a ditch by the road to rest out of the wind. The odd truck passed us, its headlights lighting up the pitch blackness. The obvious plan was to hitchhike to Tangiers but we had to be careful about who we flagged down seeing as our situation was a little . . . unusual. Any official bod was bound to be suspicious and ask tricky questions. I was contemplating our quandary when I glanced round at Gemma. I couldn't bear how miserable and cold she looked. It was me who'd got her into this mess and I wasn't going to let her suffer further. So I decided that we should risk it . . . or rather that she should. Everyone knows that girls are more likely to get a lift when hitchhiking, especially a beautiful girl at night who seems to be either participating in her own personal wet T-shirt competition or smuggling peanuts.

'Honey, erm, I think you should probably get up by the side of the road when we see the next truck coming along and stick your thumb out. It's all we can do.'

'Let me get this straight . . . you get to relax down here out of the wind whilst I freeze my arse off flashing my tits at any passing rapist in the hope that he'll deign to pick me up. Is that your plan?'

'Well, yes, that's about the size of it. But look, you only have to go up there when we actually see a vehicle coming our way and you know that they're much more likely to stop for a girl than a geezer.'

She thought about it for a few seconds. A chilly breeze was picking up, night was approaching and the land was starting to cool down. Hundreds of stars were beginning to appear above us. The silence was only occasionally broken by the far-off barking of some wild dog. Both of us were shivering. Gemma had a look of incredulity sketched on her face.

'Christ, I can't believe you've got me doing this. You drag me all the way from fucking Ladbroke Grove to fucking Africa and then get me to sort us out a lift too. Honestly, if I'd known . . .' She was on a roll. I had to interrupt her.

'Hon, if I could do it myself I would . . . anyway, look, there's a truck coming our way right now and it's heading west which means towards Tangiers, so get your cute arse up there now and stick your thumb out!' I had been checking out my very damp map of Europe a few minutes before, and had also surmised that west was probably in the direction of the spot where the sun had just set. Gemma stared with vague disbelief at my attempt to be macho and assertive but, after a couple of sulky seconds, trudged up the bank to the side of the road and lifted a weary hand.

Unbelievably, the first lorry she flagged down stopped. The bedraggled desperate look obviously pays dividends. The driver leant over and opened the passenger door to his cabin. Of course, as soon as he'd done so I scrambled up the bank carrying both bags. The driver, a wrinkly old guy with about three teeth, looked a little disappointed when he saw me but was sufficiently kind not to simply drive off despite the fact that the deal had changed somewhat. I grabbed Gemma and ran round to his side of the truck.

'*Monsieur, vous êtes très gentil. Est-ce que vous allez jusqu'à Tangiers?*'

'*Oui.*'

'*Fantastique. Vous avez assez d'espace pour nous deux?*'

'*Oui.*'

'*Formidable. Allons-y. Je vous remercie, monsieur.*'

The old A level French was coming out again and despite probably about seven grammatical errors and an accent like that of a pissed-up Scouser with a lisp, he knew what we were after. We climbed into his cabin and squeezed in next to him. I sat between Gemma and the old geezer just to make sure there'd be no wandering hands. As we set off a huge smile spread across my face. I looked across at Gemma and she was grinning like the Cheshire Cat too. We were going to be in Tangiers in less than two hours and were now in a warm, wind-free space. Fucking brilliant!

We were dropped off close to Tangiers's bustling centre by our man. He had proved to be quite a character. He'd told us stories about the battle against the French and how he'd lost a few members of his family during the war for independence. On leaving him we expressed our gratitude with genuine emotion. Then Gemma and I checked into the first hotel we could find. They allowed us to change some of our sterling into Moroccan dirham and the room only cost the equivalent of about seven pounds a night. Although it was horrific and the bed smelt as though incontinent old ladies had been the principal guests before us, we were both asleep within seconds.

We awoke to the sounds of a busy day. People were shouting at each other, motorbikes were buzzing around, cars were sounding their horns and hawkers were selling their wares. The bright sun was streaming in through the gap in the cheap and nasty curtains and was already heating up the room. The first priority, at least for me, was to try to remind Gemma that we were supposed to be a couple and that certain enjoyable bonding practices were usually associated with such a relationship. I had been breathing in her delicious fragrance for minutes and I had sensed my temperature rising ever since I'd woken up. I desperately wanted to feel we were together again. I craved her soft warmth. I wanted to lose myself once again in her beautiful brown eyes as we became one. Basically, I had to seal the deal soon or my swollen balls were going to explode.

Gemma was lying on her front with her head turned away from me. Slowly but surely I edged closer to her until my body lay ever so slightly over hers. Then I carefully put my arm round her and held her, hoping she'd feel me next to her. She just lay there breathing gently. So I decided to move my hand up and down her body to wake her up.

I did . . . and she wasn't happy about it.

'Oi . . . what are you doing? Christ, I was having the most

amazing dream. I was in a valley, riding some kind of weird tiger . . . I suppose it must be because we're in Africa, eh?'

'Honey, tigers aren't from Africa, they're from India.' I smirked, pathetically taking pleasure from one of the rare occasions I'd outwitted her. I immediately regretted choosing that particular moment to be a smartarse.

'Oh, you know what I mean. For fuck's sake, I've just woken up – I don't need your sarky bollocks.' I could see my hopes of getting down to business disintegrating like ash in the wind. The tingle of anticipation in my loins disappeared, and I lay there for a few minutes cursing my stupidity. Gemma was giving me the silent treatment. Even though her head was turned I could sense a grouchy snarl distorting her beautiful face. I decided to quit while behind and got up and took a shower. All I could think about as the tepid water hit my face was how long I would be denied my conjugal rights. This forced abstinence was getting ridiculous. When the fuck was she going to forgive me?

I told a still mildly pissed-off Gemma over a croissant and coffee that after a quick shop in the souk for some new threads we should head straight to Marrakech. This time, she didn't even question the logic of visiting some dodgy carpet seller who might or might not sell passports. It could have just been a continuation of the silent treatment. But maybe it was because my plans had somehow so far proved themselves to be vaguely sensible and Gemma was beginning to think I was full of smart moves. It was a pity I was about to prove her totally wrong.

Whilst we were checking out some particularly unfashionable shirts at one of the market stalls a short, skinny lad of about seventeen sidled up to me and asked if I wanted 'some kif... some mariwanna'. Now, I've always liked a smoke and proper Moroccan hash is legendary, so without even thinking I said, 'Yeah, all right.' I immediately received a disapproving look from Gemma but decided to hold firm on this one. The prospect of getting my grubby mitts on some red seal or double zero had me virtually salivating with desire.

'Look, what's the problem? We're just tourists, remember? No one's after us here. Look, I've done loads of travelling. This is Cool and the Gang.'

'OK, sir? I go get for you. Forty dirham, please.'

'No way, mate. You must think I was born yesterday. You get the gear and then I'll pay you.'

'OK, sir. No problem.'

'Listen Gemma, you carry on shopping and I'll sort this out. Let's meet back at that place we had coffee at in about twenty minutes, all right?'

'All right, but I think this is a totally unnecessary risk.'

'Chill out. It's going to be fine.'

Gemma left me and started looking around the stalls. After about five minutes the lad returned and told me to walk with him. I presumed that he didn't want to do the transaction openly, which was fair enough. We went down a small alley and he took out the gear. It was about two-eighths of fine-smelling red seal hash and I was buying it for about four quid. Touch! I handed him the wonga and turned round. Just before I reached the end of the alleyway two big guys in smart clothes appeared and started walking towards me. Was it my imagination or were they both staring at me? Fuck. I'd put the puff in my pocket, and to throw it away now would look suspicious.

'Excuse me, we are police. Could we speak, please?'

Oh, shit! I could feel the colour drain from my face. My heart began pumping away. My stomach turned to water. Shit, this was blatantly a set-up. The young lad behind me clearly had an arrangement with the local coppers to trap dumbass tourists like me. He'd either told them where to intercept us by mobile or had just grabbed them from some nearby café. I'd heard about this scam. It's the oldest trick in the book and happens day in day out in any third world city whenever idiots like me go looking for drugs. However, the difference between me and most dickheads who fall for it is that they've probably got passports and generally aren't wanted for at least one murder back home. I felt like a total prick. I was shitting myself.

'Erm, what seems to be the problem, ossifer?' I spluttered. I was doing my best to be calm but it was hard. My voice was cracking with fear. I was almost as worried about having to explain this screw-up to Gemma as I was about how I was going to extricate myself from this potentially lethal situation.

'We believe you have something illegal on you. Please empty your pockets.' His English was suspiciously good. It was as if he'd done this a few times before.

I didn't know what to do. The other pig grabbed the young lad behind me, who was pretending to cry his eyes out. His acting was so appalling it was embarrassing. I was tempted to ask him to stop since we all knew what was going on here.

'Erm, do you mean this, officer? I'm so sorry, I thought it was legal in this country.' I had decided to just pull out the hash. I needed to get this over and done with ASAP. I needed to get back to Gemma before she sussed out my horrific stupidity.

'No, this very illegal. You, I'm afraid, in very big trouble. Come with us now to police station.' He put his hand on my shoulder and started manoeuvring me towards the main street.

My heart was really racing now. I could feel my armpits getting damp with sweat. I couldn't stop my panic-stricken brain envisioning me as the only honky in an overcrowded shithole of a rat-infested Moroccan prison. I had to be cool. I'd been nicked before in India and Tanzania and it was usually dealable with. A little bit of baksheesh should sort it out. That's why I preferred being done in places like Africa and Asia – you knew where you stood with the cops out here. They just wanted cash. They were certainly more 'honest' than their European or American brothers. I'd been done for drugs in Ibiza, at Glastonbury and in Hyde Park and actually been obliged to fill out various forms, but surely out here it would be a twenty-quid hit and a polite 'On yer way'. Unless, that is, I happened to have encountered some serious, diligent motherfuckers.

'Look, in my country we have on-the-spot fines for this kind of thing. In my country you pay a hundred dirham to the policeman and it's OK. Maybe that's how it works here too, no?' I had used the old 'on-the-spot fine' line before. It helps the copper keep face when he's blatantly taking a bribe off you.

'Now listen to me. You Europeans do not run this country any more. This amount of hashish is two years minimum in prison in this country.' Oh, fuck! I had even more vivid visions of the next couple of years of my sorry life. They weren't pretty.

'Look, when I said a hundred dirham I meant a hundred dollars . . . each.'

'My friend. You pay me and my colleague a thousand dollars and we let you off.' Oh, shit. They were going for the big score. They could smell my fear and had probably got lucky with some rich Yank dingbat tourists in the past. I had to be strong. I only had two hundred dollars in my wallet, as well as about fifty dollars' worth of dirham. The rest was in my bag and with Gemma. I'd try to blag them back. It was the only way.

'Listen, officer, I'm not a rich tourist. I am poor tourist. I only have this money on me. This is all I have in this country. If you need more, then we must go to police station and discuss it with your superiors.' I had taken out my wallet and removed all the cash. I was hoping that the sight of so much dosh would blind them and mean that they wouldn't take it any further.

There was a tangible pause. The policemen both looked at each other. One of them grabbed the notes off me and began counting them. Finally, he said, 'Look, boy, you have more money. Where you stay?'

'I stay at Bellevue Hotel just by market. You welcome to come with me to room. You see I have no more money. After you take this . . . well, now I must go to British embassy to get money from them so I can go home. I not joke, I promise.' For some reason, I was speaking in a strange staccato fashion with a kind of mock Moroccan accent and a distinct lack of definite articles, as if that would make me better understood. It probably had the opposite effect as these characters spoke perfect English. In fact, they probably thought I was taking the mick.

Still, I could see that they were beginning to buy my bullshit. The hotel we'd stayed in the previous night was so cheap and nasty that only a poverty-stricken backpacker would dream of going there. Mentioning the British embassy with a panic-stricken look on my face must also have been convincing.

'OK. But do not come back to this city. We do not like drug users in Tangiers.'

And with that they turned round and walked off. They still held the 'dealer' by the shoulder, and he was still pretending to cry his eyes out.

I breathed a sigh of relief. If they'd taken me back to the hotel and looked in my bag they'd have got a few thousand pounds. If they'd nicked me I'd probably have been sent back to England to be either arrested or murdered – potentially both. I took a deep breath, steadied myself and started walking towards the café where I was to meet Gemma. I decided I wouldn't waste her time by telling her what had just happened . . . no need to worry her unnecessarily.

It was whilst I was sitting at the table outside the café, nursing an espresso, that I suddenly realised I'd just been royally conned. Those weren't fucking coppers at all! I'd never seen any ID. I'd just assumed that they were who they said they were because they were big mothers and wore smart clothes. In my panic, I'd never questioned them. Fuck me, that has to be about the best scam in town.

Still, it didn't matter. I was alive and free and only two hundred and fifty dollars the poorer. More important, Gemma need never know how I'd just had the living piss ripped out of me.

'What's going on? You look a little lost in thought there.' Her words made me jump a little.

'Oh, nothing. Just thinking about our next moves. By the way, I decided not to get any puff from that geezer. It was rubbish. Fucking henna, basically. Anyway, you're right. We probably shouldn't do anything illegal that could get us in trouble.'

Gemma looked at me with a slightly raised eyebrow. I was convinced she could tell something was going on, that I wasn't giving her the full story. 'Really? Sounds like complete bollocks to me but I can't be bothered to get into it. Let's go to the bus station and get a coach to Marrakech. Once we're there I'll feel a lot safer.'

'Yeah, let's do that. We're on the final leg of the journey now,' I said confidently.

I still didn't have a clue whether we were doing the right thing or not.

Forty

'IT'S THIS WAY . . . WELL, I could have sworn it was this way.' We'd arrived at another strangely familiar crossroads.

'Steve, you're fucking lost and you fucking know you are.' Gemma spat out her words in frustration.

'I'm not, honey. I swear I know exactly where we are and where the carpet shop is.' Of course I didn't have the faintest idea.

'Well, I swear that we've been past that butcher's before. I'd recognise that goat's head and tripe sculpture anywhere.'

'Please, honey, just chill. We're gonna get to the shop any minute, you'll see.'

It had taken almost nine hours by bus to get to Marrakech. As soon as we'd arrived we'd taken a taxi to the hotel I'd stayed in before heading off to climb Toubkal. It was fairly standard but it took dollars and was only about two hundred metres from the west entrance to the Medina – the walled, ancient part of Marrakech. After a decent kip, another failed attempt to shag Gemma and a continental breakfast that was almost good enough to eat we set off on our mission to get new identities. Of course, I had assured Gemma that I remembered exactly where the carpet seller was and, truth be told, I thought I did. However, those narrow cobbled streets were like a maze. Things weren't going quite as smoothly as I'd hoped.

We passed another crossroads that looked strangely familiar.

'We've been here before too.' Bollocks, she was completely correct. We were lost but I couldn't bear to admit it.

'Nah . . . it's this way, pretty damn sure this time. I recognise that . . . that bicycle repair shop and that geezer doing dentistry on the street. It's definitely down here.' In truth, I had simply selected the only alleyway I couldn't remember having been down before that morning.

'Really? Well, if you're wrong . . .'

I cut her off by walking swiftly up the narrow alley. A group of three shrouded women passed us by. A couple of old chaps wearing the traditional hooded robes sat on a doorstep chatting away. Suddenly, I saw the sign to the carpet seller pointing up some creaky, dusty stairs on the right of our alley. I could barely conceal my joy though I tried my best not to seem astonished at my good fortune.

'Honey, here we are. I told you I knew where it was. Follow me and accept the simple fact that I am a fucking genius!' I was failing abominably to cover my own shock at having found ourselves at our desired destination. Whether

Gemma realised it or not, she had the good grace to say nothing.

We climbed the stairs, walked through an ancient wooden doorway and entered a dusty, spacious room which had a wonderful musty smell and contained hundreds of carpets rolled up on shelves around the walls. A guy sat at a desk at the end of the room looking through some large notepads, probably doing the books or something. As I got close I could see it was the same geezer I'd dealt with before. I'd have recognised that glass eye and shifty look anywhere. He spoke first.

'Hello again! Mr Jones, no? From Wales, no?' My God, these guys were outstanding salesmen. I hadn't seen this bloke for almost a year and he remembered my name and some of the inane details about my life that I'd unwarily divulged during my last visit.

'That's right . . . and you're . . . you're Muhammad?' I was struggling a bit here to return the compliment, but then I hadn't come out of our last encounter having ripped off some confused tourist by selling him a hundred-dollar carpet for three times its value.

'No sir, my name Muwaffaq. Please do not worry, very difficult name for tourist. How I help you, sir? You want buy another beautiful carpet?'

'Actually no, not this time.' Muwaffaq's face dropped. 'Actually, we're after something different. Do you remember the last time I was here you offered to buy my passport? Well—'

'Oh sir, you want to sell passport? No problem. Like last time I give five hundred dollar . . .'

'Well, erm, this time I'd actually like to buy a passport . . . in fact, two . . . with photos of me and my girlfriend in them. We . . . want to travel on aeroplanes with them and we don't want to be stopped.'

Muwaffaq's face lit up. 'Well sir, you know this is expensive. *Very* expensive. It is not just cost of passports – which as you know is at five hundred dollars minimum. It is also cost of best forger in Marrakech . . . who happens to be my brother-in-law. I think it is British passports you need . . . and, so sorry, but those are most expensive, my friend.'

Gemma was looking more and more distraught each time Muwaffaq mentioned the word 'expensive'. We only had about eight and a half thousand pounds and five thousand dollars and euros to our name and we still had to buy air tickets to wherever our next destination was.

'OK, well, how much will they be?'

'Sir, since you good customer I give you good price.' I could see his brain working overtime. He was assessing how desperate I was whilst trying to analyse the possibility of my going to someone else to do this dirty transaction. He was almost certainly a smart enough salesman to understand that I didn't know anyone else and that any tourist looking to obtain a new identity was pretty damn desperate.

'Sir, I think it cost for you, for two British passport with good forgery, two thousand dollar each. I am sorry but this first and final price.'

I looked at him. I knew no one else in this town. I tried to barter but simply received an adamant shake of the head in return. We had no choice but to accept his price. I would simply have to dig deep and put the Panther's dollars to good use.

'OK,' I said. Gemma immediately elbowed me.

'Steve, that's way too much.'

'Gemma, we just don't have a choice, OK? We're gonna do this. We've gotta do this. I've got some dollars I took off that guy I beat up back in Tarifa so I'm paying, OK?' Gemma looked a bit confused at this but shut up.

'OK, Muwaffaq, that's cool with us. How about we give you half the cash now and half on delivery?'

'Yes, this no problem. You go get photos from shop round corner now and then bring here. I afraid names you have not of your choice . . . they must be same or similar to ones already on passport . . . understand? Also, please when you have photos taken do something bit different with hair . . . maybe put tissue in to fill up cheeks, OK? You cannot look same in photos as you look now – that would be very . . . suspicious.'

'Fine.' Just as long as these passports hadn't been nicked off a Balamunguthan Ratnaike or Fujitso Hashimoto we might get away with it, I thought.

We went and had our passport photos taken after we'd made minor adjustments to our appearance. I spiked my hair up and put on the glasses I'd bought in London. Gemma plumped her cheeks with some tissues and tied her bob back in a little rat's tail. After a few attempts we were satisfied with our photos and returned with them to Muwaffaq's shop. I peeled off twenty hundred-dollar bills from the roll I'd taken off the Panther and handed them to our potential saviour. Although they'd got wet on our crossing to Africa they hadn't been ruined. Muwaffaq took them greedily and counted them again. He had a big, fat smile on his face. Although he was clearly dodgy his one good eye seemed kind and he had a gentle manner. I trusted him.

'You come back this time tomorrow and we see who you are to become, eh?' He was smiling away as if we'd just done the most normal thing in the world. Gemma and I left feeling as if we might just have bought our freedom. It seemed we were on the final stage of this hideous ordeal.

That night Gemma and I shared a beautiful lamb tagine on the second-storey balcony of a restaurant overlooking the central square of the Medina. Beneath us acrobats were jumping around, snakes were being charmed and fire was being breathed. The haunting sound of the snake charmers' flutes and the smell of incense filled the air. The constant hypnotic sound of beating drums was occasionally interrupted by a braying donkey. Fires lit up the central square and their smoke drifted off into the sky. It was magical and, as we held hands, we both felt happy for the first time for many days. We weren't out of the woods yet but we'd made it so far. We looked into each other's eyes with joy. We were facing the final hurdle now. I wanted to drink a toast to our good fortune but our restaurant, like most in the Medina, didn't sell alcohol.

After a postprandial pot of mint tea, we wandered hand in hand down dark, quiet side streets back to our hotel. Once there, we nestled into a quiet corner of the bar and shared a few vodka and tonics. Gemma seemed relaxed. She was laughing at my inane gags and her eyes were wide with excitement. The smoky, twilight romance of this medieval town had got to both of us and our immediate future now seemed to promise more of an adventure than a nightmare. We were going to get away . . . we were going to be OK. I squeezed her hand and stroked her back. She put her hand on my knee and gazed into my eyes. I began to feel sure that the love that had been sleeping for so long had been reawakened. We stayed for one last drink, talking excitedly about what we'd get up to in our new life. The old Gemma, at once gently mocking yet full of love, was back. I could hardly contain my joy and neither could she. My heart was racing and for once it wasn't with fear. My whole body was trembling with anticipation.

After she'd downed the last mouthful of her drink, Gemma grabbed me and led me to the lift, where she pulled me towards her and our mouths met. We kissed passionately and within seconds my excitement was all too obvious. The lift arrived at our floor but we hardly noticed until the doors started closing. I wedged them open and we virtually ran to our room. Within seconds we were naked and . . . it was beautiful. Passionate yet relaxed, exciting yet calm . . . so, so worth waiting for. The love I felt for her as we lay in each other's arms was stronger than ever. I stroked her back until I sensed she was asleep. I couldn't wait to wake up and feel myself inside her again. She was my girl again. We were together again.

Everything was perfect . . . what could possibly go wrong?

Forty-One

'FRANÇOIS CHEVALIER? FRANÇOIS BLEEDING CHEVALIER? Are you taking the effing piss? This is a fucking *French* passport, my fine feathered friend. I asked for a fucking *British* one. This is not cool . . . not cool at all!'

'So sorry, sir, but this only passport possible we could use. You see how well my brother-in-law put photo in, yes?'

'Yeah, that's just fucking great but I ain't French and if I'm asked questions other than where the fucking cathedral is or whether I'd like a fucking ham sandwich I'm gonna be in big fucking trouble.' I could feel myself getting redder and redder.

'So sorry, mister, but this is all we could do with so little time. You could pretend be deaf or not able speak, no?'

'Christ, mate, any pig worth his salt would see through that shit in about three fucking seconds.'

'Steve, calm down. Your French isn't that bad and you usually don't have to speak when going through customs. You just show them your passport and smile sweetly. Look, once we're out of Morocco and other French-speaking countries it shouldn't be a problem anyway. The fact is that Muwaffaq has just organised two perfectly good passports for us in under twenty-four hours, as he said he would. Look, mine is absolutely perfect. It's British, the photo looks absolutely fine and I even like my new name: Crystal Wood – how cool is that?'

'Yeah, fine for you. How am I supposed to convince everyone I'm French? Put on a ridiculous "'allo 'allo!" accent and tell any sucker dumb enough to listen to me that my countrymen invented sex?'

'Yeah, that should do it!' Gemma was actually laughing. Muwaffaq, who'd looked a bit worried before, was smiling now, realising that he was still going to get the other half of his money.

'Christ, this is not what I was after. Are you sure you haven't got any other passports?'

'So sorry, mister, but if you want another you wait many days.'

'Shit! OK, here's the cash, but I ain't happy. If I'm ever back here I want a proper discount on one of your moody kilims, all right?' I was laughing a little now too, but I didn't know why. I think I was just happy to have some ID. Now all we had to do was take a plane to Bombay and hope that no one asked me a single question in French for the whole journey. Whilst I might be able to respond, the chances of anyone's not seeing through my English accent seemed extremely remote. I could claim to have been brought up in

England but that was bound to rouse suspicion. I had to think about this or we could fall flat on our faces within sight of the finishing line.

The bandage round my neck looked fairly professional. Gemma had done a pretty damn good job. Maybe I was being too cautious but there was no way I was going to pretend to be French, especially not in French-speaking Morocco. My accent would definitely be a dead giveaway. My first plan had been to take Muwaffaq's advice and pretend to be dumb, but that was just too obvious. Over yet another cup of mint tea Gemma and I had decided that the trick was to pretend that a wasp had stung my neck on the morning of the flight and that I was a little allergic and subsequently couldn't speak. I thought that perhaps I should compose a note in French saying something like *Une guêpe a piqué la gorge* that I could show to nosy customs officials and the like but I concluded that might actually raise questions rather than answer them. We decided that I should buy a couple of French novels and guidebooks to put in my bag and that Gemma, my 'English girlfriend', should do all the explaining were it to come to that.

Four wonderful, happy, loving days after the purchase of our passports Gemma and I were walking through Marrakech airport towards our check-in. We had bought two cheap and cheerful tickets to Moscow using the Russian airline Aeroflot. At Moscow airport we were to have a wait of seven hours and then take another Aeroflot flight to Mumbai,

India. The travel agent had sorted out an Indian visa for us but before we worried about getting to India we needed to find out whether our passports showed up as stolen or lost on the airline's computers.

We waited in the Aeroflot queue. We'd bought bigger rucksacks and had spent the previous day buying toiletries, books and more clothes to fill them with. Our half-full little rucksacks were just not the kind of thing travellers going from Marrakech to India would be sporting. We had to reduce all potential suspicion and look as 'normal' as possible, and that meant decent-sized rucksacks that actually had enough shit in them to convince an official that we were engaged in a round-the-world travelling adventure. In the circumstances, I was sure Nick would forgive me for ditching the one I had borrowed from him.

There were now just two people ahead of us in the queue. My heart was beginning to pound. Not only were we about to find out our fate but I couldn't involve myself in negotiations, due to my bandage. If there was any bull-shitting to be done it was now up to Gemma to supply it. I squeezed her hand, probably a little too hard. She looked round at me, and I smiled nervously at her. She attempted to smile back. The old Russian couple in front of us walked away towards departures. We shuffled forward. The lady behind the desk looked up and smiled. Gemma passed her both our passports, and our tickets. Her hands were shaking ever so slightly.

The lady looked at our documents and very quickly

seemed fully satisfied. She printed out our boarding cards and attached labels to our checked-in luggage, which was then promptly sent away on a conveyer belt. She smiled sweetly, returned our passports and signalled for the next passengers to approach her. Fucking tremendous! We were past the first barrier. I think Gemma could sense my feeling of relief. As we walked away, she clearly felt the need to shatter my illusion of success.

'I hate to say this, honey, but that was never going to be the problem. The problem we face is passport control. Those are the guys who'll study these passports of ours properly. We're not even close to being out of the woods yet.'

She had a point. My feeling of euphoria rapidly disappeared as we approached the gate to departures. In front of it were four booths, each containing a nasty-looking official. They were bound to see through our false documentation. We were, without doubt, doomed.

We waited in the queue. After what seemed like an eternity we reached its end. A woman, the most fierce-looking of a pretty fierce bunch, beckoned us over to her booth. She looked like Bond villain Rosa Klebb, but not quite as tender or compassionate. We tried to look as calm as possible as we approached her booth. My shoe caught in the floor and I almost stumbled. Not cool. She held her hand out whilst staring directly at us. Her glare could have melted pig iron from fifty yards. Gemma handed her both passports.

Rosa looked at my passport first. She examined the

photo. She looked up at me. She examined my photo again. She looked back at me. We'd at least made sure we weren't wearing the same clothes we'd been photographed in. After what seemed like an eternity she put it down. She did the same with Gemma's. She appeared satisfied with hers too. So far, so good.

But then she began looking in mine for something. She flicked through the pages one by one, intermittently licking her thumb and forefinger as she did so. Christ! I hoped she didn't ask me about any of the places I'd theoretically been to. Then she picked up Gemma's and gave it the same treatment, and I realised we'd made a mistake. A big fucking mistake. Muwaffaq had explained that he never recycled his dodgy passports in under a year, to minimise the risk of their still being looked for when their new owners wanted to leave the country. There would be no recent entry visa stamp into Morocco in either passport. We hadn't thought of that. We were surely doomed. Images of me being taken away to a back room and interrogated by some nasty *Midnight Express* copper with a bad attitude began to fill my head. I was sweating more than the air temperature justified.

Rosa started speaking to me in French. I pointed at my neck bandage and then at Gemma. My finger was shaking. Gemma said as calmly as she could, 'A wasp has stung his neck. He finds it painful to talk. Please tell me if there is a problem, but in English please . . . I don't speak French.'

'So, I cannot find entry visa stamps this year in these passports. Please tell me . . . how did you enter Morocco?

Stamps are made at all entry points into Morocco.' She was staring straight into Gemma's eyes as she said this. I could tell she was seeking out any signs of mendacity.

'Oh, God, I knew this might be a problem. You said it might too, didn't you, François?' Gemma was tutting in a convincingly natural way. 'Basically . . . the thing is, we came on a tourist boat from Algeciras in Spain to Tangiers about ten days ago. We were supposed to go back on the same day. The passport guy's ink pad had obviously dried up by the time we reached him and when we told him we were heading back to Spain that day he didn't seem too bothered about stamping our passports. However, we loved Tangiers so much that we decided to stay. We're travelling the world, we're gonna get married soon and this is our last adventure before settling down. We sometimes do spontaneous things. That's the whole point of travelling. I knew that this might cause problems and I felt bad because my fiancé got quite upset about it. And when his neck got stung by a wasp this morning I felt even worse. But that's what happened – we got a boat from Spain to Tangiers and I'm sure we weren't the only ones who didn't get a stamp that day.'

She might have been rambling a bit but Gemma's bullshit was impressively persuasive. I wasn't quite sure what to make of the marriage bit, though. Was that for my benefit? Was it to try to appeal to Rosa's romantic streak? If so, judging by the woman's bulldog countenance, I suspect she was wasting her time. We both waited expectantly. I was squeezing my jaw together just to stop my teeth chattering.

I could see that Gemma was trying to appear as calm as possible. She was succeeding, better than I was. What a girl!

The lady in the booth looked through both passports again. She looked up at us again. She picked up the telephone next to her. Oh, fuck, we're done for now. She began to speak into the receiver. I couldn't hear what she said. All I knew was that this wasn't going as smoothly as I'd hoped. After what seemed like ages she put the phone down. She gave one last look at our passports and then . . . and then she stamped them and handed them back. *She handed them back!*

Calmly, Gemma said, 'Thank you,' and I nodded my appreciation. Rosa simply motioned us away. We walked past her. We really were all right. Mumbai, here we come! Goa, here we come! Freedom, here we fucking come!

Forty-Two

GABRIEL STARED IN DISBELIEF AT the photocopy of the article from *El País* that his servant had handed him. It was a short piece that concisely described the basic facts of the murder. The headline simply said 'Man Shot in Tarifa Guesthouse'. The description of the anonymous victim as 'bald, tall, athletic . . . possibly of Middle Eastern origin' confirmed all Gabriel's worst fears. He had suspected something was wrong when he had not received any recent updates from his favourite contract killer, but this was a complete surprise. Gabriel clenched his fists until the knuckles turned white. The longer this stupid child evaded him the more he wanted him dead. Every extra hour Steve Jones lived was a personal insult to him and the empire he had so painstakingly built up.

He pondered the situation. Things were out of control. He had to be decisive. He stared across his vast acreage from the comfort of his favourite Spanish colonial chair. It was dusk, the golden hour – his preferred time of day. A time of peace and tranquillity. But Gabriel felt far from calm. Everything he had built up could be lost in days. After several more minutes of introspection he decided he had no choice. He would call Pedro.

Gabriel motioned for his servant to bring him the telephone. He took out his diary, found Pedro's number and dialled it. He knew that Pedro was to be contacted as infrequently as possible and that calling him at this hour would not be appreciated. Still, desperate times called for desperate measures.

After six rings Gabriel heard an angry voice at the other end of the line. 'Yes, who is it?'

'Your *amigo*,' was all that Gabriel needed to say.

Pedro stood up immediately, excused himself from his table and marched towards the corridor, straightening his dinner jacket with his free hand as he did so. The chatter of the hundred or so seated guests soon faded away. As soon as he had found a discreet corner and was sure that his conversation could not be heard he spoke again.

'Signor, it is always a pleasure to speak to you . . . but I thought we had agreed only to use this number in emergencies.'

'This is emergency. The little problem we discussed one week ago has still not been resolved. Indeed, the solution that we sent to Spain has himself been . . . "resolved". This boy could be extremely costly to both of us. I need you to use all your contacts to remedy this situation.'

'My God . . . he still hasn't been dealt with? OK, it's time to sort this out once and for all. I have friends in MI5 and they have friends in Interpol. Please send a coded email to my favoured confidential address detailing everything. Our friend doesn't have much money, he is travelling with his girlfriend and he makes mistakes ... we'll find him soon enough.' Pedro was trying to sound confident and sure of himself, but occasionally his voice betrayed a certain nervousness. He hated direct contact with Gabriel, who even from several thousand miles had the ability to scare him.

'Let us hope so. By the way, be sure to thank your daughter for her help in this matter. Without her we would have completely lost the trail.' Peter Saint's mouth dropped but before he could ask what exactly Gabriel meant he heard the click of the receiver being replaced. He looked into the distance for a few seconds, listening to the dial tone, and then called his daughter.

'Hi, Daddy. What's up?'

'Jane, I've just heard from our Colombian friend that you helped him out recently. Why the *hell* didn't you tell me about this? What the *hell* are you doing getting directly involved in this without my say-so? Do you have a *clue* how dangerous these people can be?'

'Sorry, Daddy. I . . . I was asked to help out and was told not to bother you. All I did was tell them where . . . our friend had rung me from. I didn't want to worry you and honestly, Daddy, I didn't put myself in any danger.'

'But Jimjam . . . don't you realise that these people can be very dangerous? You saw what happened to Chuck . . . Please, never, ever do anything like this again without asking me, OK, baby?'

'Daddy, you got me that job at Geldlust so I could keep an eye on things. I'm a big girl now and what I did didn't put me in harm's way. But OK, henceforth I promise I'll tell you everything that's going on. Anyway, how is the Mansion House dinner going?'

'Christ almighty! It's the dullest thing I've ever been to. Regulators, politicians and investment bankers really have to be the most appalling people in the world! I wouldn't trust any of these gangsters as far as I could throw them. Still, I'd better get back. But, darling, promise me you'll never get directly involved in our . . . sideline again without my permission, OK?'

'I promise. Bye-bye, Daddy.'

Jane stared at her mobile for a second. Her father worried too much – had done so ever since her mother had died when she was only nine. Despite the fact that certain liars from her mother's family claimed that it was Peter's gambling and womanising that had pushed his wife to suicide, she loved him unconditionally. She had no siblings and over the years had formed a bond with her father of such strength that nothing would ever break it. They were a team, and Peter always shared everything with her. Some of her friends had told her that their relationship was 'unnatural' or 'too close' but she didn't care, and neither did he. She knew that

Peter had never remarried because there was not enough room in his heart for two women, and when she turned into a beautiful version of his former wife they had grown even closer. They would laugh and flirt with each other over lunch at Le Caprice every Wednesday happy in the knowledge that their fellow diners assumed that she was the dapper older man's youthful mistress.

Jane reclined in her chair and thought back to the first time her father had told her about his money-making enterprise. He had visited her at Oxford just after she'd finished her final exam. He'd met her outside the hall with a bottle of champagne in one hand and two glasses in the other. After a joyful walk round Oxford's beautiful town centre passing the bottle back and forth between them, ignoring the stares from the numerous tourist groups they passed, he took her down a cobbled lane that ended up at a riverside pub he'd frequented regularly when he had been a student at Queen's thirty years before. He sat her down in a dingy corner and, after a long pause, asked her what career she would like to pursue. Jane had looked lovingly into her father's eyes, smiled and said that all she'd ever wanted to do was follow him into the City. Peter smiled. He stood up, went to the bar and bought them both a double whisky. On his return he took a long, deep breath and quietly delivered a speech he'd been preparing for weeks.

He told her about his gambling problem and how it had led to his becoming embroiled in Chuck's activities. Whilst he had met Chuck at various City events over the years their real relationship had been formed over the blackjack and baccarat tables of Crockfords – the oldest private gaming club in the world. Of course, as Peter became an ever more important figure in the City establishment, Chuck had done his best to ingratiate himself with him. It was when Peter's gambling had got completely out of control and lost him nearly everything that Chuck had made his move. He was commiserating with Peter over a glut of whisky sodas at Annabel's about the latter's need to sell his Kensington home when he first tentatively broached the subject of making some money on the side. Initially, Peter had been sceptical and he'd even feigned disgust at the 'sideline', as Chuck had repeatedly called it. But successive angry letters from his officious bank manager chipped away at Peter's defences and eventually he called Chuck to 'have a little chat about . . . that proposition'.

Jane had looked adoringly at her father. She had been captivated by his story. Her father explained that within months of signing up he had become a key member of the team and after merely a year had become more important than Chuck. The rewards were instant and massive and the risks were negligible. Peter always avoided getting his hands too dirty and each promotion through the ranks of the Square Mile made him ever more vital to operations. He had always been useful because of his powerful contacts, but on becoming London's chief financial regulator he had become invaluable. He was now informed of every proposed regulatory investigation and hence was able to tell his paymasters about all potential issues, and to stymie any threats with impunity. After Peter's appointment as Chief Executive of the FSA Gabriel began to use London exclusively to launder all his dirty money.

After Peter had explained about his 'sideline' he had asked his loving daughter if she'd like a job at Chuck's bank to help him out and make sure there were no 'complications'. He told her that Chuck would find a role for her and that there'd be no need for 'silly things like interviews'. All she would have to do was keep a close eye on everyone in the department and pretend to all her colleagues that she was a diligent, conventional banker. He'd make sure that there was never any direct connection between her and the 'sideline' in the unlikely event that things ever got out of hand. Without a second's hesitation Jane had agreed. What could be more fun than working closely with her father and doing something . . . a little naughty? Their underhand dealings would just tighten their relationship even more.

After Chuck's death they had held an emergency meeting to discuss what to do. His murder had shocked them both but they had vowed not to panic. They would have to be smart and careful from now on – that was all. When Jane had been asked directly for a little favour by the Colombians she had jumped to the challenge. She would show her dad that she could handle herself. She would show the Colombians that she was a dependable and useful asset. But most of all she would make sure that her idiotic, egotistical boss got his comeuppance. Steve was the only thing that threatened her and her father's life together. There was no way in hell that she'd let his meddling ruin everything.

She would do whatever it took to make sure nothing ever changed for her and her daddy.

Forty-Three

THE SUNLIGHT AND THE HEAT woke me at about ten o'clock, as it always did. I lay there for a few minutes, gathering myself, my eyes only half open. A few joints just before bed always made things a little fuzzy at this early hour. I looked around. Gemma wasn't there. Probably at yoga or maybe she was at her studio. I slowly pulled myself out of bed and meandered to the bathroom. A quick shower and then a difficult choice – head off to Orangina for a full English breakfast or take the healthier option at the Shore Bar. Tricky. This required some thought. Maybe a bifta would help. I picked up my stash box and donned my shades. I turned on the stereo and Jimmy Cliff's 'Many Rivers to Cross' soon filled the air. I shuffled off to the balcony and carefully eased myself into the huge hammock. I slowly rolled a charas jay on my stomach and lay there puffing on it until it was dead. I occasionally pulled on the string that I'd attached to the wall to get the hammock swinging without expending any major effort. Once the joint was finished I didn't feel like doing anything in particular and our cat was sleeping on my lap. Why move when this was sheer bliss? I'd had over a year of sheer bliss. It just doesn't get any better than this, I thought.

After perhaps ten more minutes staring at the ceiling hypnotising myself with gentle swings generated by leisurely pulls on the string I decided to act decisively. I stood up unsteadily and put on a pair of shorts, a T-shirt and my flip-flops. I picked up my bike keys and strolled over to my Enfield, which was, as always, parked just in front of our house. Oh, beautiful . . . the journey to the Shore Bar was going to be almost as wonderful as the fresh juice and muesli and curd that I would enjoy on arrival. Soon I was racing along raised narrow roads with fields on either side in the late morning sun wondering where it had all gone so very right. I couldn't help but have a broad grin across my face as the warm air whistled past me. A few water buffaloes lazed in the water on either side of the road. I passed a couple of hippies I knew and raised my left hand in acknowledgement. I went down the narrow paths leading to the Shore Bar, parked up next to the other bikes and cruised in via the back entrance. I gave a thumbs-up to Richard, the owner, who was already chugging a beer, and took a seat at my usual table at the front overlooking the beach. 'Blue Lines' by Massive Attack was playing quietly in the background. It was high tide and the Arabian Sea lay no more than thirty feet from my table. Only the crashing sound of the occasional wave punctuated the calm. The sea looked tempting. I wondered about going in for a swim immediately but decided that a fresh pineapple juice was the priority. Santosh, the waiter, came and asked how I was. 'Same as yesterday, Santosh, damn good . . . *damn* good!' I gave my order, lay back in my chair and stared at a few beautiful bikini-clad tourists below me. It just doesn't get any better than this, I thought again, for about the millionth time that year. Another day in fucking paradise.

A blissful thirteen months had passed since we'd touched down in Mumbai at the beginning of October 2007. The twelve-hour coach journey down to Panjim hadn't been much fun but neither of us could be dealing with the risk that taking another plane might have entailed. We'd arrived and I smelt the familiar smells that a dozen previous visits had ingrained in my brain – exotic spices, cow pats, motorbike fumes and coconut oil. We took a cab to my friend Alex's house near Anjuna beach and, although he was somewhat surprised to see us since usually I gave him fair warning, he welcomed us both with open arms. He hadn't heard about any of the shit that had happened. I loved that fact . . . that our notoriety hadn't spread as far as India. I explained to him over a few Kingfishers at the local bar the somewhat unusual situation we found ourselves in and like a true friend he put us up for a couple of days before we settled in elsewhere. He helped us find a place to stay – a beautiful, cosy bungalow about five minutes' ride from Anjuna beach. We organised a six-month lease which set us back the princely sum of eight hundred quid and nestled in. Soon

Geraint Anderson

Gemma had decorated our love nest with her own art and an assortment of drapes and ornaments bought from Anjuna's weekly flea market, and turned a house into a home. Within a month or two we were settled into a wonderful existence and had begun to forget about our hideous experience. Quite often, usually when high, my mind floated back to some dreadful incident but by talking about things we managed to deal with what we'd been through. At night, just before I drifted off to sleep, the image of the Panther's contorted deathly grimace often re-entered my mind but usually it merely took a look across at Gemma's serene face to dispel the appalling picture. After about a month I told Gemma the real story of that particular encounter. To her credit, she took it remarkably well.

Our life was simple. Gemma spent her days painting in her studio and learning yoga. She also made sculptures out of wood, which she sold at Anjuna's Wednesday flea market. I got high a lot and occasionally did a little yoga at the Brahmani centre near Granpa's. I sold a little bit of puff to make money but wasn't really what you'd call a dealer – just a middleman who traded with friends. Sometimes we'd go to parties in Shiva Valley and dance the night away on acid and MDMA or K, but no more than every couple of months. We ate simple, healthy food and swam a lot. If I was feeling particularly energetic I'd do some boxing training down at Chapora. When the weather became too hot in April we headed to the mountains of Nepal where we extended our tourist visa for another six months. We then spent a little time in the Indian Himalayas in a remote valley near Manali living a remarkably sedate life. In early September, just as the monsoon was ending, we came back to our humble abode – using trains and buses because flying still gave us the willies.

Our love had blossomed into something I'd never experienced before. The trauma of those days in late 2007 had bonded us in a way that no other experience could have. We trusted each other and we never found ourselves feeling bored with our conversation or our adventures. Sometimes we ate out at the posher restaurants Goa had to offer like La Plage or Sublime, but most nights we'd cook simple food and enjoy it alone on our terrace with a bottle of dubious Indian wine. Within weeks of settling into our new routine we found ourselves thanking the gods for our good fortune. Rarely a week went by when we didn't tell each other that our calamity was the best thing that could have happened to us. We were in love, had made great friends and didn't have to get up early to do a job we hated. Admittedly, we had had to rename ourselves Crystal and François just in case, but no one we met seemed to suspect anything. We lived in a tropical paradise, had false passports and enough money to get by on – what could possibly go wrong?

Of course, on our arrival I'd been forever checking out the internet for news of the investigation into Chuck's murder, and that of the Panther. Soon we became old news. There seemed to be no major developments. We weren't exactly Bonnie and Clyde, then. In time I found myself more interested in what was going on in financial markets across the world. It looked as if fate had forced me to leave the City at just the right time. I pictured my former colleagues receiving piss-poor bonuses or losing their jobs altogether and, whilst I took no pleasure in their reduced circumstances, I could only conclude that it was merely the result of their own misdeeds. Anyway, perhaps if they lost their jobs they'd go and find something more fulfilling to do with their lives. Frankly, nothing that had happened since my departure surprised me – Jérôme Kerviel's alleged €4.9 billion trading loss, the fall of Lehmans and the near self-destruction of capitalism. They all seemed strangely inevitable and merely a symptom of the madness that had gripped the world in recent times. The 25-year bull market had reached crisis point and it was payback time. The party was well and truly over and the hangover looked as if it was going to make most of the others in living memory feel like a gentle walk in the park. We bankers had been living in a fantasy world of endless prosperity and fathomless greed without any thought of the long-term consequences of our actions. Gordon Brown hit the nail on the head when he called my period in the City 'the age of irresponsibility'. I didn't miss any of it. We Cityboys had created a mess and the whole world was suffering. It made telling people that I had been a drug dealer in my former life all the more palatable. Drug dealers were deemed a far more salubrious group than bankers by people out here, and who could blame them? Any more than they could blame those who had decided to see out the recession sitting here on a tropical beach enjoying a Kingfisher beer or twenty? The ones I couldn't understand were the people who felt they had to endure precious years of their all too short lives in the depressing drizzly cold of a credit-crunched Britain. We had hardly any cash but I'd never been happier.

We managed to keep in contact with our parents via various cunning methods. Neither of us wanted our folks to worry about us but we obviously didn't want to give any hints to PC Plod regarding our whereabouts. I either sent a letter to Nick with one for my folks enclosed to be posted to them from London or I gave Alex stuff to post when he went back to Blighty on one of his intermittent visits. The letters explained that we were in South America and extremely happy. It seemed sensible to lie ... at least regarding the former claim. There was little chance that our parents would do anything to shop us but there was every chance that the letters they received were being vetted by the rozzers. Of course, it was all one-way traffic since we never heard from them, but occasionally I'd get Alex to ask his dad, who had met my parents a few times, how they were and he'd report back. Unsurprisingly, they were both pretty upset about what had happened, particularly my mother, but they believed my story and were comforted by the knowledge that we were alive and well.

I'd also sent letters detailing my version of events to Jane and her father via Alex. Both sent answering emails to an address I'd asked Nick to set up for me, which I occasionally checked at internet cafés. They assured me that they were looking into my accusations and kept insisting that I should come back and see them so that they could help me clear my name. They also explained that talking to the police directly would not be a good idea because the latter were convinced we were guilty. When nothing had happened after a year of occasional interaction with Jane and her father, Gemma and I were becoming increasingly frustrated with them, but they carried on reassuring me and I couldn't help but feel that, with their help, I'd eventually be exonerated. Of course, that didn't mean that I'd ever be able to rest easy, but at least I wouldn't have the police to worry about.

Anyway, after finishing off my curd and muesli on that particular day in October 2008 I smoked another joint and casually moseyed on down to the beach to catch a few rays. It was whilst I was relaxing on my sarong that I noticed two guys hassling an old hippy called Dave . . .

Forty-Four

I WAS HURTLING NORTH ALONG the dirt track parallel to Anjuna beach. The beautiful calm of the last thirteen months already seemed like a distant memory. Our little paradise had become our potential cemetery. I had to reach Gemma and get her out of here immediately. My feeling of total panic was multiplied tenfold by the industrial strength joint I'd smoked with such enthusiasm just moments before everything disintegrated.

Still, I knew the paths I was motoring down like the back of my hand and that was definitely an advantage. But I could hear the bikes of my would-be assassins screaming close behind me. My Enfield was a slow, heavy bike and those fuckers had chosen nippy little Japanese numbers much more suited to this kind of shit. They were blatantly gaining on me and I was already going way too quickly for this old bike on these sandy dirt tracks. I skidded badly twice when taking corners too fast and had to keep shouting so that shopkeepers, tourists and the odd long-horned Brahman cow knew that I was coming at them like a bat out of hell. I received occasional expletives from locals and tourists alike but there was no time to explain my behaviour.

I finally arrived at the beginning of the main Anjuna to Mapusa road and as I turned inland risked a glance to my right. They were both coming at me and were sufficiently close for me to see the insane, hateful looks in their eyes. These malicious cunts had been hunting me for the last thirteen months. Fuck, they were persistent. They'd probably been told by their boss that they weren't to return without my head on a platter. Clearly, I was to be tracked down and killed no matter what the time or expense. I had most definitely crossed the wrong guy when I pulled that insane stunt all those months ago.

As I raced inland I received yet more insults from people on the road. I just continued at full throttle, passing astonished tourists on scooters and Indians crammed into Ambassador taxis. I looked in my wing mirror and saw my two hunters no more than seventy feet behind me. I simply couldn't risk driving home. There was every chance I'd not be able to lose them before I got there.

So, instead of turning left at Starkos junction as I normally would I continued up the road as fast as I could without endangering my life and the lives of everyone in front of me. I was still screaming continually so that people were aware of my presence. The locals must have thought that I was stark raving mad, whilst I suspect that the dreadlocked long-term travellers presumed I'd taken far too much acid. I reached the crossroads and turned right towards Baga beach, I'm not sure why. Perhaps it was to get as far from our house and Gemma as possible.

As I turned towards Baga I suddenly remembered something about this road that could be to my advantage. There was a set of 'rumblers' just after a sharp bend in the road in about five hundred metres. 'Rumblers' were the most ridiculous 'traffic safety' innovation Goa possessed. They were like sleeping policemen but came close together in threes and were much steeper. In theory, they existed to force you to slow right down, almost to a stop, in front of schools and so forth. In reality, their location seemed fairly random and I had no doubt that they caused many more accidents than they prevented. I myself had been a victim of this absurd traffic calming measure on several occasions, though admittedly only when I was off my nut on wonk after some all-night party. The beauty of this particular set of 'rumblers' was that they did not have the white warning markings that most possessed and they were just after a bend so you didn't see them until you were almost on them. My mate Alex had mashed his knees early on during his time in Goa when he had come off at this very place, and had warned me about them on several occasions. I knew where they were and I knew you had to either slow right down and clunk your way over them or use the sandy bit on either side of them to avoid potential nastiness. I also knew that my hunters were in all likelihood oblivious of all this.

I raced towards the bend in the road as fast as my bike

could take me. As soon as I turned and was out of Diego and Juan's sight I squeezed the brakes and veered off the tarmac on to the thin sandy patch as a thousand locals and long-termers had done before. I was going way too fast for this manoeuvre and my back wheel began fishtailing badly in the sand, but somehow I managed to stay upright. I passed by the rumblers and remounted the road, pulling back on the throttle as I did so. By the time my two would-be killers came round the bend I was on the road again and back up to fifty miles an hour. To them it must have looked as if I'd simply continued racing down the road, though I was now a bit closer than before. They accelerated towards me, smelling blood.

I heard the screech of brakes seconds later and looked in my wing mirror. They must have seen the rumblers just metres before hitting them and slowed down way too late. Despite the relief I felt on seeing both bikes crash spectacularly and both riders sliding along the tarmac, I couldn't help but squirm and grit my teeth as I imagined the pain they must be feeling as they tumbled along the road. I slowed down a little and turned my head. That must have hurt a lot. To my amazement, and despite the damage that their knees and shoulders must have suffered, both were trying to stand up. I pulled back the throttle and after another fifty metres or so looked in the wing mirror again. Although Diego and Juan were now almost out of view I could see that one of them was already up and limping towards his bike.

Forty-Five

'**W**E HAVE TO GO AND *we have to go right now!*' It had taken about fifteen minutes to drive home along the back route and Gemma was having an early afternoon kip when I disturbed her. I'd come crashing through the front door and shaken her awake.

'What? What's going on?' She had the somewhat spaced-out air that she always had after she'd just been woken up.

'Those two fucks . . . that's what's going on. They've fucking found us!'

'Christ! Fuck! Shit! What happened?'

'No time to explain. I don't know how close they are. For all I know they could be here any minute. Just come right now. We're going to Alex's.'

Gemma didn't say a word. The look of sheer wide-eyed sweaty panic on my face was all she needed to see. She put on her clothes and grabbed her bag and within a minute we were racing inland towards Alex's house. The air rushed by, making my eyes stream.

'Keep your eyes peeled. Those fuckers are round here somewhere. If they see us we can't go to Alex's. We'll just keep driving south . . . all the way to Karnataka if necessary.'

'It's those same two? The ones that kidnapped me? They've come all the way here to kill us?'

'Yep – fucking Tweedledee and Tweedledum have followed us here. Unfuckingbelievable!'

'Christ! What the fuck are we going to do?'

'First things first. Let's get to Alex's and analyse our options. Probably best if we don't explain what's happened. He might not be too pleased to know that we've potentially put his missus and son in danger.'

After another five minutes of careful driving, with Gemma constantly turning her head to see if our two long-lost pals were around, we arrived at Alex's. Fortunately, his girlfriend Virginia was home, and she welcomed us in and gave us a cup of fresh coffee in the kitchen before going to look after her screaming one year old who had just woken up and needed feeding. It had taken several minutes for my shakes to subside but Virginia had seemed oblivious. Gemma and I departed to the terrace to discuss our 'strategy'.

'OK, they know we're in Goa and they know we're local. They're determined. They ain't going to give up easily, having come all this way and spent all this time finding us. It won't take them long to locate our pad. If they focus their efforts on Anjuna and show enough people our photo they'll find the bungalow soon enough. We've been stupid. We got complacent. We thought we were safe. We were wrong.'

'How did they find us?'

'Fucked if I know. Anyway, we need to get out of here.' In fact, I suspected they came to Goa because I'd made it fairly clear in several of my newspaper columns that Goa was my favoured holiday destination, but I didn't want to tell Gemma that for fear of severe retribution.

'I'll tell you exactly how they knew ... maybe it's something to do with the fact that you've been here twelve times before and have mentioned that fact in your column a few times. You wouldn't have to be a rocket scientist to work out that this might just be your favoured hiding place.'

'Shit. Perhaps you're right. Maybe coming to Goa wasn't such a smart move. But anyway, how they found us ain't important ... what's important is what are we going to do now?'

'Well, we've got about six hundred quid to our name and we've left our passports at the house.'

'Oh, *shit*! That wasn't smart.'

'Yeah, and if I hadn't been half asleep when you dragged me out I reckon I would have remembered them. Steve, you're not thinking. Are you back on the morning joints? I thought we agreed no hash before six.'

'Yeah ... no ... yeah, OK. I had a joint this morning, maybe a couple, but again that's not really relevant. We've got to get those passports and we've got to leave Goa, possibly India. We just need to find the same kind of chilled beachy set-up elsewhere ... perhaps Thailand or Bali or bleeding Guatemala ... anywhere but Europe.'

'But are you happy to go back to the house? They could be waiting there right now.'

'OK, I tell you what I'll do. I'll wait until it's dark, then borrow some of Alex's clothes and that ridiculous hat he loves and wear that moody pair of glasses I've got. I'll drive there on Virginia's scooter and case the joint. If there's no one around I'll run in, grab a bunch of stuff and be out of there quick as a flash.'

'God, are you sure? Couldn't we just go on the run without passports?'

'Babe, it's the only way. It will probably take them a little time to find out exactly where we live. We won't be able to get new passports with the money we have and without them we're doomed. They check them every bleeding five minutes in this country. Please, please don't worry. Everything's going to be just fine.' I hoped she didn't realise that if I'd actually believed that, I probably wouldn't have been tapping my foot on the floor like a nervous maniac.

Six hours later I said goodbye to Gemma on Alex's porch. There was something definitely poignant about that embrace. In fact, there was something worryingly final about the whole thing. She hugged me with tears in her eyes. 'I love you' was all she said as I got on Virginia's scooter. The whole thing might have been vaguely cool and romantic had I not resembled some kind of two-bit loser who'd fallen out of a charity shop. The clothes I'd borrowed off Alex were about three sizes too big and, frankly, his ethnic Afghan hat shouldn't be worn this side of the Himalayas, let alone by a westerner driving a pink scooter. Still, I had a job to do. I could handle looking preposterous if it reduced the chances of getting my liver carved out.

I rode towards my destiny, my heart pumping away. The wait had been awful, though pretending to Alex and Virginia that everything was just fine and dandy had somehow made it bearable. They had invited us to stay the night, and I had spent time playing with their son. I wondered if Gemma and I would ever have the chance to create something so beautiful.

I parked the scooter about fifty yards from the bungalow, being sure to leave it turned round in case I needed to beat a hasty retreat back to Alex's. I walked slowly towards the house, all my senses on high alert. My eyes kept darting from one side of the street to the other as I checked for my potential murderers. When I was about seventy feet from the house I suddenly remembered the little back passage that would allow me to creep round to the rear of the bungalow without being seen from the road. I'd forgotten about it until then, having only used it once when out looking for our cat. I still wouldn't be able to get into the house unseen, as the only entrance was at the front, but it would be an unexpected approach that would make me less conspicuous to any murderous Colombians who happened to be watching.

I crept down the dark passageway, seeing a piece of wood with a nail in it and instinctively picking it up . . . just in case.

Broken bits of glass and rotten sticks occasionally broke underfoot, making an unwelcome racket. Each time this happened I stopped dead in my tracks to see if anything stirred, and each time all I was greeted by was shadows and silence. The only sound was that of my heart, pounding away in double-quick time. Finally, I reached the side of our house. I could now survey the whole area in front of my gaff from behind a bush with virtually no fear of being seen.

Everything looked fine. There were a few tourists in the bar opposite chatting and having a laugh. The market stalls were still out and about and, as usual, lacking customers. Everything looked exactly as it should. I was just about to head out to the front door when I suddenly saw them – two shadowy figures at the very rear of the bar. They were shrouded in darkness and I only spotted them because one had taken a drag on a cigarette, illuminating his face briefly as he did so. His eyes had only been revealed for a second but I knew exactly who it was in that instant. It was the tall thin one. The one who never spoke. The really scary one. Next to him was the now unmistakable silhouette of his squat *amigo*.

So, they'd found our house. They were waiting patiently for us to return like a couple of spiders expecting a fly. I remember thinking I bet they were really fucked off with us. *We've forced them to traipse around the globe looking for us. Their boss is undoubtedly underwhelmed by their performance to date. I've sprayed Mace in both their faces, kicked the shit out of Lee Van Cleef and made them both have motorbike crashes. I've lied to them, outsmarted them and humiliated them*. They weren't just going to kill me if they found us, they were going to get medieval on my bony arse. They were going to do things to me that would make the Spanish Inquisition plead for restraint. Shit, I needed to think really long and hard about how much we needed those passports.

After a few minutes of surreptitiously clocking their moves, which basically involved smoking tabs, the odd sip from a Kingfisher beer and the occasional rubbing of a bruised limb, I decided to act. These boys were on my turf now and were about to find out what a Goan welcome was all about.

I crept back down the passageway and walked back to Virginia's bike. I couldn't help turning round and looking over my shoulder every few seconds but I managed to reach the pink monstrosity without a problem. I started her up and rode reasonably calmly the few miles to Calangute. It was a hideous package tourist beach but what mattered was that it had a dodgy late night chemist's I knew all too well that would still be open. I wandered in and, somewhat to my surprise, was welcomed like a long-lost friend by the owner, Krishna. He knew from my previous visits that I wasn't here for a few aspirin and a tube of toothpaste; he was well aware that I was going to invest heavily in the strongest pharmaceuticals this fine country had to offer.

'So nice to see you again, sir. How can I help you?'

I always enjoyed this part of the game. 'Well, Krishna, I've got a few issues that need sorting and I think you might just be the man to help me out. First of all, I've got a horse that badly needs an operation so I will be needing some of your finest horse tranquilliser . . . that's right, ketamine. About two hundred mils should do the trick.'

'Ah, yes. Your horse often needs operations, does it not? Such a shame, but you are very kind to it. Other owners would have got rid of it by now.'

'Ah . . . correct. Next, my family are going to travel to the UK tomorrow and all eight of us are extremely nervous flyers. So I'll be needing thirty tablets of tetrazepam and twenty of Rohypnol.' I wasn't going to actually need all that but it was always nice to have some around in case of a rainy day.

'They are extremely nervous passengers, your large family. Such a shame . . . particularly since they have to fly here so often.'

'That's right. It's a crying shame. Anyway, that should do it for the moment, though I can't promise that my horse won't need another operation at any minute.'

'What about some Viagra for your grandparents, who seem to visit every few weeks?'

'No thanks. They're not coming for a few months.'

'Of course. So . . . that will be seven hundred and fifty rupees.' I'd just bought enough drugs to knock out the Chinese army and it had cost just over a tenner. You've got to love this country!

Next I made a quick visit to my favourite dealer, Jonno, who lived only a mile from our house. As always, he was lying in his hammock on his porch smoking a fat joint and staring at the stars. He was about forty, Australian, and had lived in Goa for almost fourteen years. His deeply lined face, vacant eyes and faded tattoos showed the effect a life of drug-fuelled sun-soaked excess could have.

I parked the bike in front of his gaff and, without getting off it, called out: 'Jonno, I need some acid right now!'

After a long pause, Jonno replied in the lugubrious, sardonic tone he always used, 'Mate, why don't you say it a bit louder? There's a bloke over in Delhi who didn't quite catch that.' Like all Aussies, the pitch of his voice rose at the end of every sentence whether he was asking a question or not.

'Sorry, sorry – I'm just a bit over-excited at the moment. Anyway, are you packing?'

'Yep, come on in. What's with the weird hat and glasses, man?'

'Don't worry about that. What have you got for me?'

'Well, I'll give you a few double-dip Hofmann trips that will knock your fucking socks off. Mate, you need to cut these bad boys in half and even then they'll still last twenty-four hours. We are talking two eighty mics each.'

'Bullshit. I'll eat two and run a fucking marathon! No, seriously, give us four then.'

'Christ, you ain't mucking around. Are you going to that party up at Ashvem?'

'Nah – just having a quiet evening in with the missus but thought I might pep it up a bit . . . you know, inject a bit of romance back into the whole thing.'

'Romance? Romance? Mate, if you can manage any romance after just one of these you can have your money back.'

'Ah, you underestimate my powers, my son.'

So, after handing over the required 1,500 rupees, I got back on my bike to execute my plan.

On the way back to the bar that housed my would-be killers I stopped at a public phone and called up Raja, the bar's owner. He had become a solid friend over the previous year and I often called him to ask him to start preparing a certain meal or do something to the house when we were on our way home from other parts of Goa. He was a westernised Indian who'd been to Britain a few times, and just a year younger than me. I'd been helping him out with his English and we'd been on a couple of benders together. We were genuine buddies. He was one of the very few people who knew my real name.

'Hi, Raja, it's me, Steve, but please don't say my name out loud.'

'Eh? Is that Steve?'

'No, no, no. Raja, listen to me very carefully. Please don't say my name again. Listen, you trust me, right?'

'Yes.'

'Well, I'm going to tell you something and I hope you can help. There are two guys right at the rear of your bar who want to hurt me. Can you see them?'

'Yes. They both look a little . . . dangerous. They've also obviously had an accident of some kind recently.'

'Yep, those are the fellers. They're waiting for me to go home so they can . . . hurt me, but I need to get into the house to pick things up. Now, I'm going to meet you at the side entrance to your kitchen in three minutes and we're going to make a little mixture of powder that you're gonna put in the next beers they order. It's nothing serious. It will just knock them out and let me get my stuff.'

'Erm . . . Steve, I not sure about doing this.'

'Raja, *please* stop saying my name! OK, we're old mates, you and me. I promise this won't harm them. Look, I'll pay you a thousand rupees if you do this for me.' The desperation in my voice must have been obvious.

'Well, that sounds OK to me. See you soon, Steve.' The cunning bugger was just waiting for a bit of baksheesh. I loved the way these guys operated.

Five minutes later I was hidden at the back of Raja's kitchen concocting a mixture of drugs that would give Keith Richards the willies. I washed up about fifty mil of liquid ketamine into a fine white powder using a saucepan lid above a pan of boiling water. Into this I crushed four Rohypnols and six tetrazepams. I then used a razor to cut four of the tabs of acid into tiny pieces. I stirred the mix together and poured it into a piece of card that I'd bent in the middle to act as a funnel when the time came. Those boys were sure gonna get more than they bargained for when they ordered their next Kingfishers.

After about ten minutes Raja came into the kitchen looking excited. 'OK, they've ordered two more beers. But listen, I always open them in front of them so how are we going to do this?'

'Don't worry about it. Open them here, but do it carefully. I'll pour in the mixture and then we'll put the caps back on. As long as you cover the cap with your hand when you open them you should be all right.'

Raja carefully removed the bottle tops and I funnelled half of the potent mix of drugs into each bottle. He then replaced the tops, and though they looked a little bent it was hardly noticeable. We then held the bottles upside down for a few seconds before placing them upright on the table and instinctively crouching down to examine the liquid. The dark brown glass was fairly opaque anyway, and the powder had pretty much dissolved completely in the beer. A few tiny scraps of the acid tabs had settled on the bottom but the Colombians wouldn't see those until it was too late . . . way too late by my reckoning.

Raja placed the bottles on a small round tray and walked out to the seating area. I watched through a gap in the rattan wall of the kitchen as he approached my would-be killers, opened the bottles in front of them and poured half the contents into two glasses. He didn't look nervous and nothing gave away the fact that he was up to no good. Raja left and the two Colombians began drinking the beer. They didn't suspect anything. Soon they were refilling their glasses. I felt a mixture of fear, excitement and pride.

All this time, Diego and Juan didn't exchange a single word. They just stared at my front door. However, about fifteen minutes after finishing the doctored beers Juan broke the silence. I couldn't exactly grasp what he said, but it was something like 'Oye, mira, anda Mickey Mouse por alli?'

Stony-faced, Diego continued to stare into the middle distance. There was a definite glazed look to his eyes. Suddenly from nowhere a smile began forming. His mouth slowly curled up at the edges and his shark-like teeth were revealed. Within seconds he was laughing hysterically. He was cracking up so heartily that other tourists were turning round and checking him out. I heard an Aussie bloke say to his mate, 'I'll have half of whatever he's had . . . no, make that a quarter.'

Juan was looking at his pal with a look of utter confusion etched all over his face. He seemed totally amazed. Mistaking a black dude with massive dreads for Mickey Mouse might have been somewhat disorientating, but it was the sight of Lee Van Cleef laughing so hard he could barely breathe that had really astounded him. He was clearly in all sorts of trouble. Despite my frayed nerves I was quite enjoying the show.

Juan had started shaking Diego and getting incredibly agitated, which just made Diego laugh even more, his face contorted into a look of insane, saucer-eyed joy. Juan was looking totally panic-stricken. He clearly didn't have a clue what was going on. Suddenly, he stopped dead. His eyes were wide open and completely terrified, and he was pointing his finger at an albino girl with a shaved head and about twenty-five earrings in her face. She looked freaky enough without the acid but poor old Juan must really have been confused. I reckon he thought he'd come face to face with the Aztec god Quetzalcoatl himself.

Suddenly, Diego's hysterics stopped as quickly as they'd begun and he slumped in his chair. Juan started desperately trying to wake him up. He was crying out in Spanish and tears were cascading down his face. He was sobbing like a little girl. All he could say was, '*Está muerto . . . está muerto . . . está muerto. Mi amor está muerto. Está muerto . . .*'

What? My Spanish wasn't up to much but it sounded like Juan had just admitted that Diego was his lover. Christ, either that acid was fucking poky or these lads had been finding lots of interesting ways to pass the time whilst they'd been on my trail. Brokeback Mountain eat your fucking heart out!

After a couple of panic-stricken minutes spent pointlessly trying to rouse his colleague/lover Juan's eyelids began to droop. Soon, he slumped back in his chair and was fast asleep too. The Colombian acid show that my wannabe killers had been putting on for their fellow tourists was officially over. Despite my pounding heart and sweaty brow, it had been one of the funniest things I'd ever seen.

Raja came in. He was in hysterics. 'Oh, Steve, did you see that? Hilarious, no?'

'Fucking funny. OK, this is the deal. I'm gonna collect all my shit and take it somewhere else. You don't need to know where. Leave these boys sleeping as long as you can. I'll bell you if I need you to do anything else. All right?'

'No problem. For a thousand rupees they can stay here all night. I'll throw in breakfast if necessary.'

'Perfect. The longer they're kipping the better.'

And with that I sidled out of the kitchen, still not daring to use the front entrance just in case they stirred. I went over to the bungalow, found our passports and packed two bags full of our most important stuff. When I left I could just make out the comatose forms of Juan and Diego. I slung one rucksack on my back and the other on my chest and rode away.

I pulled up in Alex's back yard and strode into his gaff like a conquering hero. Gemma had got up and was waiting in the hallway.

'Steve . . . you're OK. I was so worried . . . you were gone so long. What happened?'

'What happened is that I dosed those boys up good and proper. Oh, they'll rue the day they crossed me . . . oh, yes! I fucked with their minds. They won't forget this holiday for a long time.' I was buzzing like a good 'un. I lifted Gemma up in my arms and started tangoing around the hallway. 'We are sorted. We can fuck off now. We'll do it tomorrow. We are free. We are laughing all the way to . . . to whatever country has got wicked weather, beautiful beaches and poky gear. That's where we're headed, baby!'

'All right, all right. But I don't know why you're so happy . . . you know we'll always be looking over our shoulders until this is sorted. How can we ever relax knowing the police and those wankers are after us?'

'What are you suggesting? That I go back there and slit their throats? Come on . . . let's leave tomorrow and think about the long-term plan when we're safe.'

'I'm just saying . . . there isn't much to celebrate. We've created a beautiful life here and now we're back on the run. I don't know how much more of this I can take. If only we could get the police to believe the real story . . . if they were off our backs we'd be much safer. They could give us new identities or something until this Gabriel bloke finally gives up the ghost. I know you've sent letters to that regulator guy but what the fuck is he up to? And anyway, we're gonna need more evidence or we'll never be truly free.'

She had a point but she was ruining my buzz. I paced off towards the terrace feeling less euphoric – a bit miffed in fact that she wasn't as happy as I was. As I went outside I passed the devil mask Alex had hanging on his wall. He wore it to every Halloween party and it was truly horrific. A red, snarling, horned monstrosity about twice the size of a normal head. He'd bought it at the flea market a few years ago. It was so scary Virginia had once asked him to take it off the wall because she thought their baby was getting freaked out by it.

As I stood outside, leaning on the balustrade and smoking a cigarette, an evil, nasty but potentially outstanding idea entered my brain. I finished the fag and walked back in. I explained my idea to Gemma and, despite early reservations, she concurred.

As soon as I'd got Gemma's say-so I phoned Raja to

check that our two chums were still out for the count. 'Steve, they look like they won't wake up until next week,' was his reply. I then borrowed a video camera off Virginia, who fortunately asked no awkward questions, and took Alex's mask from the wall. I also borrowed a long dark red dress from Virginia, explaining that I wanted to show it to a tailor to get one made for Gemma, and prepared to set off back to the scene of the crime.

Gemma and I had a slightly less emotional goodbye this time and soon I was racing back to Raja's bar. It was near closing time when I arrived and only one couple remained. I explained to Raja that as soon as they had buggered off and there was no one on the road we were going to transport one of our new pals to my house. He initially disagreed, saying I was crazy, but another two thousand rupees soon changed his mind. He also lent me some rope and a can of paraffin.

I went back to the bungalow and prepared a room for what was surely going to be a horrific experience – for me, but especially for Juan. I took all the dark red and orange-coloured drapes and bedspreads we had and hung them on the walls of the small guest bedroom. My heart was pounding hard and I wondered whether the idea was ridiculous – the product of a crazed brain, sent mad by the recent stress and one too many joints. I tried to ignore my doubts.

When I went back to Raja's there was no one around. I peeped out at Juan and Diego, who were still sleeping like babies. Raja asked his two staff to leave early. They obeyed, looking happy to be going home at a decent hour.

I crept out with Raja not far behind me and approached the Colombians from behind, a kitchen knife in my hand. They looked completely unconscious but I couldn't risk being unarmed. They were both wearing bum bags, and I carefully undid the clasps from behind and slid them off. Then I checked their shorts pockets, my heart pounding. Juan's contained a dangerous-looking serrated knife in a leather scabbard. Diego had something heavy in his, which was difficult to remove until I got a pair of scissors from Raja and cut the pocket open. Oh yes. A gun. An old-school snub-nosed six-shooter. I put it in my pocket and scuttled back to the kitchen to check out the contents of their bags. I nabbed their money, their bike keys and their passports. My wannabe assassins were called Juan Rodriguez and Diego Velazquez and both were from Colombia. Those were the two men who'd made my life hell. I threw both passports in the fire. That would make their globe-trotting hunt for me a little more complicated.

The next part of the plan was trickier. Raja and I went back outside and gingerly approached my foes. After satisfying ourselves that they were still out of it I picked up Juan's feet while Raja grabbed him under the shoulders. He was short but he was heavy. We began staggering towards my house trying desperately not to drop him. I'd left the door ajar but the walk across the road was no fun at all. We were both struggling badly. We were also frantically looking from side to side just in case there was anyone around. Thankfully, we were alone. We hobbled up the steps and I guided us into the newly adorned guest bedroom, where we lowered Juan as gently as we could on to the bare concrete floor in the corner. I tied Juan's arms behind his back, then tied his legs together at the ankles. For good measure I wrapped a few coils of rope around his chest and upper arms. I wasn't going to take any chances.

I told Raja to tie Diego to his chair and tie his feet together too. It would be easier to deal with just one of them and I didn't need Lee Van Cleef, whose silence had made me assume he couldn't speak English. Raja followed my instructions. For two thousand rupees I probably could have asked him to dance an Irish jig non-stop for twenty-four hours and he would have said 'No problem'. Raja left and closed the front door behind him. I couldn't see his face but I had little doubt he was somewhat confused by all this. It didn't matter. I got a bucket of water from the bathroom and placed it by the guest room door, then set up Virginia's video camera in the doorway and covered it with some purple cloth so that only the lens peeped out. I focused it on his face so that his bonds weren't visible, and pressed record. I thought his upcoming 'testimony' would be less convincing if it was clear that he was a prisoner. Then I surrounded Juan with a stream of paraffin and placed a box of matches on the floor. Finally, I put on Virginia's dark red dress and fitted Alex's devil mask on my face.

OK. Here goes.

I took out Gemma's iPod and started playing some Goan trance that was so filthy, any right-minded person would take a shower on hearing it. Soon its deep, scary bass line filled the whole house. I took a long, deep breath and then picked up the bucket and threw its contents at Juan's face. He stirred and started mumbling something in Spanish. I slapped his cheeks until he finally looked up at my devil face. Then I backed off, out of view of the video camera, struck a match and lit the semicircle of paraffin that surrounded him.

The man was groggy but he was still obviously tripping his nuts off. In fact, he was probably peaking. His pupils were totally dilated and he had a look of complete and utter horror on his face. He tried to move but found he couldn't budge an inch. He didn't seem to understand where he was, who he was and why he couldn't move. He stared at me in my diabolical outfit and his eyes widened to the point of popping.

Juan had just woken up to find himself in hell. The demonic bass line was pumping and the fire and brimstone were raging. Not only was he in hell but he was with the main man himself – Satan, Mephistopheles, Beelzebub, Lucifer, the Lord of the Flies . . . call him what you will, he was definitely here. Now I had to act like I'd never acted before and hope he didn't question why the devil spoke in English with a London accent. I made my voice as deep and menacing as I could and began my spiel.

'You, Juan Rodriguez, are dead. You are in hell. You will suffer for eternity for your sins.' My devil voice was straight out of a Hammer House of Horror film but this was no time to be subtle.

'No, please, no . . . *no! No!*' He was absolutely shitting

himself. I have never seen anyone more scared in all my life. A softer part of me almost felt sorry for him. But there was no room for sympathy. I suspected that a combination of his Catholic upbringing and his numerous sins were making this whole episode all the more believable . . . and all the more horrific.

'You have only one chance to leave this pit of fire. Confess your sins. Tell me of the evil you have done and maybe I will let you go to the other place.'

'*Ay, por Dios!* Please, I so sorry. I have been bad man, but . . . but—'

'No excuses. Confess your sins. Starting with the most recent. Why did you kill Chuck Johnson?'

'I no kill him. My . . . friend Diego. He slit his throat. He had to die. My boss Don Llosa made us do it. It not me . . . *It not me!*' Fortunately, Juan didn't question Beelzebub's poor information.

'Where and when did Diego kill Chuck Johnson?'

'About one year ago. He killed him in a park in London. Santa Maria . . . please have mercy.'

'You will receive mercy if you tell the truth. Why did Don Llosa want Chuck Johnson dead?'

'Because . . . because he failed . . . I not sure. He tell us to kill and we kill. I know it not right. I know we bad. I pray to God each night to forgive me.'

'And what about Steve Jones . . . why did you seek him?'

'Don Llosa tell us to get him and Señor Saint tell us to go to India to find him . . .'

What? What the *fuck?* Suddenly, everything became crystal clear. The penny well and truly dropped. All at once, the constant procrastination we'd faced from Peter Saint made sense. The non-stop excuses for inaction revealed themselves as simply attempts to string me along. My God! If Peter Saint was involved then maybe so was Jane. I thought back to Jane's efforts to meet up with me in London after I'd gone on the run. I recalled how she kept asking me where I was and how she urged me to not get the police involved. I thought of the way she had kept me on the phone at Tarifa. My God! It all made sense now. She'd never fancied me . . . just kept an eye on me and used me. She'd played me like a fiddle. The conniving bitch!

After a few minutes of horrified recollections I pulled myself together. I needed to get back in character. I continued questioning Juan about Gabriel's organisation, the money laundering, the cocaine business and Peter Saint's role. His utter horror never receded but he managed to answer my questions despite it. It looked as if he really and truly believed he was in hell. If the acid I'd fed him was as strong as Jonno said I wasn't surprised. He had no idea what was going on. He'd obviously never tripped before and had just woken up in a truly demonic situation. The ruse was working.

After I'd got everything I wanted I said, 'I will leave you now to think about your fate but I'm afraid it doesn't look good. I think you will be alone in this room for eternity. Goodbye, Juan, for I have other sinners to talk to – mainly bankers of course! My work never stops. It is the way of the world. But before I go I will smother your lies with this.'

I held up a ripped piece of sarong that would act as a gag: I didn't want his cries to alert the neighbours. The 'hell fire' had long since gone out and I was able to approach him. Despite his struggles I wrapped the cloth around his head and into his mouth and tied it tightly at the back. Then I left, closing the door behind me and leaving him in total darkness. If there was no God and no devil then I had done their work. If he didn't end up stark raving mad after this experience I strongly suspected his killing days were over. I had meted out God's justice. I had been a divine judge and, for once, had made sure that the bad man was punished.

As soon as I was in the corridor I let out a huge sigh of relief. That was the weirdest thing I'd ever done but it had worked. The British police would now have something other than my testimony to prove I was innocent and Peter Saint and his devious bitch of a daughter would surely be investigated too. OK, the pigs might be a little bemused by my methods but the video would corroborate the other evidence I would provide – the printed out emails I'd send them, and Gemma's testimony.

I carefully packed up the camera and took off my costume, putting both into my bag. Then I walked back to Raja and together we hauled the comatose body of Diego over to my house. He didn't look likely to wake for some time, so we untied him before I removed anything that would show them that Gemma and I had lived there. I wanted them to wake up without a clue as to what had happened and with no indication of my role in it. With luck Juan would think the whole thing was just a vivid nightmare, with a bit of bondage thrown in.

Outside, I shook Raja's hand. I told him to profess total ignorance if our two pals asked him about what had happened. I told him to say that he had only met me once or twice if he was questioned. I also asked him to go and check on them next day if they hadn't reappeared. I couldn't handle the blood of two more people on my hands. That was their gig, not mine.

On the way home I had no smile on my face. What I had done was nothing less than torture, albeit psychological. I was not proud of my actions. I arrived at Alex's and was once again greeted with tears by Gemma. We shared a couple of beers but few words were spoken. When I told her about Peter and Jane she didn't seem fazed. She just closed her eyes, looked at the ground and shook her head. Neither of us slept that night. The next day, we would leave for pastures new and we had no idea what would happen. We would restart our lives on another beach in another country – that was all we knew. We would try to forget all that had happened once again.

There was just one thing left to do before we started our new lives.

Forty-Six

From: Steve Jones (cityboy69@hotmail.co.uk)
Sent: 13 November 2008 09:34:43
To: Gabriel.llosa007@hotmail.com.co; jane.saint@gmail.com;
peter_saint@btinternet.com

For the personal attention of Señor Gabriel Llosa, Miss Jane Saint and Mr Peter Saint.

I trust you are all well. I am pleased to report that, despite your best efforts, I am.

Please find attached an AVI file that contains an excerpt from a short film I recently shot. In this film you will see your friend Juan confessing that his colleague Diego murdered Chuck and naming you, Gabriel, as the boss who ordered the killing. He goes on to tell the viewer a little about your organisation and the roles you play in it, Peter and Jane Saint.

I have sent the complete film to two friends in London along with various files that confirm Chuck was involved in money laundering at Geldlust bank. I have sent these same friends a document detailing everything I know about your operation. They also have all the evidence I could find that you, Peter and Jane Saint, were involved. You both know full well that if the police receive even a hint that you're connected to this scam they will start nosing around and will inevitably find proof of your crimes.

I propose a deal – you promise to stop sending people to kill me and I promise never to release any of the information I have about you. My approach henceforward is going to be fucking simple – if I even smell a Colombian ever again then I will send my journalist friends at *thelondonpaper* and the police everything I have. Believe me, I've got a Cityboy column already written up that's going to win me the fucking Pulitzer – should it ever be released. Be aware that if anything unfortunate happens to me then my friends in the UK will send the police everything I have sent them. I have committed to contacting them every month and if those emails stop they will release the evidence forthwith. You'd all better fucking pray I don't eat a dodgy prawn over the next decade or two.

I hope you all see the logic of my deal. I am currently no threat to any of you and, unless aggravated, will remain so. Gabriel, whilst you may still seek to avenge the death of the man the bloggers call the Panther, please understand that revenge is not a financially rational motivation. Indeed, my death will have a profoundly negative impact on your wealth and the physical well-being of your two colleagues in London.

Let us not allow emotions to affect our behaviour – this is, after all, just business.

Yours, Steve

It was Gemma who decided that we needed to send an email to our relentless foes and take the battle to them. I had initially thought that we should simply send the police all the evidence we had but Gemma had argued convincingly that Gabriel would definitely continue to pursue us if we did that – out of sheer spite if nothing else. No, we would use our knowledge (and the pretence that we had more evidence than we actually did) to threaten them and make our continued existence a rational business choice.

So far it seems to be paying off.

Epilogue

WHEN I LOOK BACK AT all that's happened it's clear that I had become hideously corrupted by the ruthless greed that had infected the whole of the City in those early years of the third millennium. By the year 2000 the world's financial centres had degenerated into get-rich-quick loony bins designed to enrich the lucky few who worked in them at the expense of everyone else. There was little difference between the way crime syndicates and certain banks acted during that period – though I suspect the former acted with greater integrity and less hypocrisy. The line between gangsterism and finance had become so blurred that many of us Cityboys thought nothing of breaking rules if it meant that more cash was destined for our already bloated silk pockets. Some chose insider trading whilst others spread false rumours or laundered money in the wild west casino that unfortunately still dominates Britain's fragile economy.

Of course, the people who inflicted the most damage

were those despicable wankers working in structured finance, their self-serving dumbass bosses and the lying scumbags at rating agencies whose boundless avarice brought capitalism to its knees. The only difference between me and those immoral cocksuckers whose short-term pursuit of wealth plunged this world into a catastrophic recession was that I was punished for my sins – I received divine retribution here on earth. However, those bankers who knowingly infected the global financial system with over a trillion dollars' worth of toxic loans are now kicking back drinking pina coladas in Barbados when they should be having the pink skin flayed from their corpulent bodies by the people whose lives they've ruined. Fate dealt me a tough blow for my wrongdoing but others, who have caused infinitely more hardship to their fellow men than I ever did, are currently sitting back counting their millions, safe in the knowledge that their crimes will never be punished. Indeed, the promised banking reforms in the UK seem to have been massively watered down and bonuses for 2010 once again reached astronomical levels. What amazes me is that the general public seems to blithely accept the continuation of a corrupt system that almost brought the global economy to its knees whilst making those who run it disgustingly wealthy. It makes me wonder whether political apathy is now so ubiquitous that rich elites can just go on screwing us all, safe in the knowledge that none of us will ever take to the streets.

Rest assured I'm now on another tropical beach – though

for obvious reasons I can't say where. Our life is very similar to that we enjoyed in Goa though cocaine no longer plays any part in it. After seeing the evil that it creates I cannot enjoy its buzz any more. Every line of that devil powder is steeped in blood and I can no longer have that on my conscience.

As I write these final words I am poor but reasonably content. Gemma and I spend our days living the simple life, though we will probably always be looking over our shoulders, wondering if Gabriel heeded our warning or whether one of his goons is scuttling up behind us, a stiletto in his hand. We may never see our families again and we know that at any moment we might have to flee elsewhere.

But still, there may be some reprieve on the horizon. Much to my surprise, we received good news from the police a few weeks ago. It seems that they are finally coming to understand I had nothing to do with Chuck's murder, and they have contacted my parents and known associates to explain that I'm free to come home. After over a year of incompetence on a truly biblical scale, their investigations combined with some impassioned pleas from my family and ex-colleagues have convinced them that I was the victim of circumstances – a minor league player in a bigger drama. Gemma and I have been seriously considering returning to the motherland, but while Gabriel lives this will almost certainly remain a distant dream.

On dark nights while Gemma lies sleeping by my side, I sometimes ponder the good times we could have together back home. We have to live from hand to mouth here, but in England we would have a great deal of cash at our disposal. I miss my family and friends much more than I expected, as does Gemma who feels increasingly homesick. Over a beer or three at the local beach bar I catch myself staring into the middle distance as I envisage a new life back in London. I remember the buzz of that great city and even, much to my surprise, the mindless giggles I used to have with my old colleagues in the Square Mile. In truth, I'd love to go back there and do something to show the world what a bunch of corrupt shysters populate the City. It would be so much fun to take revenge on the banks that have ruined so many lives, seemingly without retribution. I'd tried to do so once via an anonymous column but maybe I could do something more direct, more dramatic. Though that would probably require entering the heart of the beast again . . .

I'm not sure if I believe in karma. Too many good people suffer and too many bad people get away with it. But I didn't. I got my comeuppance. I just hope that one day those guilty bankers who've destroyed the lives of millions get theirs.

Then, maybe, I'll start believing in karma.

Dr. Yes

Bateman

You don't say no to Dr. Yes, the charismatic plastic surgeon on the fast track to fame and fortune. But when the wife of obscure and paranoid crime writer Augustine Wogan disappears shortly after entering his exclusive clinic, Mystery Man, the Small Bookseller with No Name, is persuaded to investigate.

Business is in the doldrums for No Alibis, Mystery Man's infamous crime bookshop. And, as fatherhood approaches, our intrepid hero is interested only in a quick buck and the chance to exploit a neglected writer. But he soon finds himself up to his neck in murder, make-up and madness – and face to face with the most gruesome serial killer . . . since the last one.

Bateman: the word on the street:

'I've been a fan of Colin Bateman ever since his first crime novel and he just seems to get better and better' Ian Rankin

'Bateman has a truly unique voice . . . he is a dark and brilliant champion of words' James Nesbitt

'Sometimes brutal, often blackly humorous and always terrific' *Observer*

978 0 7553 7861 6

headline